THIRST FOR SALT

MADELAINE LUCAS

ONEWORLD

A Oneworld Book

First published in the United Kingdom and Ireland by Oneworld Publications, 2023

p. vii: Robert Hass, "Meditation at Lagunitas" from *Praise*. Copyright 1979 by
Robert Hass. Reprinted with the permission of HarperCollins Publishers, Inc.
Marilynne Robinson, *Housekeeping* used by permission of Faber and Faber Ltd.

ISBN 978-0-86154-649-7
eISBN 978-0-86154-475-2

Printed and bound in Great Britain by Clays Ltd, Elcograf S.p.A

Oneworld Publications
10 Bloomsbury Street
London WC1B 3SR
England

Stay up to date with the latest books,
special offers, and exclusive content from
Oneworld with our newsletter

Sign up on our website
oneworld-publications.com

MIX
Paper from
responsible sources
FSC® C018072

For my parents, for telling me stories.
And for Robert, for beginning a new story with me.

To crave and to have are as like as a thing and its shadow.
—Marilynne Robinson, *Housekeeping*

Longing, we say, because desire is full
of endless distances.

—Robert Hass, 'Meditation at Lagunitas'

ONE

Today I saw a picture of Jude with a child. Not one of the fair-haired nieces I remembered from photographs around the Old House, who would be grown by now, but a dark-haired little girl. Three or four years old. Still soft-cheeked, straight hair cropped at her chin, a short fringe that looked home-trimmed. Eyes so brown they were almost black. A Cupid's bow mouth, stained with berries at the creases. Jude's lips.

The photograph had been featured in an article about a portrait prize for capturing contemporary Australian life. The artist herself was unfamiliar to me, but it had come up when I searched Jude's name. Such a long time since I'd seen or heard from him, though sometimes, lonely and between lovers, I looked him up online. There was never much to find—Jude had remained a great resister of technology, it seemed, in the time we'd been apart, preserving his privacy and his solitude. Within a few years of the fire, he had all but disappeared. But then this: Jude and his daughter overlooking a green valley at a farm or vineyard. Mountains behind them, blueing with distance. Somewhere in Tasmania. Low grey fog lingering above the hills like a memory of smoke.

It was something in the way he held her—that's how I knew she was his. Not composed and smiling, the way you would be when holding someone else's child to show that everyone is having a good time. They were caught off guard, Jude with his back to the camera and the girl in his arms—she was peering over his shoulder at whoever was taking the picture. He'd turned, just at the moment the shutter fell. His lips parted, as if about to speak.

His face had aged, skin creased and papery at the corners of his eyes and the folds of his neck, which looked sunburned and tender, his hair cut shorter now. If I am thirty-seven, Jude would be fifty-five. Old, perhaps, to be a first-time father, and he did look tired, a dark patch beneath each eye like a stain, a new vulnerability to his expression.

It was a beautiful photograph, and I was surprised how much that hurt. The greens lush and saturated, like a country fresh with rain, colour so rich I could almost taste the earth, the water in the air. The little girl's expression, solemn and soft. The art of it, the intimacy of that gaze. Briefly, it seemed like I had stumbled across an image from another life. That what I had seen was none other than the unrealised possibility of our long-ago love.

You're hung up on the past, my mother said to me earlier tonight. Why carry all that around with you?

We were standing in the kitchen of her house in the Blue Mountains and I was watching her attempt to slice through a lime with a butter knife. I remembered this feeling from when

I was younger—we had moved so often when I was growing up that in the process of packing up or unpacking, we were always missing some essential tool for whatever task was at hand. Things got lost along the way. We made do with what we had.

I'd been trying to describe what it felt like to be back here, staying in her spare room again after living overseas for so long. It was like time collapsed along with distance, I said, though I'd had the sense not to mention Jude or the photograph. She hadn't understood. She thought I was talking about something else.

You can still have a baby if you want one, she said, sawing bluntly at the fruit. Isn't that what the doctor said?

In New York, I'd sent plastic vials of my blood in the mail to a clinic in Manhattan. I was asking a question about fertility, which is to ask a question about time. My results had come back indicative of a *diminished ovarian reserve*. In my confusion, my shock, I heard *reserve* and thought of reservoirs, of lakes, of rivers, depleting natural resources, my body like a body of water. Without asking any further questions I hung up on the specialist mid-sentence and called my mother. Come home, she'd urged, get a second opinion. There's no shame in coming home, you know.

My latest teaching appointment was finishing up for the summer and I was soon to vacate the studio I was subletting from a professor on sabbatical, most of my belongings already housed in a storage facility in Queens. Okay, I'd said to my mother, but only for a little while, to see her and my brother. I wasn't planning to stay.

In the few days I've been back she has hardly left the subject of children alone. Each morning, more pamphlets appear beside the coffeepot from various donation banks and Chinese herbalists and, once, a psychic. But the fact remains that for me to have a baby now would likely be difficult and expensive, if not altogether impossible, and I'm not sure I want to go through with any of it alone.

This was something I could not easily explain to my mother, who raised me and then, twelve years later, Henry, with little intervention from our respective fathers. Seeing the photograph of Jude had articulated something that was painful to admit—some part of me had not given up the dream I'd had when I was twenty-four of having a baby with a man I loved and raising it together. Mother, father and child—a family of three. It made the possibility of motherhood feel far from me now—as far away as my time at Sailors Beach with Jude and King, our beloved long-dead dog. Those days of homemaking, lovemaking, housekeeping remained the closest I'd come. How could I not be hung up on the past, I wanted to say to my mother, when so many things I'd loved had been left behind there?

Now, I sit beneath the lamp in the spare room at the desk that once belonged to my grandmother, drawn back to it by that same compulsion I've had since childhood to write things down, to document. It's late, but my body keeps New York time. This is what happens when you break with one life to live another—it causes a doubling. Knowing eleven at night here is seven in the morning there. Some part of you is always in conversation with that other self.

Perhaps my mother is right. I've carried it all with me for too long. I need to find a place to put it all down. For so long I have lived like the woman in the parable, looking back to see whatever ruins lay behind me. If I had remained at Sailors Beach and had a child with Jude, if I had married him, as I once imagined I would, my bridal train would have been made of salt and sand.

When we met, Jude and I had marvelled at the symmetry of our ages. Written down in my diary—*24 42*—they looked like a palindrome or a postcode from an outer Sydney suburb. It's hard to remember now that I was once that girl, lying in the sand in my red swimsuit and swimming late into the day. *Sharkbait*, he called me.

I had gone down south on a holiday with my mother that summer to Sailors Beach. A watery place, surrounded by the bay on one side and the Pacific Ocean on the other, a place we had not visited since I was a child. It would be just the two of us again, for the first time since my younger brother was born. Our family an ever-tangling web and men the loose threads left hanging, but not our Henry, not yet. Man of the house, we teased, though he was still a boy then, only twelve. He belonged to us except for the month of January, gone fishing with his father up north, and we hoped he would return uncorrupted by the silent, absent ways of all the other men who passed in and out of our lives.

Back then, my mother had only recently moved to her house in the Mountains, and though she often said she was used to life without a man around—preferred it, even—being at home without a child was something else, and I think she did not like the idea of spending weeks in the new place alone. She was repainting, she'd told me when she called a few weeks before the New Year, and the fumes were giving her a headache. Plus, there was something about the way the tree branches scraped at the windows in the hot breeze. The smell of paint, the heat—it played tricks on her mind. She had seen the garden hose coiled on the concrete back steps take the shape of a brown snake baking in the sun, right beside her boots.

Though my mother is older now and has settled, she has always had a tendency to talk of houses the way other people talk about lovers: This is it this time, I've found the one, I can feel it. Her wandering eye for a Victorian terrace, or an ageing Australian bungalow built in the California style. All her new beginnings took the shape of freshly painted walls, a roof under which nothing bad had ever happened. No wine spilled on the carpet, no fist-shaped hole through the drywall. I think she liked the work of it—ripping up a garden gone to seed, peeling back flaking wallpaper, stripping the paint from the floors to reveal a dusty golden pine or wide boards of solid Tasmanian oak. The strength it takes to bring an old house back from the brink of ruin, bringing in the light, the air. Water and seeds out for the birds. That kind of work, she said, it makes you believe that change is possible. You can see the difference you made, and all for the better too.

That was my mother—dreaming in blueprints, ever since I was conceived beneath the bare wooden bones of an unfinished house on a construction site in suburban Melbourne where my father worked as a labourer during the day and slept sometimes, after hours. She was in her last year of art school then and living in her childhood home, so my parents made love in sawdust, a blue tarpaulin slapping against the empty frame in the winter wind that blew in sharp off the Tasman Sea, moon shining through the crossbeams. Brushing sawdust from their hair. My parents separated sometime between my third and fourth birthdays—young enough for me to have few memories of them together, but I had my mother's stories, repeated over the years until they gained the quality of myth.

Besides, she had continued over the phone while I sat in my bedroom in Sydney, I'm sure you could use a break, a sea change. You hardly left the library all last year.

I was living in the Inner West of the city then with two girls from university, in a Victorian terrace house that faced away from the sun. I'd turned in my thesis a month earlier, in November, and was soon to be, at last, a graduate.

I had enjoyed the rituals of research, sitting in air-conditioned reading rooms in companionable scholarly silence with the other young women who frequented the art library, though it was possible to go a whole day without speaking to anyone. Both my housemates worked nights—Petra at a Greek restaurant and Bonnie at an art-house cinema—and I often got home after they had left. Also, I was often sick. Pallid from months indoors, blue shadows under my eyes from lack of sleep, paper cuts on my cold, dry hands. Trailing a bar heater room to room. Living on tea and honey and oranges, and thin soups I stretched to last a week on my meagre student's allowance. Whenever it rained, the house filled with water, the walls soaked through. Pots and pans made musical sounds in the kitchen where the ceiling leaked, and damp bloomed in my room. I went to sleep in sweaters, two blankets on my bed. Swaddled, said Bonnie, but Petra had ideas for a different cure. The body is constituted by other bodies, she said, quoting some theorist she was reading. Activated by touch. What you need is a good root.

That's your answer to everything, I said, and Bonnie clucked, God! You make it sound about as romantic as fixing the kitchen sink.

My mother also questioned my solitary habits—though they shouldn't have surprised her. I'd been a quiet child, and a dreamy, introspective adolescent. You tend to your loneliness like a garden, she'd said once during my last year of university, and on her trips to the city she began to buy me potted plants, bring me flowers and cuttings from her yard. But who, I wanted to ask, could I have learned that from?

Still, I wasn't offended by her suggestion that I hadn't been doing so well at looking after myself. I was always touched by my mother's worry in a way I sensed was unusual. She had been twenty-four when I was born, the same age I would turn on our trip to Sailors Beach that summer, and we often joked that we had raised each other like two sisters, runaways.

Our holiday, I agreed, would be a pause—between my life as a student and whatever would happen next. I was on the edge of something, I felt sure. I could sense it, as one catches the scent of salt on the wind when the ocean draws near, before it comes into view. The year ahead stretched out before me like a lacuna in my still-young life, and it was this space that Jude would walk right into.

The week of my twenty-fourth birthday, we drove south. Past the empty roadside restaurants, retirement villages and funeral parlours on the outskirts of the city and through a repetition of small coastal towns, their supermarkets and motor inns all clustered by the road. Beyond that, bush.

Finally, the road narrowed and Sailors Beach was announced by a reduced speed limit and an Anglican church on the corner with a billboard that read: *Need a new life? God accepts trade-ins.* At the turnoff from the highway, a sign out my window made a claim to the whitest sand outside Hawaii.

My mother had rented an old whaler's cottage for the month, a weatherboard painted pale yellow. It sat one street back from the water, on a rise, with a scrubby patch of lawn out the front. Blue hydrangeas, red bottlebrush trees and flowering gum attracted lorikeets in the afternoons.

The beach was made from the lip of the bay, which let out into the South Pacific Ocean, and we could see it there from the small verandah, beyond the other flat-roofed rentals, square fibro shacks and new, glassy modern houses. On our first evening, we shelled and ate prawns with our fingers, dipping our hands in a bowl of warm water and lemon, and toasted with prosecco in plastic picnic flutes, out on the porch.

Isn't it funny, my mother said, to think that when I was your age, you were born.

I was looking out at the horizon. At a certain time down south, sea and sky seem to merge, to kiss. Mirroring each other, like lovers do. Above and below, one expanse of silver blue. I'd never known that kind of love—where all boundaries disappeared. Her observation had troubled me. I'm not a woman, I'm a child, I thought, on some romantic getaway with my mother. I finished my drink in one swallow.

I'm going for a swim, I said, and though it was growing late and we'd been drinking and the tide was coming in, my mother was not the kind to tell me not to. There had been times when I'd wished this was otherwise—that she might have offered me some words of warning, a gentle caution.

I made my way to an isolated cove, where the shore bordered the dense bushland of the national park. The beach, at dusk, was empty, the air cooling after the heat of the day. Small fish in the shallows darted along the sandy floor. In the high season, such privacy was rare, and I took it as a gift. There was no wind, no waves. I was sheltered there.

I lay on my back, floating, and my irritation dissolved. Thinking of what Petra said about the way that touch contours a body by making its boundaries known, and maybe what I wanted, what I longed for, lying there with the ocean outlining mine, was to be held in the way you're supposed to be when you're no longer a child.

I was high and free and lonely. I closed my eyes, felt the tug of the water beneath me. Imagining the movement was the Earth in motion and I could feel it turning.

The cool shock of the blue. Movement, water, salt, light, heat. I began every day that way, my first week at Sailors Beach. Rising up with the waves and kicking down into the depths, into those sudden cold patches where the sun didn't reach. Patterns of light on the surface, shadows passing above, water darkening. The fear, sometimes, of something brushing past my leg—a tangle of kelp, or a lone gull landing beside me. Rocks seemed to quiver on the silty bed below, and once, I caught sight of a silver ray. Henry would have loved that, I thought. At twelve, he was fascinated by marine life, a wall of tanks tinted his bedroom at my mother's a neon blue. He'd sent me a picture of himself on my birthday, sitting on the edge of a boat, one hand in the shape of the rock 'n' roll sign. *About to go diving with hammerheads*, his message read. Already, my baby brother was becoming braver than me. I preferred to keep my eyes closed when I went swimming, moving blindly stroke by stroke. Happier not to know what might be out there, circling.

My mother was more concerned about the way our pale skin burned in the sun. From the waves, I could spot her on the beach with her wide-brimmed hat, dark sunglasses and linen shawl wrapped around her shoulders.

I'm glad, she said, as we walked along the beach together one morning, that I was a punk for most of my youth, when tanning was all the rage. The girls at my school used to lie on their lawns on tinfoil, slathered in coconut oil, like they were nothing but meat. So many women my age look withered now. Overdone.

Unlike my mother, I wanted to burn, water drying off my body in the heat—once my favourite vice. It felt good in the way a minor transgression can, like taking a drag of a cigarette or kissing a stranger. I liked the sting of it, standing under the cool needles of the outdoor shower at the end of the day, rinsing the sand from my feet. The freckles I'd had as a child, long dormant, appearing again on my arms and across the bridge of my nose. I thought of them as light mapped on the skin. Evidence of where I'd been touched by the sun.

While my mother retreated inside to rest during the hottest part of the day, I stayed on the beach in the afternoons, swimming out alone, past the breakers. Each day a little further as I gained confidence. Pushing my limits out in the deep.

Don't you worry about sharks? she said, when I came back to the cabin with my shoulders pinked, a fine crust of salt dried on the hairs of my arms and eyebrows. You wouldn't want to be out there on your period. They smell it, you know. The blood. Like dogs can.

Jude, too, would warn me: If you ever meet one out there, look it in the eye. Never turn your back on a shark. And I'd laughed at what seemed like a strange code between animal and man. One, therefore, that didn't apply to me, a girl from the city, a stranger to his town.

Thirteen years have passed since then, and from this distance, it's tempting to substitute the weary father in the photograph, daughter in arms, for the younger man of that summer, when what I'm trying to do is remember us as we were.

The first time I saw Jude, we were in the water.

One afternoon towards the end of that first week, I became aware of a movement a short distance away from me while I was swimming. There was the sound of a body cutting through the waves with a swift stroke. Strong arms, browned by sun, emerging out of all that blue. The swimmer surfaced a few feet ahead of me, shaking hair darkened by water from his face. He kept his distance, but nodded.

We were out beyond where the waves were breaking, and at that time of day, the wind was low and the water relatively still. I lay back, kicking lightly to stay afloat, thinking he'd soon pass me by. But he stayed there, treading water, watching me. Watching my legs rising with the ocean's gentle swell. His lips curled and eyes focusing. Curious.

I suppose I'd been playing, the way I did sometimes when I was out there alone—making arcs, pointing my feet like a dancer—because in the water I could love my body the way I never did on land. In the water, I was graceful, a light and buoyant thing.

I knew this to be my better self, the most fully alive, my lungs filling with air, salt tangling my hair and making my eyes brighter like after sex or after crying, sunlight catching the water beading on my shins.

Although we can never really know how we are perceived by others—especially those who come, in time, to love us, those initial impressions overlaid with the knowledge of later intimacies—I believe it came down to the fact that we were in water, that he saw me first that way. On the beach, or walking along the one main street in town, I would have been concealed. I was shy, and I wore my shyness like a cloak that obscured me from view, and as a consequence, any advances I made carried a certain intensity that, I sensed, was unnerving—as if I'd abruptly revealed myself. And though I did not give myself up easily, was guarded and slow to trust, I was also painfully earnest. My young face had an openness that tended to reveal too much, and this, I knew, could be strangely intimidating in the way vulnerability sometimes is. I was not casual, especially with men, raised as I was in a world of women—all-girls' schooling and a single mother—and even throughout university, it showed.

None of this mattered in the water. Out there we had no need of speaking. Still, he kept his distance that day in the deep, swimming neither closer nor further away, and later I would remember this as an example of Jude's ambivalence. Sun bright as a flare, I closed my eyes, saw his face like an indelible print on the backs of my eyelids. When I opened them, he caught my gaze, held it. Suddenly, it seemed we were no longer playing a game. It was a challenge, and I faltered, breaking away, turning and swimming quickly back towards land.

Lying on the sand, I could hear my heart, louder than the rush of waves tossing themselves at the beach. With such abandon, I thought. The tide goes on, throwing itself again and again at the shore.

The next afternoon, lying on the beach with my eyes closed against the sun, a shadow fell across my face and there was Jude. Standing above me and blocking my light. He told me he'd seen me swimming.

I had pulled the straps of my swimsuit down to try and even out the pale stripes it left on my shoulders, and when I sat up, I held it flat against my chest with one hand so it wouldn't slip. He looked at me the way he had in the deep—as if he could see through to the core of me, burning away all that was not essential, the way the high noon sun burns up all the water in the morning air. No man had ever looked at me that way before.

You look good in the water, said Jude. Or it might have been, *you're* good in the water. His voice lost against the waves and playful shrieks of children, testing their courage. Running to the edge of the shore until the tide chased them back again.

Standing in front of me, dressed and dripping, I recognised him from around the town. I'd noticed him in the coffee shop across the street one morning—the ease with which he leaned across the counter, talking closely with the waitress. On land he was tall, and always wore proper clothes—boots and dark jeans, a thin button-down shirt with sleeves rolled up to the elbow, rabbit felt hat perched high on his head. Not like the other customers, who came in wearing board shorts and bikinis, feet caked in sand and trailing seawater. I could tell he belonged in this place in a way most people didn't, that he was the kind of man who was good with waitresses and bartenders and shopkeepers, knew how to charm them. Making small talk about the weather and the tides. Tipping his hat in the street to the sun-beaten locals in a fashion much older than he was, imitating the manners of an earlier generation of dairy farmers and fishermen and sheepshearers' sons.

But how old exactly? I'd never been a good guesser of ages, and I can no longer easily recall the way I saw him as a stranger. His face would become more familiar to me than my own father's—the crease between his brows that reminded me of a cowboy in an old movie, bump on the bridge of his nose where it might once have been broken, though that day as he stood in front of me, wet hair wilting the collar of his shirt, patch of damp above his breast pocket like an ink stain, I could only guess how—a drunken fall, a fistfight, some feat of athletics long ago. He was handsome, though not in the way I imagined he would have been when he was younger. Burned-out look around the eyes, deep-set and slate that day, though I'd learn in time that they were changeable. Like moods, like weather.

There's a name for your kind, you know, he said.

What kind is that?

Out all day, swimming till sundown. Round here we call them sharkbait.

He told me I had to be careful—that if I got into trouble out there, there was nobody on hand who could save me. These are unpatrolled waters, he said. No lifeguards for miles.

I know that, I said, regretting the edge that came into my voice when I felt shy. Petulant and sullen, like a teenager. I learned to swim here when I was young.

Compared to some of us, you're still young, he said. A joke, lightness in his voice.

Well, younger, then.

But it had been a long time, I thought, since we'd come to this beach, the three of us—my mother, my father and I. It was one of my earliest memories—my father lifting me from the waves, teaching me which ones to jump over and which to dive under, so I wouldn't get knocked down. Trusting his arms would be there to pull me up if it got too rough. Those three seconds of tumult, tossed upside down and under, before he yanked me out, calling me his *little fish on the line*, and held me coughing against his chest. Salt-stung and rashed by sand, but saved. I would never be that young again.

You from the city, then? he said.

I nodded. Sydney.

And what do you do up there?

I pulled up the straps of my swimsuit, shifted to shade my eyes with my hand. I told him that since I'd finished university in November, I'd been working at a bookstore café by a beach on the east side of the city.

Bondi Beach was crowded with bodies browning in the sun, tourists staying where the waves were waist-high, never going out too deep, afraid of what might lurk beneath the dark and choppy water. Sand hot and grainy and yellow. Burned your feet to walk across it. It was not like Sailors, where bush grew around the fringes of the shore, making it feel sheltered, secluded. Down south, the sand was soft and white as caster sugar, and you could scoop up handfuls of seawater, pool it in your cupped palms, and watch it run clear as it slipped through your fingers.

It was a second-hand bookshop, I told him, but despite the carefully curated shelf of first editions, hardcover copies of *To Kill a Mockingbird* and *The Bell Jar* wrapped in plastic and priced in the hundreds, most of the customers were backpackers looking for cheap beach reads and an internet connection. Books changed hands as these travellers swapped cities and hostel beds, and their paperbacks returned to us a little more worn, dog-eared and waterlogged, sand caught in the creases of their cracked spines.

At work, I was surrounded by these temporary visitors and before long I'd begun to dream of being one of them, spending more of my shifts alphabetising the guidebooks in the travel section. Whatever plans I had at the start of that year were vague and revolved mainly around departure, of touring European cities by train. There was a dignity, I imagined, to this kind of passage, more romantic than the transience I'd grown up with and offering the kind of higher purpose I believed in—the purpose of experience, of extending oneself to gain knowledge. These books, I often thought, as I stacked the two-dollar cart on the sidewalk full of new donations, they've seen more of the world than I have—although I did not say that then, to Jude.

Ah! he said. A bookstore. So, you do want to be a writer.

What makes you think that?

Well, you brought Duras to the beach. He gestured to the book beside me, stripped of its dust jacket. My library copy of *The Lover*. Blue cloth cover growing hot in the sun, gold lettering glinting in the light. Only a writer would bring Duras to the beach.

I don't know what I want to be, I said. In the moment, it felt true.

He raised his eyebrows, as if I had revealed something personal. I wasn't like him, I knew. I had no easy way with strangers. Always giving away too much, or saying too little. It seemed clear I had missed some essential lesson. I was not like the children at the shore's edge, testing the waters, wetting their toes, knowing the right time to rush forward and when to back away. It was easier, I thought, when we'd been swimming. There was no need for conversation then. Navigating the waves was intuitive, there was a rhythm to it—I knew when to use strength and when to surrender, when to rise over or dive beneath. In the waves I could lie back and trust that they would hold me. I could let myself be held.

Well, he said, what did you study?

Oh, you know. Literature, art history. Practical things.

A romantic, then.

Not particularly vocational though, is it? Hence the bookstore. At least for now.

In any case, he said, the lightness in his voice returning, you really ought to know better. I mean, as a bookseller. Salt, sand, wet hands. Bad for books, you know? Warps the pages. I work with antiques myself, at a place in town. Deal with furniture mainly, so personally I'm more concerned with water rings.

Was I trying then, as I looked up at him, squinting against the sun, to picture his body tauter, leaner, hair golden from a youth spent outdoors? Or did that come later? Wondering if his face would have once been round and boyish, or square-cut—the kind of beauty I found boring, simple and above all, unapproachable. I always liked a mutt, a stray, he would joke with me that winter, the day we found King on the beach and took him home. I thought of the line from my book, lying beside me on my towel. *I prefer your face as it is now. Ravaged.*

Would it be wrong to say that I liked Jude—wanted him—as he came to me? As he was then, standing on the shore, long white feet sinking in the sand. Hair a shade lighter now that it was drying in the sun, a few strands of silver catching the light. Curling a little where it was damp at the ends, just long enough to tuck behind his ears.

Well, he said, see you around, Sharkbait. Try not to get eaten alive.

I watched as he turned and walked back across the beach in long, slow strides towards the bush track that led to the main road. Leaving two large footprints where he'd stood above me, casting his tall shadow.

That night, I dreamed of him. The Man from the Deep. Dreams not of sex but of other kinds of intimacy. I was touching his face. Feeling the bump of the bridge of his nose with the soft tips of my fingers. Tracing the delicate folds of his eyelids, his lips, the corners of his mouth. Moving my hand across the plane of his brow.

In the dream, we were standing together in a drowned house. Somewhere on the second floor, a pipe had burst and dirty water rushed down the stairs, filling the empty room around us like a basin. Both of us were dressed in layers of warm, heavy clothes that obscured the shape of our bodies. It was difficult to lift my arms towards him, weighed down by wool and water. I pushed my face into his chest, rubbed my cheek against the rough weave of his coat. The water was rising and he was the only warm, dry place. I put my arms around his neck, wrapped my legs around his waist. Climbing him, like a child. I took his head in my hands, cradled it against my chest, kissed his hair where it was greying at the crown and temples.

I woke naked, twisted in white sheets, nightgown up around my neck. What had I seen to make me dream that way? Veins on his arms, the few dark curls on his chest above his low-buttoned shirt. Elegant feet, pale and long. As sleep dragged me back again, I felt the heat press against me like a second skin, heard the ocean outside my window like a lover's breath. Everything suddenly unbearably erotic, alive.

I looked for him on the beach the next morning while my mother fussed with our towels, shaking them out, weighing them down with our books and sandals.

Beside us, two women were kneeling beneath a white beach umbrella. A mother in her sixties applying sunscreen to her grown daughter's back, the daughter's belly swollen like a spherical fruit, a perfect globe rising beneath her black swimsuit. The younger woman looked tired, blinking her eyes slowly open and closed against the light, while her mother's hands moved across her back—brisk, but tender. Something in her actions made me feel she was impatient, ready to be done with it, this mothering, and pass the task on to the next generation.

Look, my mother said, that will be us one day.

I suppose she meant that one day I might be pregnant, that I would become a mother and she a grandmother—what she saw as the natural and inevitable progression of things—but what struck me then, as I watched the two women, and what continued to haunt, was the absence of men.

Yes, except you'd still have Henry at home, I reminded her. He'd be a teenage uncle. And with any luck, I might even have a boyfriend by then.

Or a husband, said my mother.

Sure, I said, one of those too. I'll take both.

Oh very funny, she said. A husband and a boyfriend, you're not that kind of girl. Of the two of us, you've always been the good one.

A few days later, on a grey morning, my mother and I drove into town to buy prawns wrapped in paper, fresh oysters, cucumbers and tomatoes and salad leaves, feta soaked in oil from the deli. While she went looking for the bottle shop, I wandered the main street. Five blocks from the playground and small public pool on the hill above the ocean to the one-screen movie theatre in the converted community hall. It had rained overnight and the whole town was damp, dripping, in a way that made it seem shabby, like someone dressed inappropriately for the weather. Racks of swimsuits, shawls, sarongs, cheap plastic sunglasses in front of the small arcade. Wind chimes and dreamcatchers swinging in the wet breeze. Smell of fried food, cooking oil, batter from the fish and chip shop. An ice cream parlour that sold candy imported from America, a candle store, signs advertising whale watching and dolphin cruises, tourists lining up by the boats along the wooden pier with digital cameras bowing their necks.

At the park end, on the ocean side, I stopped in front of a window advertising *Old Wares*, peering through the filmy glass. Remembering what Jude had said about wood and water rings.

Inside the shop, the knell of small brass bells above the doorway and the usual odd collection of forgotten or discarded things. Tarnished souvenir spoons from country towns around Australia, from the Ten Dollar Town Motel in Gulgong to the ski fields of Bright, Victoria. Out-of-date annuals and almanacs and manuals for housekeeping. Hand-stitched doilies and a crate of vinyl records marked down to five dollars—*Tommy* by The Who, *Tubular Bells*, Duane Eddy *Twistin' 'N' Twangin'*. Rounds of soap wrapped in wax paper stacked on the counter. A few yellowed classics, *Jane Eyre* and *Persuasion*, paperback editions printed for high school required reading on thin paper in thick bleeding type. Tea sets cracked or chipped or missing pieces, jars filled with wax and wicks to make decorative candles.

I was hunting around for a rack of clothes—second-hand silk or lace dresses I might find for cheaper than in the city. My captive consumptive look, Jude would later tease, for my way of swanning around the house in slips. Splinters snagging the delicate fabric.

Further in, a second room held furniture stacked in tall towers. Dressers and elegant end tables poised on three legs. A wicker chair with a wide, round back, the shape of a throne. A vanity with a spotted mirror that opened in three parts, like a jewellery box I'd had when I was a girl. It had been a gift from my father. You turned a key at the back and when you opened it, a tiny dancer twirled to 'As Time Goes By'.

There were secretary desks, dining sets and chairs stacked upon tables made from rustic timber I'd later be able to identify as blond pinewood or oak or ash or maple. Iron bedposts leaning against one wall. Armoires and chests of drawers with pretty porcelain handles that reminded me of my mother's house and all the antiques we'd inherited from my grandmother, Sylvia, who had been able to recognise period and style from sight alone. Gifted in assessing the correct value of things. Always won at the horseraces and at auction houses. Lucky in those pursuits, if not in others, like love.

In the corner stood a writing desk like the one she had left to me. Dark wood, with a worn leather top. The hidden drawers had fascinated me as a child. My grandmother had kept sweets in them—red-and-white-striped peppermints and Butter-Menthols in waxy paper squares, cool from their life in the dark and tasting faintly of wood—next to nips from aeroplanes and hotel minibars, gin and cognac bottles sticky with lint. Letters from her first love bound with ribbons beside my mother's girlhood ballet shoes.

The one in the shop had trick drawers, sealed shut, but carefully I lifted the lid. Inside, a black pearly button rolled back like an eye, came to rest by a stray needle and thread. Relics of its former life.

A door shut down the back of the shop and I jumped, snapping the top down. Jude emerged from another room, bringing with him the smell of varnish and wood stain. Similar to my mother's painting turpentine I remembered from when I was a child, but vaguely citrus-scented, syrupy. Like oranges soaked in alcohol.

Sharkbait, he said, and my face burned. Remembering my dream. How easy it had been to reach out and touch his face. The coarse texture of his hair when I ran my hands through it, his rough woollen coat against my cheek. The heavy warmth of his body like something that could fold over me, weigh me down. My palms itched. I buried my hands in my pockets.

You don't strike me as someone in the market for antiques, he said. Wiping his hands with a checked cloth, wringing it between his fingers.

I was walking past. This is your shop?

More or less. Belongs to an old couple, but they don't get down here much these days. My workshop's out the back. They give it to me cheap for keeping an eye on the place for them.

So, you live down here?

I do, most don't, he said. It's a tourist town.

Must really empty out once the season's over, I said. Quiet.

Oh, but it's better then. Come back in the winter sometime, then you'll see.

He seemed softer in that cool dark room, the dusty light. Creases around his eyes when he smiled, like someone who might laugh often and easily.

I heard the bells by the door and turned to see my mother, her arms loaded with paper parcels, plastic shopping bags hanging from her wrists. There you are! she said, beaming at me. Don't you just love that peacock chair? We used to have one like that when you were little, until someone climbed up on it at a party, put their foot right through the seat. I was devastated. It had been a wedding present from my mother.

Now, here is a woman who appreciates antiques, said Jude, and I noticed the way his voice changed, brightened. Smooth and honey-toned, the voice of a practised salesman.

This one's made of rattan, he was saying, resting his hand on the back of the chair. The natural palm stems are much better quality than any of that synthetic stuff. Hardly had to work on it at all. Traditionally, they were given to celebrate a marriage, or a birth.

Trust my mother to have known the traditional thing, she said. Always was good at that. First anniversary paper, second year cotton, then leather. And then is it silk? Never quite got that far, myself.

My mother has always made easy small talk with strangers, genuinely curious about the lives of others. She stood there cradling our parcels of seafood, gripping the wine by the neck, plastic bag full of vegetables digging into her wrist, but she spoke so casually while I waited empty-handed, watching condensation drip down the crisp green bottle. Their conversation slipped into an easy groove, the boundaries more recognisable—he a local craftsman and she a customer from out of town.

He was a failed actor, he joked. All his years in the theatre spent behind the scenes in the lighting booth or painting and building sets, he never made it to the stage, but it taught him skills he could use, and I could hear it then, an actor's elocution— that rich conviction that made him so difficult to argue with. Carpentry his father's trade, picked up in earnest later in life, after he moved down south. Fixed up an old house here by himself. Now he spent his time finding pieces to repair and sell, driving to auction houses and estate sales and op shops, though often the real treasures, he said, were found dumped on the side of the road or in a back alleyway. Made his own furniture, too, from recycled wood and timber bought cheap at the tip.

Together they spoke about rising property prices in Sydney trickling down the coast, the new highway that would bypass the smaller towns, putting a strain on the local businesses that depended on the passer-by, the daytripper. The best place to buy fresh fish and how oysters were always better if you bought them closed up in their shells, shucked them yourself with a knife. Like turning a key in a lock, he said. Miming the action with his hands.

Not a bad price on the chair by the way, if you're interested.

He draped his arm across its curved back. Gently possessive, proud of what he had. I would feel the power of this when we walked through town with King that winter—Jude, the dog and I, parading.

My mother waved the offer away. I've got no need for one now, she said. But who knows, maybe I'll get to buy one for my own daughter one day. Continue the tradition.

Smoothing my hair then, like she did when I was a little girl, knots catching on the rings on her fingers.

Ouch, I said quietly, shaking my head and moving out of her reach.

Well, I hope you'll be back, said Jude. Both of you. His eyes levelling with mine.

He likes you, said my mother, as we walked back towards the car park.

No he doesn't, I said quickly.

Jude was closer to my mother's age than he was to my own. It pained me to think that he should have been interested in her.

Older men have always been interested in you, she said. Remember that time at the supermarket?

This was a story my mother often used to tell when I was younger. She seems to have retired it now—perhaps it seems less relevant now that I am in my thirties, or maybe she is aware that it could imply that I, too, am *past my prime*, as she would say. But in the story, I am still a child, and I've just had my hair cut at a salon in the shopping centre that gives discounts to kids and students and pensioners. Gone was the long hair of my girlhood, the new layered style grazing my collarbones, and I felt, for the first time, grown-up. We were in the fruit and vegetable aisle when, according to my mother, a man—old enough to be my father—looked me up and down while I stood beside her in my pink singlet and denim pedal pushers, filling a plastic bag with peaches, the soft hairs on my arms rising against the air-conditioned chill.

How old were you then? she said, as she unlocked the door to the car and loaded our shopping into the back seat.

I was only twelve, I said. Not even old enough to wear a bra, and getting my hair done at a place called Just Cutz, with a *z*. You had Henry in a stroller. He was probably looking at you, that man. Trying to figure out how you could possibly be old enough to have a daughter my age.

I'd become accustomed to this over the years, growing up with my mother. Teased by the boys in primary school, who made lewd gestures when she wasn't looking, picking me up in her black leather shorts and sheer lacy blouses, singing along loudly to 'Linger' by the Cranberries on the stereo. Butchers and grocers who winked at us, joking, You two could be sisters, or This must be your babysitter. She laughed quickly in a way that made her whole body shake. Motherhood had done nothing to blunt her desirability, even with Henry on her hip, and though as a teenager I would covet her clothes, her wardrobe of second-hand suede and snakeskin and fur, as a girl I had gone through a phase of being punctilious and prim. *My little puritan*, she called me, when I scolded her to stop smoking or to put a jacket on. It was of great importance to me when I was ten or eleven years old, to never give anyone a reason to laugh at me behind my back the way the boys had laughed at my mother.

You didn't notice, she went on. You weren't aware of men then, but I knew you would be soon. I remember thinking, That's it for me. It starts so much younger than you think.

What does?

Oh, you know. *Nature.* All of it. Not that I mind, these days, she said, raking her fingers through her hair, blowing wild in the salt breeze. Takes some of the pressure off me. When you have a daughter one day, you'll see.

Across the street, I could see the bay, our whaler's cottage somewhere on the other side. I watched a family dragging kayaks to the shore, and two people on paddleboards gliding across the flat surface. From a distance, it looked like they'd found a way of walking on water. I felt this way at times at Sailors—that magic might be possible there. I couldn't see our rented cabin, or any of the other beach houses. The bush grew thick around the shore, and for a brief moment I could imagine that all the streets and houses disappeared in our absence, and only rematerialised when we drew near.

How old is he, do you think? my mother said, as she settled herself into the driver's side, fixed her lipstick in the rear-view mirror.

Who?

The man from the shop.

How should I know? We don't know each other.

You seemed to get along.

You were the one doing all the talking, asking for his life story.

Oh well, he seems a bit old for you, anyway, she said. Isn't that just the way it goes? Too young for me, too old for you. Drumming her fingers on the steering wheel, as if she had made up her mind.

That night, I ran a bath and watched my body turning pink in the hot milky water, listening to another storm roll in and break across the bay. Rain on the tin roof, hesitant at first, and then thunder like something finally cracking open.

I thought of the conversation I'd had with my mother earlier about Jude. Whatever passed between us in the shop, she had felt it, and I wondered if it had bothered her—as a parent, or another woman, or both. I regretted this—firstly because I sensed that she would never be in favour of him, and also because I did not wish to eclipse my mother, even if it was, as she said, only natural. There was a sadness in this, that was perhaps the sadness of all grown daughters, for it forced me to admit that she was growing older too, and I did not want to reckon with the vulnerability that would come with her ageing.

And yet, we were both adults, and I felt for the first time deserving of a love that was not my mother's.

To recall the past is to unravel the tendrils of a bluebottle jelly-fish, map the welts left on my back and throat that summer, now long healed, though my body remembers them still.

Jude was there the day I stumbled from the waves, stinging. We had become friendly, the Man from the Deep and I, in the way you do with locals in small towns. Stay a few nights longer than most tourists and you become a little more familiar, a little less anonymous. Though I was too shy at first to call him by his name. Greeting him gruffly on the street, in the coffee shop. Returning his Hello or G'morning with a tight-lipped smile and one hand raised. Halfway between a halt and a wave.

The water was rough and dark that day, clotted with seaweed and kelp stirred up by the storms. Beach mostly emptied out, the way it would be in the winter, wind tossing a fine mist of sand along the shore. How quickly the sea can change overnight. Not really beach weather, my mother had said earlier, looking out from our verandah at the low clouds knitting together, but I had always loved to swim in summer rain. The silent sound of it hitting the ocean, small drops lost against the swell. Water above and below.

Running through the waves and diving under, I didn't see the bluebottle there in the water. Needles of pain flared up around my neck when I broke the surface. Shallow-lunged panic. Thinking at first that the swelling was my throat closing up, all breath squeezing out of me, I pushed myself towards the shore but was pulled further out in the swell. I saw it then—its translucent body floating between the waves. Plastic-bag blue. Strange somatic shape like a bladder or a kidney or a sexual organ, tentacles like threads of blue blood.

Somehow, I was swept towards land, and fell on my knees in the shallows. Instinctively I looked for my mother, though I knew she was back at the cabin, taking her afternoon rest.

Down at the other end of the beach, a family picked their way across the rock pools where kids collected silver crabs and scooped out small fish on sunnier days. It was just the three of them—two parents and a small child, red buckets bright against the grey. Too far away to hear me if I called to them over the waves.

I stood up, stumbled. Saw trees bending back against the warm wind and a tall figure emerging from the bush track. Already recognising his long-legged gait, unhurried stride. He was coming closer at a steady pace. Coming to me. Taking my elbow, looking me over while I stood there, shivering. Gritting sand between my teeth to stop myself from saying *please*. All the want in me rushing forward with the waves breaking around our feet. Waterline rising up the legs of his dark jeans, light rain pockmarking the sand.

Your boots are getting wet, I said.

Come on, he said. Come with me.

I followed him as he led the way up the overgrown track to the main street, holding back the branches as he walked ahead so they wouldn't catch my face. Later I would remember this—the feeling that he was clearing a path for me. Smell of tea tree and damp earth as we cut through the bush. Wet leaves and cool silt soft underfoot. Digging my nails into my palms, warm tears welling but not letting them spill, wiping my nose with the back of my hand. I didn't want him to see me cry, on top of it all. How much younger I'd seem then—too young. Just another girl from the city, hapless in the natural world. *Sharkbait*, like he'd said. I wanted to belong at Sailors Beach the way he did, calling trees, clouds, birds by name. From the beginning, I wanted us to be equals, I wanted to know all the things he knew—an impossible wish, but a true one.

As we walked down the track towards his house, I hugged my arms against my chest because I had nothing else to cover me—I'd left all my things on the beach.

I hardly remember my first impression of the house. Tripping inside, eyes adjusting to the dark. Knocking over paperbacks stacked by the door. Watching Jude's broad back disappear down the hall, shirt stuck to his skin with sweat. Peach-coloured cotton that looked soft. Focusing on his shoulder blades, the curve of his neck, to take my mind from the bluebottle stings rising in a rash around my throat.

Then through to the kitchen, which I would come to think of as the heart of his home. Muted light through the big glass windows that looked out onto thin and towering gum trees, trunks pale and blanched as if they'd been stripped. And outside, the wooden porch where I would spread my arms to make a cross, Jude's hands on my waist, his lips on my ear. Teaching me how to feed the birds.

Sit up here, he said, knocking on the large wooden table that dominated the room, wide as a bed but longer. Surface flawed and knotted, the grain maintaining the impression of whatever tree it had come from, but smooth against the back of my legs.

Can't remember the last time somebody got stung by a blue-bottle at Sailors. We don't get them much down here, he said. Water's always been too cold, but of course, all that's changing now.

I watched him move around the room—opening and closing cupboards, dousing a rag in vinegar over the sink, taking two beers from the fridge, brown glass bottles clinking together as he gripped them by their necks in one hand. Aware that I was near naked in the middle of his kitchen, swimsuit clinging to my damp body. Dripping water from my long hair onto the floor.

He opened our beers against the tabletop, the edge of it etched with little grooves where it had been bitten by the teeth of other bottle caps.

You don't care that it leaves a mark?

Not on the things I'm going to keep, he said. Furniture is for living in. Can't be too precious about it. A bit of wear adds character, shows you your habits, the pressure you put on things. You can tell a lot about a person from a chair, or their kitchen table.

I ran my hand along the wood grain as if it were a flank, a broad back.

Let me see, he said, and I lifted my chin so he could look. You must have swum right into the little bastard. Look here—

He pointed below my ear, across my throat and down my back. Tracing the sweep of the stings without touching me.

Hot water and vinegar should do it.

He handed me the cloth and I pressed its wet warmth against my neck. Feeling my pulse beneath, my quick-moving blood. With every blue flare of pain, my body flushed with heat and I was sure that he could feel it. Standing between my legs, close enough for me to feel his breath on my face. Crease of concern between his brows.

I kissed him then. A sudden movement, catching his lip with my teeth. The smell of beer and vinegar between us. He blinked back at me, surprised, and I wasn't sure if it was the fact of the kiss or that I had been so abrupt about it.

Sorry, I said.

Are you? he said, and when he turned from me, walked back towards the sink, I feared I'd made him angry or offended him somehow. Thinking, what would I tell my mother? That he'd been a good nurse, taking the cloth from me and rinsing it again under hot running water, wringing it out between his hands.

Here, he said. Let me.

He moved across my shoulder blades and down my back, pressing gently in all the places I couldn't reach. The kiss had been a mistake, I was sure, and he was polite not to mention it again and embarrass me further, but I turned my face away in shame. Some fire had worked its way through my bloodstream, that was all. It could have been the venom. It could have been desire. The fierce blue sting of it.

There, he said, and tossed the cloth on the floor where it landed with a dull, wet thud. One strap of my swimsuit had slipped from my shoulder and he lifted it with one finger.

Tell me, he said. Do you always wear this?

Teasing. Fixing it back in place. Lingering at my collarbone, grazing it with the back of his hand.

And then we were all lips kissing, teeth biting, hands pulling and tangling through hair. Shucking him from his shirt, digging my nails into his back. He kissed me between all the places I was stung. Blisters lighting up with his touch but the pain subsiding, making way for something new.

Later, I would ask Jude what he was doing on the beach that day when he found me all stung up on the shore.

Looking for you, he said.

And why were you looking for me?

The narrative would change, depending on the mood. Sometimes it was, Because I wanted to fuck you, his hand sliding up my leg, beneath my dress, reaching for my underwear. I found language like that blunt and crude and yet it thrilled me.

But mostly the answer was, I wanted to talk with you. Without your mother around.

And why did you want to talk with me?

Always the beggar for his love. I was like the desperate ocean, wearing away at him. The ceaseless questioning of the tide to the shore that I heard from our bedroom window all winter long. Asking, Do you love me? Do you love me?

And his answer, which never quite satisfied: If I didn't, would I still be here in bed with you?

It's not so easy, I'd tried on one occasion to explain, to tell what keeps people together, what makes them fall apart. You can leave someone and still love them. You can lie with someone and never love them at all.

So many nights I remember like that in his brass bed with the one bare bulb above. Our warmest place, with King down the end dreaming whatever it is that dogs dream. Black liquid night outside our window, wind whistling through the gaps in the wooden house, ocean just beyond. The feeling that nothing else existed, that we were outside of time, the way all lovers wish themselves to be.

I could tell I made you nervous and I liked that, said Jude, on another one of those nights. You were so shy. And it had been such a long time since anyone had been like that around me. It was sweet. Brought back some old teenage feeling. Didn't think I'd ever know that kind of thing again.

Did you think anything would happen between us?

Never expected you'd be so bold, he said. Stripping off your things in the middle of my kitchen.

Well, I needed a distraction—from my bluestings.

I was only joking. It's okay, you know, just to want someone. Nothing to be ashamed about.

I know that, I said, but I felt injured. Wondering again, how many women? In the back seats of cars parked on country highways, in the acrid stalls of pub toilets with hands pressed against graffitied walls—*For a good time call*—or sheltered by trees in a park or a graveyard or down on the beach in a quiet cove in the sand.

I've never done anything like that before, I said. Nothing like this has ever happened to me.

Me neither, he said, and it felt like a victory—to give him something new.

But then I remembered all those years between us, a gap wide enough to fall into. Eighteen years—a whole adolescence, a coming of age.

It's really true for me, I insisted. I wish you could fall in love for the first time again. Or that you'd never loved anybody else before me and neither had I.

He laughed and said, Oh, trust me. I was a pretty shitty boyfriend. And anyway, every time is like the first time. That's the beauty of love. Love erases.

I didn't know the violence of it then—that erasure. I liked the idea of Jude made into a clean slate for me, my touch negating all others', so sure then I would be the one, the last, to make an indelible mark. I wanted so badly for it to be true. That we might be like two virgins.

The next morning, I sat beside my mother in the car while we wound around the bay, which, on the map, made the shape of an ear with a tear-shaped island off the coast like a jewel earring. We were going to see the lighthouse on the cape—or what was left of it anyway, which was not much, she told me, but stones and rubble.

Yesterday's weather had cleared, and I did not want to lie on the sand waiting to spot Jude among the other swimmers, walking out of the water, flicking wet hair from his eyes, or standing on the shore rubbing his face with a towel. Remembering the rough texture of his kiss grazing my mouth and chin. I'd rushed away from him so quickly afterwards, saying, I have to go, my mother's waiting, and he'd laughed. His wooden house, the A-frame peak dwarfed by towering gums, was only up the other end of the hill from our cabin, on the edge of the bush, but it seemed inaccessible to me, like a house in a dream. It was a one-time thing, I felt sure.

We had taken up our usual positions—my mother at the wheel and me, her navigator. I had only recently got my licence and she had been encouraging, paying for lessons at a driving school. But there was something about our living together—even temporarily, in that rented house by the beach—that made us revert to our old roles. I was her only passenger again, like when I was small.

On the way to the ruins, I asked my mother questions about love. I was put in mind of it because of something she had said earlier, describing her work at the Maritime Museum, where she'd been commissioned to produce a series of illustrations for an exhibition on the lighthouses of the New South Wales coast. It suits me, she'd said, packing her sketching tools and digital camera, because I've always felt something like a lighthouse keeper's daughter. And I had imagined that to be a lonely, captive feeling.

What I wanted to know from my mother was how to reconcile the fact that some people never find love. I am sure I said it that way, *find*, like a miraculous, unintentional discovery, as if love were a stone in the sand. But to be found also implies that something lost has been returned to its place of belonging, and what did I know about love and stones? I was still holding out for a kind of love that felt like homecoming.

It's just one of those things, my mother said. Like trying to explain why bad things happen to good people.

It seemed easy, I said, to understand why the bitter and selfish and cruel might remain loveless. But, strangely, weren't they sometimes the most loved? Those who did not know how to love back. Why did we feel compelled to keep on giving?

I remembered the artist I'd studied who had once sat in a gallery and invited the audience to, one by one, cut a piece from her clothes. Some people took a tiny snip from somewhere inconspicuous—a hemline or a sleeve—while others sheared her suit away at the seams, snipping the straps of her underwear until she was stripped bare, exposed. Yes, I thought. Love could be something like that.

I think we like the idea that people can learn from each other and change, my mother said. That we might sort of break each other in, like horses.

All my mother's relationship advice has something to do with animals: *Always date men who've had pets because it proves they know how to look after something* and *A bird in the hand is worth two in the bush*, things like that.

You might be right, I said. Maybe love could be a learned thing.

My mother was leaning over the wheel, lifting up out of her seat a little to check her blind spot as we rounded a corner. She was concentrating on the road, or her mind was elsewhere, or perhaps she was afraid she couldn't give me the answers that I wanted. Her responses grew vague. She said that we all want to believe people can change, that it's possible all our mistakes might lead to learning to love better, but in her experience what they say about old dogs and new tricks is just about right.

There are no second chances, the only do-overs you get are with someone new. Look out the window there, she said then, at the lake.

On my side was the beach, and on hers, a flat expanse of water like a silver disc dotted with black swans, dark hooked necks like one half of a love heart. Once thought to be an impossible thing, existing in the minds of Europeans only as a metaphor. Until they came here, the great Down Under underbelly of the world where water drained anticlockwise and the seasons were reversed. Spring in September, smelling of jasmine and rain. Winter in July. Trees grey-green and dry all the year. Brittle, easy to burn.

This is right near the turnoff to Swan Lake, my mother said. On the other side of that water there, and a little bit further south, that's where we came to stay when Henry was little. Remember? How old were you then?

About to turn thirteen.

We had fun for a minute there, didn't we? The four of us. You loved the cabins. They were like little dollhouses, all matching.

I remembered the dunes—my mother leading the way through the scrubland in her hat and sunglasses, Henry not yet a year old, riding high in the carrier on his father's shoulders. Small enough to sit on my lap as we slid down the sand on flattened fruit boxes. You could see the ocean from up there, on the highest point of the hill. Holding my brother tight against my chest, his laughter as we gained speed, rushing towards but never reaching the blue. Mornings spent swimming in the lake. Teenagers, older than me, setting off fireworks after midnight. And the little fibro cabins, six of them clustered around the inlet, each painted in a different pastel colour and decorated in a fifties style, with matching sugar and coffee jars, knitted tea cosies. Prints of watercolour ballerinas framed on the walls. Surrounded by nothing but bush and bodies of water. Silt and soil damp beneath bare feet. Gardens of wild blue hydrangeas, the size of human heads. My mother holding my shoulder beneath a lamp while my brother slept, squeezing a tick from my arm with a pair of beauty tweezers. We played at being a different kind of family that summer, stitching ourselves together into the roles of mother, father, daughter, son. Sutures showing only in the gulf between my age and Henry's, which hinted at some long-ago rupture, an entire childhood, almost, between us. I was a small girl at the tail end of twelve, skinny and breastless, knock-knees and crowded teeth. Smiling with my mouth closed. When people asked my age and my mother wasn't in earshot, I said that I was nine.

But time caught up with us. By sixteen I was too embarrassed to hold Henry's hand in public. It was the way people stared at us when I was minding him. We both looked like our mother, which meant we looked alike, though I had dark hair and brows where he was fair. From our ages some did not guess brother and sister. My thick black eyeliner, steely gaze, the way I hunched my shoulders as if in shame—it looked like teenage motherhood. Called *whore* and *bastard* by an old man drinking from a bottle in a brown paper bag, sitting on the church steps beside the supermarket where I waited in my school skirt, Henry on my tartaned hip. Virgin Mary in blue plaid, white socks sliding down shins, waiting for our mother to bring the car around from the car park.

It's a lie that swans always mate for life, you know, my mother said. They're not as monogamous as they're famed to be. I watched a documentary about it on the ABC one night, *The Truth about Swans*.

I wanted to know what happened to the children, the cygnets, in this animal divorce. Were they abandoned in the separation, or did the swans continue to co-parent while mating with others?

You know, my mother said, it didn't say. I don't think it happens when there's kids involved. I mean, eggs, babies. I think it's only when there's a problem with nesting. If they can breed, they stay together. Unless one mate dies, in which case, I don't know. Maybe the babies learn to fend for themselves.

So, my mother said, after we'd driven in silence awhile. You seeing someone back in the city, then?

I'm not seeing anyone back in the city, I said. Looking out the window, picking at the small splinter left in the flesh of my palm where I'd lifted myself up on Jude's kitchen table.

Are you? Seeing anyone up in the Mountains, I mean.

Oh no, my mother said. I mean, I have a few well-meaning *gentleman callers*. Neighbourly types, mainly. See me in the drive and help with the shopping bags, or pop around to give me the heads-up about storms and fires. Offer to rake the leaves from the gutter for me, that sort of thing. But they seem so . . . what's the word? Old, I guess. They seem old. Time does more damage to men, in the end—at least the single ones. They just seem to go to ruin, unless someone's looking after them.

Maybe you should go younger, I said. You could pass. You're not even fifty.

Fifty! God, how awful, she said, and winced. I don't feel fifty. We should make a deal. How about, I won't see anyone younger than you, if you don't see anyone older than me. Sound fair?

Gee, I should hope so, I said, though I knew I was cutting it fine with Jude. Old enough to be— but not letting myself finish the thought. For the first time it occurred to me that he could have kids somewhere, might be married—though there was no ring, or discernible line where a long-worn wedding band might once have been. At some point I'd started checking for these things, a compulsion to look at every left hand. As if it could help me figure out the logic of who was married and who was not, but there wasn't any that I could see.

Is it true about Sylvia? I said then, reminded always by rings and fingers of a story my mother told about her mother. *Sylvia.* She'd made me call her by her first name because she'd felt too young to be a grandmother when I was born, and she would have been, I realised, only a few years older than my mother was that summer at Sailors.

After your dad left, did she really do it? Lop off her own finger, I mean.

That's what she always told us, my mother said. Her hands had swollen so much over the years she couldn't get the ring over the knuckle. She said one day she couldn't stand to look at it anymore. Though it could have been an accident, I suppose. Out in the country, chopping wood or something. We were at the snow with Dad that weekend, skiing with him and with his young wife. They were newly married then, still thinking it fun to play family with us kids. But I always believed Mum about the ring. No reason not to, though I guess she could have been making a joke of it. Always had a strange sense of humour. Anyway, I think that story felt more true to her. Don't you remember her metal finger? You were afraid of it as a baby. She had this habit of tapping it against the table when she was thinking. Used to make you cry.

I remember, I said. Or at least I think I do. It was like a suit of armour. It didn't bend where the joint should have been.

I think I would have stuck with the ring myself, my mother said. Rather than cut off my own finger. You'd think that would be the more traumatic thing.

I guess it's different, I said, because she did it to herself. She chose it.

She chose the ring once too, my mother said.

I knew the story of my mother's first memory so well it had almost become my own. Sitting between her two brothers in the back seat of the yellow Volvo on their way from Melbourne to their property on the Mornington Peninsula, pulled off to the side of the road, while my grandmother stood hoisting a rock in her hands above the near-dead thing. They'd hit it, that blur of grey-brown fur now slick with blood—once wallaby—and while her brothers laughed and made jokes about eating roadkill pie, my mother howled, stiff-limbed, knees and elbows locked in panic, great rasping breaths stringy with spit and mucus, hot tears on her red face, body turned to board and lungs expanding, filling up with her first experience of grief. My grandmother had turned to her and snapped, Tell me. What would be the crueller thing?

She stopped her screaming then, shut her mouth, sniffled. Trembling. But in the end, she won. Because inside the pouch had been a baby, still breathing, still warm. My grandmother unbuttoned her blouse and wrapped the creature in it, handed it to her daughter to hold while they drove to the animal hospital in the next town. Trucks and cars honking when they passed on the highway because there was my grandmother at the wheel, driving one-handed, smoking out the window, in her underwire. String of pearls around her neck, smear of blood on her jodhpurs where she'd wiped her hands after handling the young. No stranger to gore. Her family kept horses and she had learned to assist with the births at fourteen, pulling the foals out of the mares by their legs. My uncles were stone-silent, mortified, while my tiny mother cradled the babe. Patted the soft grey fur. Felt the fragile heart beating against her chest as she rocked it in her arms. Hushed it with soothing words she imagined a gentle mama might say. Shh, baby. You're my baby now. Go to sleep, baby. That's when she knew, she told me, that she wanted children. At four years old in her braids and dress made from Liberty fabric, she already knew.

It changes things though, my mother said then. Children do. Afterwards, all that stuff is different.

Dating, you mean? And love?

I mean, you can't even imagine it. Sometimes it feels like my capacity for love is spent, all used up on you and Henry. See, the thing is, it seems so romantic at the time—like *the most* romantic thing you could do—have a baby with someone. To give that to them. But once you do, it kind of eclipses everything. You think you're ready for it, but you're not. That kind of love? It's terrifying.

The lighthouse was close to a navy base, and as we approached, we passed cadets on the road in grey camouflage. Tall and lanky boys who looked hardly any older than my twelve-year-old brother. They ran drills on the far end of Sailors Beach. When I lay in the sand, I could see the ships in the distance, the encampment out on the point.

We parked in a dirt lot at the edge of the cliff, car wheels grinding on the gravel road. Outside, rocks and scrub and saltbush trees until the land cut away. Wind off the cove throwing grit and tangling hair. Making us silent. I could hear the waves below even when I couldn't see them.

From a distance, the lighthouse looked jagged, like a broken tooth. But you could imagine the tower there, where it had once stood, and if you didn't know you were looking at the ruins—that the navy had blown it up after a better beacon was built on the opposite shore—you might think it was only under construction. Demolished turret and sandstone rubble fenced off behind bars.

On a plaque, an acknowledgement of the traditional custodians of the land. Land that was stolen, occupied, returned in an act of reconciliation, renamed in a recovered tongue. In the regional Dhurga language, it translated to something like Bay of Plenty. Signs warning visitors about unstable ground.

My mother walked ahead, taking pictures with her digital camera. The job she had at the museum was new—something she'd applied for and taken up now that Henry was getting close to high school, needing less. When I was small, she didn't work, and then, after we left my father, she switched between temporary jobs with children or plants or animals. Working part-time in a flower shop, cutting stems, moving bouquets between buckets of water, de-thorning the roses. Washing and clipping elegant dogs, who went home in better cars to bigger houses than we did. Or being paid to look after other people's children at a local nursery. The jealousy I felt in that year I was shuffled off to school, while those other kids got to spend the day with my mother.

Later, weekends spent selling clothes at the markets in Sydney. Waking up in the early dark, and falling asleep again in the back of the car on piles of silk and denim and faux fur while my mother drove. It was a cobbled-together life, most of our things second-hand or borrowed, but my mother had her limits. There were some things she would never do for money: sex stuff, nursing, waitressing. Too gory, she said, to all of that. Though once, when she was a student, before she met my father, she had posed as an artist's model for one of her teachers. Tied up by the wrists to a wooden cross in the nude. A naked, female Christ. Left there for an hour while the artist went out to score. She shrugged when she told me this story—that was Melbourne, she said, that was the eighties—but made me promise not to tell my brother because he didn't need to think of his mother like that. *His* mother, I often thought, had become a woman so different from the one who had raised me.

I walked around the headland, away from the lighthouse, to look down at the sea below. Wrecking waters. Something violent, I always thought, about the edge of a cliff. All that rock hacked away by salt and water and time. Rougher out here, near the open ocean, than down at Sailors, Jude's beach. Already thinking of it as something that belonged to him because he had fixed up a house and made a life here, and I was only a visitor. Tourist town, he'd said, but home to him.

Near a trail leading to a camping ground was a mounted sign showing a picture of the lighthouse when it was first completed. Grim-faced Victorians in black and white, sitting on the grass in front of the lodging houses. Lounging in the sun but looking already long dead, in the way that early photographs seem to make ghosts of the living. In the picture, bungalows with wooden verandahs and picket fences marking crooked boundaries like a line of matches stuck in the sand. All vanished now. The bush had reclaimed what had been hacked away.

The sign also told a story about two teenagers from early lighthouse families, daughter of the chief and daughter of the assistant. Sixteen and nineteen in the winter of 1887. Near women.

They had been playing a game, these two girls, had broken into a fisherman's hut down on the cove in a dare or desire to be close to a man other than their fathers, to look through this stranger-man's things. The smell of brine and leather making blood quicken and hands quiver. Sand blowing in through the open door. House creaking in the wind like the sound of boot leather.

The chief's daughter dressed up in the fisherman's clothes for a laugh—his hat, too big, fell over her eyes, and his coat sleeves slipped over her slender wrists. She picked up the rifle he kept by the door, as they all did, living so isolated out on the edge. The bullet struck the assistant's girl in the temple. Tripped and it went off, the chief's daughter told the court. All in an instant.

There was no further mention on the sign of the fisherman or the murderess. No details of what happened to her after—whether she moved away or married or lived out the rest of her days on that cliff's edge—nothing, except that she was acquitted at trial, since she'd meant no harm. Only skylarking, declared the judge, and no one living to deny it.

I imagined suicide pacts made in pinkie promises, love triangles—but enough of ruins and islands and the dead. In the palm of my hand, I held a message from Jude, telling me he was at home, that he'd done enough work for the day. The door was open if I happened to be passing by. He used his mobile only for emergencies, he'd told me the day before, *fair warning*, and so I felt in that moment that he needed me. *Where are you?* the message said, and that, too, seemed like a kind of loving. Wanting me to be near, or at least to know how far.

I looked around for my mother, but she had remained on the other side of the cliff's rise, where I could no longer see her. Brief swell of panic—a childhood feeling—at my mother moving out of sight. As though, if I took my eyes off her, she would disappear.

But as I rounded the cove and began to pick my way back along the worn trail, towards the lighthouse, I could see her there on a low wall, sketching. Black hair tucked into the red windbreaker zipped to her chin, a few strands picked up and tousled loose by the wind.

It is hard to explain to people who meet her now that my mother used to be a different kind of woman. I wondered sometimes if Henry could even imagine it—aviator sunglasses staring down the highway, red-painted nails bitten to the quick, cigarette burning in her right hand while she steered with her left. In the car her mother's daughter, despite it all. Hair dyed copper from a thick paste that smelled of mud and earth and left rust-coloured rings around the bathtubs of our rented rooms. All the men who came to visit, leaving behind their humble offerings—flowers and wine bottles and wooden stringed instruments shaped like strange fruits. Mandolins and banjos and parlour guitars rounded like pumpkins or papayas or chestnuts—objects for my mother to sketch, and though they were given to her to play, her fingertips remained soft. And then there was the night we came home to find the necks snapped, guitars with their bodies kicked in and splintering wood. Broken bottles and shattered glass, a rock through the window, my mother's silk dresses ripped up and thrown in a heap on the floor.

Desire, I was only beginning to understand that day at the ruins, comes in many forms, and some of them are violent. We learn this in the stories we are told about love. Struck by an angel's arrow or drugged by a loveflower, desire wounds, and I had felt its blue sting. The thought of him all day, like pushing on a bruise.

By the time I reached my mother, she'd finished her sketch of the lighthouse, its tumbled tower. No light now to give.

They built in the wrong place, she said. Did you notice how it looked out in the wrong direction? Facing the open sea, instead of the mouth of the cove. Caused more harm than good. Ships got their signals crossed, and so they tore it down, built a better one at Point Perpendicular. I suppose that's the one I should be drawing, but I always find the ruins more interesting.

What is it about her and me, I wonder, that has always drawn us to these kinds of places? Something lonely deep down in the bone. A marrowed loneliness, passed down womb to womb. We wanted to believe, my mother and I, that love could restore what was beyond repair, and if not, at least let us walk around in the wreckage.

Maybe to be a lighthouse keeper's daughter is to live a reckless, freewheeling life. Dwelling on the threshold between abandon and abandonment, perched above the ocean's violence, a father's job to light the way for those travelling through the dark, not yours.

But no father can protect his daughters from growing up and becoming the kinds of women who are bold enough to enter the houses of strange and solitary men. There is nothing that can protect them from the high wild loneliness of such a life or the desires that come with it. What you might do for a way out.

The relief of Jude's house—its musty darkness and cool interior. White sheets on his brass bed at the top of the A-frame. Sloping walls and bare dark-wood bones. Dust falling from the rafters and afternoon light filtering in through the dirty glass windows. His smell of salt and tobacco and orange timber stain. Dressing beneath the covers, reaching to the floor for my underwear— cotton and lace curled from being tossed by his hand.

I told him how I'd been out on the cape that afternoon, that I'd seen a tiny island in the distance, and a broken lighthouse on the hills like a toppled crown. It was a false beacon, I said. Built facing the wrong direction.

No man is an island, said Jude, musing. John Donne said that.

No man is an island, but every woman is, I replied. I said that. And then, steeling myself:

So, then. You married?

Surprised when he laughed, too embarrassed to ask what was so funny. Trying to appear seasoned, brave, lying in his bed with the sheets tucked up under my arms.

Shouldn't you have asked me that before?

I'm asking now, aren't I?

No, he said. I'm not married. Would it have mattered if I was?

I wanted to tell him yes, of course it would have mattered, that I wouldn't be there in his bed, but I no longer knew if that was true. People acted selfishly, betrayed and abandoned one another—that was common. I'd never done anything truly bad or transgressive, but I worried this was not because of a strong moral foundation or sense of virtue. I was no better than anyone else, I feared. It was not that I lacked those kinds of desires, but I was afraid that if I acted on them, they would undo me. In a world without boundaries, I could lose myself.

That afternoon we played a game of trust. Jude and I, out on the porch. He showed me how, if you stood with your arms out, the birds would alight along your arms and shoulders. The trees were alive with them in the summertime down south—brightly coloured parrots, rainbow lorikeets, pink-throated galahs. The birds are so tame down here, they'll eat right out of your hand, he said. Splitting the dimpled skin of an orange with his thumb, breaking it apart into segments. He pressed a piece of spoiled fruit into my hands and taught me how to feed the birds.

At first I was afraid of their sharp claws near the crook of my neck, the way their feathers grazed my jaw, the beating of so many wings. I shut my eyes, scrunched my shoulders up by my ears.

I don't like birds, I said. Too flighty. Too nervous.

But then Jude's hands on my waist. Closing the distance between our two bodies. Holding me steady while the birds settled on my shoulders. Waves broke beyond the blue gums and bloodwoods that framed his porch—I could hear the rush and sigh of them.

They'll be afraid if you're afraid, he said. But if you trust them, they'll trust you.

I can see that what I am doing here, sitting at my grandmother's writing desk in my mother's spare room, is trying to create my own portrait of the man I'd known thirteen years ago. Call it *Portrait of the Man Before He Was a Father. Portrait of the Lover Before the House of Love Burned Down.* The human hand, I learned in one of my art history classes, is one of the most difficult shapes for an artist to master, but I can tell you about Jude's long fingers—beautiful and slender, strong, decisive. Piano-playing fingers, though he'd never learned. The way he rolled his cigarettes with such care. Peel of lemon kept in his leather smoking pouch to keep the tobacco from drying out. Lining pinches of Champion Blue along the little white rolling paper, filter sticking out the corner of his mouth, brow creased in concentration because he was far-sighted but refused to get his vision tested. But you'd look sexy with glasses, I'd argue with him that winter. Glasses, he insisted, are for old folks, love. You calling me old?

It became another game between us. I would shake my head and say, *No*. Would never. Climbing into his lap, kissing the hollow below his ear. By then I knew all the ways to make him feel young. And maybe I liked it—reading him the menus in dimly lit restaurants on the few real dates we bothered with. It felt good that he needed me for something, that there were things I had over him too—like my twenty-twenty vision, and time. Although time, as Jude liked to say, *time is on nobody's side.*

But then, his nails—cut short, but tobacco-stained, thin rim of dirt or dust beneath, cuticles ragged and growing up over the crescent. That was Jude. Everything about him was careful up to a point, beyond which he seemed to care no more. Hands roughened by woodworking, dry and scarred in places by the paring knife. I searched his palms, trying to tell our future, but they only told stories about his past.

My mother hardly got in the water during our stay at Sailors Beach. She has never liked to get her hair wet, complaining it grows heavy and takes hours to dry. She was afraid of the way the sand sucked out from beneath her feet, and of the waves that crashed against her body, flapping her arms in the shallows in a way that struck me as girlish. It's too rough, she'd say, or too cold, or I'm afraid of sharks. You know only yesterday they spotted a bronze whaler on the next beach over?

I'd always seen my mother as a pioneer—forging ahead while I trailed after her, trying to make sure nothing got left behind. As a child, I'd imagined her as something diffuse, like vapour or air.

Necessary, and all around me, but somehow elusive, ungraspable. As if she might slip through my hands the way she had my father's, and all the men who came after. And though I'd often wished she would become more cautious, I found myself unsettled by her new timidity. Seeing snakes in the shadows, shark fins in the blue, her fear of sunburn and sleeping in the house alone. Now I was the one leading her by the hand into the water. Keeping an eye on her if she drifted out too far, calling her back down the beach away from where the waves dragged and ripped. Although maybe this, too, was the natural way of things. From child to mother to child again. For the first time, I felt a need to establish a life outside her purview, a life that was mine alone.

At twenty-four I was a late bloomer to rebellion. My mother had never made any rules for me growing up, and so I'd never had need of breaking them. Her own upbringing had been strict, disciplined, Sylvia being of the generation that believed children should be seen and not heard. Sometimes, when I think of her girlhood, I am reminded how unlike it was to my own. For my mother, our bohemian, transient life was a rejection of all the things she had been taught to want. For her, it was a choice.

Perhaps my mother felt that all those curfews and strictures had only served to push her away, or maybe from her own experience she knew how easily they were foiled anyway, climbing out windows into the waiting arms and cars of various boys and men.

Or perhaps she had been lenient because during my adolescence she had embarked on another project of motherhood. Henry still small and entirely dependent on her. Compared to a baby, a teenage daughter was grown. In high school, I was serious and studious, but I found kindred company in the other girls who liked to spend their lunch hours in the art rooms, clay beneath their fingernails, listening to the radio while they spun the pottery wheel and I wrote in my notebook. Also, there was the curiosity of my mother—beautiful, and relatively young in comparison to the other parents, which earned me a certain amount of respect from my peers. Those years had passed untroubled—partly, I think, because of my own inclinations and partly because I sensed that my mother lacked the capacity to worry about me if I did become reckless.

Still, I took to duplicity with an aptitude that surprised me. All my years of quiet solitude, it seemed that's what they were for. When I told my mother I was going for an evening swim or had spent the afternoon reading, she didn't question me, though if she'd looked she would have seen I'd made hardly any progress with *The Lover*. For more than a week, my bookmark had remained firmly in place. I read the same lines over and over at the end of the day, too tired from sun, from sex, from swimming. *I say I've always been sad. That I can see the same sadness in the photos of myself when I was small. That today, recognising it as the sadness I've always had, I could almost call it by my own name, it's so like me.* And maybe I recognised myself in those lines, thinking of my own childhood, the raised-by-wolves look I had in certain pictures from the years after my mother left my father. But it was summer, and I did not want to read any more about pain, about sadness. I was occupied, for the first time in my life, by pleasure.

Together, my mother and I walked on the beach in the mornings, and after she returned to the cabin, I was free to spend my afternoons with Jude. Taking the path beneath the tall blue shadows of the eucalyptus trees that led from the beach to his yard. Knocking on the glass of the back window.

Cool drink? he'd say.

And I'd nod.

By our last week at Sailors, there were white lines across my back from the strings of my swimsuit. Burned, said Jude, pressing his fingertips against my thigh and lifting them off again, watching a pale print rise back against the pink. We were lying in his bed eating cut squares of mango sprinkled with lime and chilli salt, staining our fingers, licking the juice from each other's faces and pulling the bits of thread from our teeth. Skins and discarded Durex beside the bed in an overflowing ashtray.

Does your mother know you smoke?

Sitting up in the brass bed and watching me dress. Smoothing out a crumpled cigarette between his fingers.

No.

Does she know about me?

No.

How do you get around that?

Good at keeping secrets, I said, slipping knickers on beneath my skirt, buttoning my blouse.

So, it would bother her, then?

The smoking? Yes. Even though I only do it sometimes, and she smoked for years when I was small.

Still, I continued, I have a whole routine. I brush my teeth, carry mints, wash my hair. Learned it from her. When I was a teenager she used to take these long showers—sometimes three or four in a day—and come out smelling of shampoo and Listerine and a perfume like crushed lilacs. Thought she was just going through a phase of being really clean—until I found her emergency pack of menthols stashed in the bathroom cupboard. As a kid, I used to tally up her cigarettes on a list stuck to the fridge, so I suppose it was only fair she started keeping it from me. What a little monster I was. Every time she quit, it was horse-riding lessons for me up on the cliffs around Malabar, overlooking the beach. You know, with the extra money we saved, we could afford it. She wanted me to learn to ride like she did as a girl, spending her weekends at my grandmother's place in the country, but it was always two weeks on, and then she'd start up again. It wasn't until she was pregnant with Henry that I thought she'd quit for good.

Henry is your brother?

Yes. Half-brother, technically. Funny to think you didn't know that.

I didn't mean would she mind about the smoking, before, said Jude. I meant about the other.

Oh. Would she mind about you? No. I don't think so. Of course not. Why would she?

Well, I am a lot older than you, in case you haven't noticed.

No, you're not. And she's not judgemental like that. She was nineteen when she met my dad—much younger than I am now—and he was ten years older. Anyway, she likes you. That time in your shop, you talked together for ages.

But you haven't told her.

No.

And you're not planning to.

I don't know, I said.

Our afternoons were stolen time, precious to me, and I maintained my old superstition that if I spoke about what I loved, it would somehow be taken from me. I wanted to keep it close inside, this feeling, to be turned over and examined only in private, at least until—until what? What was I waiting for, perched on the edge of his bed? Some confirmation that it might be something more. Always wary because I sensed my capacity for loving was bottomless. I thought then that unlike me, Jude trusted easily, believed in the kindness of strangers, left his door unlocked and open for anyone to walk right in.

I know how it is, he said, his tone shifting. Voice warm and low. Intimate again. You like it this way. Sneaking around.

And it seemed to me he was offering a way out, and so I shrugged, nodded.

Say nothing more, he said, reaching for me. Arms around my waist, pulling me back to bed, unbuttoning again. Saved from having to explain, I kissed him to stop talk, to stop thought. I took the cigarette from his hand, and we passed it between us, blowing smoke rings into each other's mouths. I closed my eyes, my head light, giddy.

You look flushed, my mother said when I got back to the cabin that evening, later than usual. Have you been out there all day?

I told her I'd fallen asleep on the beach. Sure the smell of him was still on me, though I'd washed under the cold showers in the car park where other tourists rinsed sand from their feet.

Too much sun, she concluded, her green eyes narrowed. You should be more careful, she said, and I promised her that I would be.

But as we learn to trust, we take more risks, and I agreed to meet Jude late on the beach, on my second-last night down south. At first I was nervous as I moved beneath him, whispering, Do you hear that? and What's that sound? Thinking I heard someone coming. Our bodies made a sound like footsteps shuffling by, rutting out a hollow in the sand.

He moved his hands around my body, under and between and inside my clothes. I wanted to come apart under his hands, for all of me to unravel like a loose thread or a tugged ribbon or a string unlaced, opened and undone. He touched me with what I can only think to describe as authority—so different from my sexual experiences so far, those incoherent collegiate fumblings. It had all been mysterious then—sex. And no skill in it. Not like with Jude, on the beach that night with the white sand singing, or in his kitchen with the doors and windows open, our voices rising to join the birds.

Afterwards, we lay on our backs side by side, sheltered by the bush on the fringes of the shore. Sand in all my seams and cool beneath bare shoulders. Light southerly stirring the trees, skimming away the day's heat. Jude turned to me, rolling onto his side. He brushed the sand from my cheek and said, Sleep with me tonight.

I thought I just did.

I don't mean fucking, he said, and I marvelled at the word in his mouth—not a curse or a blunt force but somehow spoken with lightness, worn in with the warmth of many years.

I mean come home with me. Spend the night. I want to be able to reach for you.

Giving my arm a squeeze.

Of course, I had longed for this. To fall asleep in his warmth, to feel that our time together for once was unlimited. But I felt guilty at the thought of abandoning my mother on a holiday that was supposed to be for the two of us, *just us girls*. I also knew that if I confessed to her then, I'd have to explain all the other days. The things I'd done while she rested through the long, hot afternoons when I was supposed to be swimming, or picking up something in town. Coming back to her dry-haired and empty-handed, saying, I only dipped my toes in, or They were out of milk at the shops.

I shook my head. I can't, I said. My mother—

You two are very close.

It was just the two of us for a long time.

I turned to him, so we were face to face, the warmth of our breath between us. Jude, I said, my hand on his cheek. I could feel the words forming in my mind—*I love you, I love you*—though in the winter, I'd come to see this as foolish. To think I could have loved him then, when I was only playing in the shallows. But I had never acted out of desire alone, and I had no other words to hold my longing.

Or maybe it just was, right from the start. Who is to say what love is or what it wants to be, the shape it takes, or how quickly it comes on? Love has always made a fool of time.

I'll see you tomorrow, I said.

Right. Tomorrow.

Standing and brushing off his jeans. Offering me his hand.

We were feeling our way in the dark, Jude and I. Walking back up the other side of the hill alone, I pictured white grains of sand falling from my body as I shook loose my dress, my hair.

On our last day at the beach, it rained. Waking to the sound of it on the tin roof like fingers drumming impatiently across a wooden desk and listening as it soon gave way to heavy, biblical rain. Everything wet and shaking, streets turned to rivers, water pooling on the road down the end of the hill.

So much for one last swim, my mother said, as I came into the living room. Catching my reflection in the mirror above the mantelpiece. My face marked with sleep, pillow creases and dark shadows. Suppose it's best that we're going home tomorrow.

Why didn't you wake me? I said. It's late. It's already eleven.

Thought maybe you slept badly too. I kept hearing things. The front light was flicking on and off. I thought someone was prowling around outside.

I didn't hear anything, I said.

It was a busy morning, and I was eager for the rituals of packing to be done with. Sweeping the sand from the floor, drying the dishes, bringing our wet towels and bathers in from the line, soaked and heavy with rain.

Slow down, would you? You're making me nervous, my mother said as I dropped a stack of plates back into the cupboard, china rattling china. What's gotten into you? You're so restless today.

I just want to get this done, so I can make the most of the day, I said. Thinking, What would Jude be doing now? I didn't know when he left for work, or on what days, whether he was an early riser or slept late. His routines and habits unknown to me then.

I knew the shape of his mouth, his rough kiss, the small white scar on his lip in the shape of a clipped fingernail that only showed when he shaved. Cat's claw, he'd tell me later, once we began to trade the stories of love and cruelty that had shaped our different childhoods on opposite sides of the city, and eighteen years apart. Reached to pet the neighbour's one when I was a kid and she lashed out.

I looked around the cabin—its white walls, the linen curtains that puffed in the breeze like sails, paintings of boats and nautical knots. This place, I knew, would not remember me. Already, most traces of my presence had been swept away and scrubbed clean. But what about Jude? I wanted to stain him, like pollen. Wanted to press into his skin, *Remember me here.*

Rushing through the rain down the street and up the other side of the hill to his door. From outside, his house had a closed-up look about it, windows dark and drawn. No rust-red truck parked patiently out the front, wheels splattered with the hard clay dirt of country roads. I wondered for the first time if it belonged to Jude. I'd taken it as another part of the landscape before, like the tall thin eucalypts or the surfboards stacked out the front of the house next door. Hadn't given it much thought, until I noticed it was gone.

I'd learned to take Jude's shortcut from the beach, down the private path he'd made by beating back the brush. He left the back door open when he was home, music drifting outside, an old album on the stereo. Strings swelling and Patsy Cline's voice full of sorrow singing 'Leavin' on Your Mind'. Drowning out the birds that gathered to feed on the bottlebrush and flowering gum and silver princess flowers. Inside, the warmth of a lived-in place, the hum and murmur of activity. Sound of a handsaw cutting its teeth into new wood. Grease-spattered frying pan left on the stove. Smell of cigarettes and bacon and reheated coffee, Bialetti coming to the boil.

For the first time, I knocked on the front door. Waited, water rolling down the sleeves of my mother's jacket. Of course, I thought, from the kitchen he wouldn't hear me over his records and the rain, so I slipped around the side passage between the house and the neighbour's fence, pushing past the bins and wet ferns and agapanthus flowers shaking their heads until I came into the yard. Scratches on my shins from stray twigs, wet leaves sticking to my boots.

At the back window, through the watery glass, I could see the empty kitchen, dishes drying on the rack, and beyond that, the big wooden table where, for the first time, we'd kissed. Strangers then, and strangers still. The door was locked—he'd left it open for me all week when he was home, but he hadn't given me a key. In his absence, the room seemed full with all the other hours he must have stood at the window, looking out from the kitchen at those same old trees, another woman's warmth against his back.

Jude had let me into his home, his bed, and this had seemed so generous that it shocked me to realise then how private he was. How rarely he spoke about himself, his life. He wore those years like the lines on his face, carrying them with him so casually. Giving me just enough of him that I wouldn't think to ask for more.

You look like a picture of the Virgin I saw once in a basilica when I lived in Spain, he'd told me one afternoon in his room when I was sitting astride him. Afternoon light and hair in my face. Golden brown, he said, like molasses. Lifting a strand and letting it fall.

You lived in Spain?

For a while. He shrugged. I was nineteen. It was another life.

I had dreamed of going to Spain that year, and all around Europe. Whenever I mentioned the idea of travelling to Jude he was encouraging, saying things like, Oh yes you must, or Everyone should get to see Europe when they're young. Always *you*, never *we*. Erasing himself from the picture, until eventually I let it go. More and more, as our relationship deepened, it began to seem like those plans had been a fantasy. Jude and Sailors Beach, that was real. He had settled there, that much was clear, and the rest of the world he dismissed with a shrug. Another time, another life. How many had there been? Far from this house by the beach.

If Jude was a house, I sensed that he held many hidden rooms. He had turned the light on in only one of them, and he'd made me feel so welcome, so warm, that I'd forgotten about all those other places left in the dark.

I feel unmoored, my mother said, back at the cabin that afternoon. Sitting down beside me on the couch, sighing. She had her hands in her lap, facing up, as if to show me they were empty. Childlike, with nails clipped short, small palms. She always said I had my father's hands, and there was a time I collected these things she told me, as if to remember—like proof—that he was a part of me too. Because when I looked in the mirror I couldn't see it, and since my mother and I were on our own again that summer—two single women, moving around each other in quiet orbit—it was easy to think sometimes it had always been the two of us, and would only ever be that way.

We're not defined by touch, I thought. It's absence that contours the body, changes the shape of it, and yet Jude walked through the world like he wasn't afraid of anything, like nothing could hurt him. I'd never known a man like that. Even my father, a tall man, had been known to stoop.

Outside it was clearing, droplets of rain running from the leaves and plucking at the tin roof. Watery and musical. Gutters turned to rivers and the ocean always in the distance so it seemed like we were surrounded by water. The kind of weather where a house becomes a boat and I could see what my mother meant—that we had been cut loose, were drifting. It was an old, familiar feeling.

There had been no word from Jude, though I had tried to reach him. Sent a message that said, *I came by*, and then, later, *Will I see you before I go?* Maybe he's driving, I thought, remembering how he'd said that was part of his job—going out to other towns, searching for pieces he could fix up or reuse, returning with old timber, hardwood floorboards and broken furniture. Abandoned things. One man's junk is another's bread and butter, as he liked to say. I started to worry then, about the weather, the wet roads. Rain that made the highways slick and the fog that slunk in low around the valleys. Funny how he hadn't mentioned he'd be gone today, left no note. It wasn't like him, I caught myself thinking, but of course, we hardly knew each other at all. The force with which I remembered this was visceral. My stomach dropped, I felt nauseous.

Come on, my mother said. No point in our moping about. It's our last night. Let's go have a drink. Let's go out.

There was only one pub in town and that night it was crowded with damp bodies. Smell of hops and beer spilled on old carpet, wet leather and flannel. It smelled like men, like my father. He had learned to drink in a dry country, during the droughts of the late sixties, the year he turned thirteen, and he never really stopped. There's always a drought somewhere, was his reasoning. Early memories of scuffing my shoes at the bar, kicking my feet from the high stool, drinking pink lemonade and watching the races on TV. Picking out the winners for my father by their names. He taught me to read that way. Blue Velvet, Lady Luck, Rain Lover. Our bets were low.

A cricket match played on a screen suspended in one corner— white figures on a vivid green field. The clicking of cue balls and ice in glasses and people cheersing their neighbours, slopping beer and whiskey and wine, water and liquor spilling onto their sleeves. Pokies blinking neon in a darkened back room. Laughter like the whole town had gathered there to seek shelter.

It's every man and his dog in here tonight, my mother said, but as I scanned the crowd—beer bellies spilling over belts and shirts sticking with sweat—I thought, no, not every man. I couldn't locate Jude among them.

While my mother went to find a table, I waited at the bar, watching a group of people playing pool in the back corner. A woman was getting ready to take her shot. There was something familiar about her. She was dressed like the men, in brown boots, a black T-shirt and dark jeans that fit close against the curve of her hips. When she leaned across the table, her body looked soft. In that group she was the only woman, but she seemed so at ease—sipping her beer, dusting the cue with chalk, stalking around to the other side of the table to get the right angle—and I think I envied that. The way she moved through men like she was parting water.

Behind the bar was a woman about my mother's age, I guessed, or slightly older, though it was hard to tell—her face aged by a life spent in the sun. Coarse blonde fringe and long hair pulled back into a ponytail, lips painted in a pink frost, skin loose around her arms. The kind of woman Jude would have known how to charm, to be easy with. He probably knew her by name. Unlike me, asking in a soft voice so she had to ask me to repeat it, Can you please tell me what kind of wines you have?

The red kind and the white kind, sweetheart.

Two glasses of red. Please. Thank you. Sorry.

Quite a scene in here tonight, isn't it? said my mother, as I set our glasses down. House red. Cheap, like the wine I drank with

Bonnie and Petra on Friday nights that left purple rings at the bottom of the coffee mugs we used as wine glasses.

In the car we had been quiet. Driving through streets wet and rivery, wheels shearing away at the deep dirty puddles. Passing the lake, its full lip quivering, spilling over. All day there'd been a feeling in my stomach like a knot in a chain—the more I worked at unpicking it, the tighter it seemed to grip. Thinking of Jude's house as I'd seen it that morning—locked up and dark. Caught the whiff of abandonment like salt on the breeze. Trees in the yard empty of birds, and I wondered where they flew to seek shelter. It seemed like something he would have known—migratory patterns, the habits of birds. He knew the tides, could explain how they were tied to the movements of the moon with an invisible thread, tracked the changes in the weather through the wind. He'd seemed so unlike the boys I'd known—calling when he said he'd call, leaving the door open for me.

In his absence, I imagined the house had revealed something about Jude's true nature—private, and unyielding in all the places I'd thought he was inviting me in.

You're quiet tonight, my mother said.

With the wine in my blood, I could have told her about it then. Bold enough and wanting, suddenly, a witness. But what words would I use to describe to my mother what we did together? Did not have the language for it. Could not look her in the eye and call it love.

It's just loud in here, I said. And I don't know. Going home tomorrow. Going back to work.

They don't pay you enough, my mother said.

I know, I said. But it's only for this year.

The bookshop closed through most of January, when the city emptied out after the holiday rush, but soon I would return to my routine of opening shifts, getting up at dawn to catch two trains and a bus across to the other side of the city from where I lived. Those early mornings alone in the cool, dusty dark had been one of the things I'd liked best about the job when I started. Music playing loud over the café stereo while I drank my coffee and took my time counting out the cash for the registers. The promise of all those books waiting to be read, passing my hands along their spines before the customers came in, titles neatly alphabetised on the shelves. There was order, everything in its place. During my shift when the shop was quiet, I wrote ideas for stories on strips of receipt paper. But the hours exhausted me. I was not, by nature, a morning person. When I returned home in the afternoons, I emptied my pockets of paper scraps into the drawers of my desk, where they collected like dry, fallen leaves, and fell asleep in the time I'd planned to spend writing. That had been the point of standing on my feet all day for minimum wage, arches aching from the heel of my boots—the flexibility of a casual job.

My mother said she was looking forward to going home to the Mountains, to Henry, to her garden.

We have to bring him with us next time, she said. It's a stupid arrangement I have with his father. Doesn't seem fair he gets to keep him for the whole summer holidays, while I get the boring school slog all year long. Sometimes I wish I could be the fun one, like I was with you. But I suppose I was much younger then. It's different this time around, being one of the older mums.

You're hardly old.

Older, she said. Not old. Still, it's a big difference. Being in your twenties, versus being in your forties. Although sometimes I feel just the same, like I haven't changed at all.

I thought of the stories she'd told me about when she was younger, all the horses of her youth. Maybe it started back then, the belief that she could outrun any feeling if she moved fast enough, and I imagined it came back to her in certain moods. The desire to ride all night, like she'd never been hurt. Boot heels digging into a warm flank, hooves pounding on the hard dirt of her mother's farm. Urging the mare forward, learning to move with the animal's body, to balance, to anticipate its leaps and intuit its moods. My mother and the mare, jumping over dry riverbeds. Trusting the horse, trusting herself, her heart growing light.

Do you miss riding? I asked her then.

What made you think of that?

I don't know. Never asked before.

I miss the horses, she said. But I couldn't do it now, I'd be scared.

You mean of falling?

She nodded. Horses can sense it, you know. The fear, it frightens them.

My mother finished her wine and looked down at her hands, chapped and red from working in the soil most of the summer.

It's funny how things work out, she said.

What things? I said.

Oh, you know. Life, everything.

I knew then that she was thinking about my father.

My father had frequented the bar where my mother worked during art school and so, as my grandmother had been fond of saying, *she might've known*. But she was young, only nineteen, and he'd seemed so unlike the other regulars, the groups of men who swept in with the after-work rush, slapping each other's backs and sucking beer foam from their lips, yelling about Collingwood versus Carlton while my father sat alone at the end of the bar, reading. He was quiet and held his liquor well, so it was hard to tell, at first, how much he drank. In the large, grey woollen overcoat he always wore, his hair slicked back behind his ears, he looked to my mother like someone from another time. It is easy, I have learned, to mistake solitude for softness, for depth. She liked being near him.

They talked about what he was reading—old pulp novels and classic mysteries, mainly, the kinds of stories that would have once been serialised in magazines, and sometimes poetry too. She told him about the paintings she was working on and began to look forward to these conversations, his nightly presence at the bar. His company made her shifts more bearable, and when he was there, the other men tended to leave her alone. Topping up his wine so he might stay a little longer—my mother the enabler. Books were his education, he told her. He'd dropped out of school at sixteen, and now he was playing catch-up. How different he must have seemed from the tennis-playing grammar-school boys she'd grown up with, sons of doctors and lawyers and stockbrokers fated to be the same. My father, for his part, looked at my mother with her ripped stockings, her second-hand clothes and mess of wild black hair, and saw her as something like a charming street urchin from an old-fashioned movie, Audrey Hepburn as a Covent Garden flower girl in *My Fair Lady*. Imagine his shock the first night he walked her home after closing time and discovered my mother lived in a white three-storey house that looked like a wedding cake, overlooking Fawkner Park—just one of the comforts she left behind when she chose a life with my father.

Theirs was an on-again, off-again kind of love. My father disappearing for months at a time, sometimes for work, sometimes for no reason at all. In the meantime there were other men, but my father always returned, and she always went back to him. This went on for four years until, abruptly, one winter, they married, in an affair largely organised and entirely paid for by my grandmother. Six months later, I was born.

When I was a child, I used to make up extraordinary stories about my father's absence. *My father was a captain and he died at sea.* For some time, I had gone to visit him in rooms in different parts of the country. Bachelors' places, like bedsits, full of other men like him. Drinkers, drifters. I never liked those places—not because of the men, who lingered in the hall, leaning against the doorframes whenever I passed. They never leered or whistled— they had their morals, obeying some code of honour to respect each other's daughters. But my father kept sad quarters, and it seemed, for a long time, that the only men I knew were broken ones, who belonged to nothing and no one. If you hadn't been there—been that girl, standing in the dim hall on the piss-stained carpet, looking into the faces of these other lost fathers and trying to recognise your own—you might have thought there was a romance to it. I met boys like that later—loved them, even—who courted poverty, donned it like a chic second-hand coat. We were teenagers and it was cool then to buy all your clothes from the Salvation Army, to live the way I'd always lived. Getting things for next to nothing, or for free. *If you had been there*, I wanted to say to these boys, in my first year of university, visiting their rented rooms full of cigarette smoke, beer cans, sleeping with them on their mattresses on the floor. *If only you had seen those other rooms.*

We had waited a long time, my mother and I, for my father to get his life together. As we moved in and out of motels, houses, we tracked him—from Broken Hill to Adelaide, down near the Bight and across the Nullarbor—while he went searching for better luck or money. For years, my mother continued to wear her ring. Until I was ten and she met Henry's father, they remained legally married. Divorces are expensive, my mother said, by way of explanation. We never had the money.

When I turned eighteen, I stopped trying to track him down. I was on my way to university, eager to leave the sadness of childhood behind, and I had the sense that these visits were too much for my father too. So, in the way of lonely people, we let each other go. In the last note he wrote me, postmarked Coober Pedy, he said with resignation that he had expected this day would come. No fight left in my father, then. *You've always been your mother's daughter*, it read. But with the looping *g*'s and sloped *s*'s, it could have been written in my own hand.

I looked around me. People were streaming into the pub now, shaking the rain from their jackets and umbrellas. From the back of the room, a sound like the sudden crack of bone—the pool cue slamming against the ball, followed by a round of laughter, cheering, and when I looked up, there was Jude. Taller than the rest, in the middle of the crowd. Hat perched atop his head like a crown. The sight of him after the day's silence was a blunt fact, like a slap. Eyes stinging. It was the feeling of a salt wind breaking open an old wound, exposing it to the elements again.

He was surrounded by people—one man handed him a beer, others clapped him on the shoulder like he was their own kin. I watched as the woman from the game of pool leaned in close to talk to him above the hum, her lips close to his ear. He turned to follow her through the crowded bar. She was leading him by the hand.

You've lost all your colour, my mother said. Isn't that the man from the shop over there? Gosh, he's a stray, isn't he?

If she had seen what I had seen—those two figures receding—and guessed that there had been something more between me and Jude than polite hellos on the beach and in the streets of that small town—if she'd known it all from the look on my face—she said nothing more about it then.

I would learn that in a crowd, Jude was never mine. He could work the room like someone with tricks in his pocket. Always knew the right story to tell, looked people in the eye when he spoke to them. There was a power in walking down the street with him, the way he carried himself like the world's beloved son, whereas I had always felt like its illegitimate daughter. He would nod to the people he passed. Hats tipped in his direction. He belonged to the whole town, and so it belonged to him. Watching him that night, I'd been reminded of my father—the way he had always been quick to pull a coin from behind my ear when I was a child, and just as quick to disappear.

And Jude, too, was gone now, out of sight. But I did not doubt that it was him—too attuned, from weeks of watching him on the beach, to how he walked into a room, the way the energy shifted, how his voice carried in the air.

I was surprised by the realisation that even if he was not reliable in the way that I'd imagined, I did not desire him any less. I could see for the first time how it might feel good to make mistakes with someone, sway together, embrace the drift. And maybe I sensed it, wanted it then. The ways we might either break each other in or burn each other up.

I found him in the smoking section, standing with a group of people, eyes red with smoke and inebriation. The words *girlfriend lover wife* rolling through my mind like poker machine reels. Of course, I'd checked his medicine cabinet—a single toothbrush, tube of toothpaste crusted around the cap, bottle of Listerine with an unbroken seal and a three-pack of soap called Imperial Leather. No evidence of women's things.

Sharkbait! he called, his voice like a boat tilting before righting itself. Didn't expect to see you here. Joking, Of all the gin joints in all the world . . . and moving away from the crowd. Hand on my arm, leading me away towards the dark mouth of the pokies room. Machines trilling in the background, our faces lit in a pale neon. Pulsing blue, green, red, pink, violet.

I came past your house today, I said.

Ah. Wasn't home. Ceiling in the shop sprung a leak, and then I really needed a beer, so. Here we are.

I sent you a message.

I'm bad with my phone, love. Anyone will tell you that.

This was a version of a fight we'd have once I moved down south. Nights when Jude came home long after I'd gone to bed. I'd lie awake listening for the sound of his truck coming up the hill, the engine's cooling hum. Waiting to hear his heavy boot tread on the stairs. Relief mixed with anger when he fell in beside me, his breath sour, our voices tight in the dark. Fighting in tense whispers, like we didn't want the dog to hear.

Where were you?

Same place as always.

I've been calling you.

Didn't hear my phone.

But you always keep it in your jacket pocket. You think, after all this time, that I don't know how you wear your jacket?

Jude, I would learn, needed not to feel bound to anyone—love with a loose leash. To return not out of obligation but of his own free will, and for me to trust that he would. To Jude, that was love. That trust. He needed my faith in him in order to feel free.

I was worried, that's all, I said, that night in the pub. You disappeared. I wanted to at least say goodbye.

I hate goodbyes, he said. Anyway, it kind of seems more like you're angry with me.

I'm not angry.

You are. I know you are. What is it that you want from me? he said. Tell me. It's exhausting, always having to guess. I mean, you do realise I have a life here. This isn't just a holiday for me. Maybe for you it's a bit of fun, something to tell your girlfriends about back home, but the things I do here actually have consequences.

I have to work. There are things in my life I can't drop. When you go home tomorrow, I still have to live here.

You're kind of patronising when you're drunk, you know that?

I'm not drunk. You've never seen me drunk. You know what your problem is? he said. You think you're delicate, but you're not.

Fuck you.

What? Are you going to tell me you never want to see me again? As if you were planning to. I know what it is to be used, love, and don't get me wrong, I didn't say I minded. But there's no need to cause a scene, pretending this all meant something more to you than it did.

I have to go—

I'd told my mother I was going to the bathroom as we were leaving, and she was waiting for me to meet her back at the car.

Let me guess, said Jude. Something to do with your mother. It's always your mother. You know, I've been thinking about it, and she doesn't strike me as the overprotective type.

She isn't, I said, confused. What does that have to do—

I mean, surely she had boyfriends when you were growing up. Wouldn't she want you to have the same?

She does. Of course she does. But this is different.

I know, he said. I'm a lot older than you. It makes people uncomfortable. Christ, it makes *me* uncomfortable.

No. That's not it. I mean, you're not my boyfriend. You never said—

Well, is that what you want?

We were silent. The rain outside seemed to amplify the sound of voices, glasses, laughter. Windows fogged with heat and moisture, collective breath. Could someone like Jude—a grown man, with a past, and a house of his own—be a boyfriend? A word that recalled teenagers holding hands and sleeping like sardines in single childhood beds.

Jude was shaking his head. Do you think I'm in the habit of this? Picking up young girls on the beach? Do you think that's something I just do? I know what it looks like, what people must think.

I don't care what people think, I said.

That's sweet, he said, but you do. Sneaking around, hiding from your mother. I get it, but I'm forty-two, for fuck's sake. And it's not great for my fragile ego either, love. Feeling like you're ashamed to be seen with me.

I was relieved to see him smile then, joking. His dry sense of humour, self-deprecating. *You always liked a mutt, a stray . . .* But I could see it, behind his eyes. Some hurt there. It had never occurred to me that I could hurt him, that even a grown man might have a heart still raw in places.

My vision of him was beginning to blur. Jude, standing in front of me on the old, sticky carpet. I was reminded of one of the times my father had come to visit me when I was a girl. His visits were few and always on his way to elsewhere. He had a miniature game of chess he kept in his pocket, because he was afraid to fly and couldn't drive, so he travelled long-distance by train, Sydney to Perth on the Indian Pacific. I didn't know the rules, but I loved the magnetic board, the tiny figures, and I did know, even at seven or eight, that a game might delay his departure, let me keep him a little longer, and so I begged to play.

I tried to mirror him, moving my pawns forward one square at a time until he cornered my king in five moves. *Checkmate.* It happened so quickly, the pieces swept away, the board closed up and slipped back into my father's coat, and then he was gone. It was that feeling—of being deep into a game I didn't know how to play because no one had taught me the rules—that came back to me then.

By the pool table, the woman from earlier was calling to Jude, saying, Hey, you're up! It's your turn to break. As she walked towards us, I could see even at a distance that she was beautiful. High cheekbones in a heart-shaped face, fine lines around the corners of her lips when she smiled. The kind of beauty that needs nothing. Unmistakably feminine, though she dressed in men's clothes.

We're all waiting for you, she said, her hand on his sleeve. Your friend can play too, if she wants.

My mother's waiting, I said. Blushing when she raised her eyebrows. Feeling twelve instead of twenty-four.

Give us a minute, would you? he said. We're in the middle of something. And God knows I need a cigarette before I let you slaughter me again.

Outside, it was raining heavily, white sheets of water running off the awning, making our conversation feel private, shrouded by rain. Both of us staring straight ahead, leaning against the brick wall, warm hum of the pub behind us. He lit a cigarette, took a long drag.

Jude, I said, is that woman your girlfriend?

I don't have a girlfriend.

Wife? Partner?

Jesus, no. What's gotten into you? You already asked if I was married. What did you think, I lied?

He took his hat off and ran one hand through his hair, then placed it back on his head. His brow, I noticed, was beaded with sweat. In the streetlight, I saw that his hair was getting longer, curling at the ends now it was growing out—as if we'd been apart weeks instead of a single day. Love had a way of doing that, I would learn. It could collapse or rearrange time the way I'd thought only art or memory could.

That's Maeve, she's an old friend, he said. She's dating a mate of mine, Willy. He left his wife and kid and moved down here a few months ago, and now they're seeing each other again. It's complicated, as you'd imagine. The three of us have known each other a long time. She's always been Willy's girl.

Maeve, with her long dark hair and silver rings on her fingers. It was hard to imagine a woman like that belonging to anyone.

But you just said Willy got married, had a kid?

He did, said Jude. But even then. It's just one of those things. You know how it is.

And of course I didn't, not really, but I nodded along with him because I wanted to seem like a woman who knew something about love and its casualties—and maybe I did. Thinking of my mother and how she would always love my father, no matter how many men and houses and children now separated her from him. She'd remained loyal in her way. In all that time she'd never remarried. As if she were still waiting for him like a teenager twenty years later, hoping for him to bring roses to her door, to take it all back. How many flowers would that take? There didn't seem to be enough in all the world.

You don't trust people easily, do you? said Jude.

I shook my head.

Why's that?

A long story.

You'll tell me then. Next time.

There will be a next time? I wasn't sure.

Now we were alone he was quieter, calmer. With every exhale, I could almost see his shoulders loosening. Still learning the way his moods would change suddenly. Anger that gathered fast and then dissipated, like the quick-moving weather in that region. He tossed his cigarette in the gutter and kissed me then. In the middle of the street, clutching at each other's clothes. Pulling at his shirt, kissing his collarbone. My back against the brick wall of the pub, warm through my shirt from days baked in the sun. Our bodies pressed together, standing on tiptoe in my boots, slipping my legs between his. I knocked his hat from his head, heard the hollow sound it made when it bounced on the pavement, pushed my hands through his hair.

At the sound of a car horn we broke apart. The same two short notes I'd heard my whole life, calling me out of friends' houses and swimming lessons and horse riding or out in the school car park. Blood rush of lips kissed raw. Shielding our eyes from the lights of my mother's car.

So, the man from the shop? she said, as I slipped into the passenger seat beside her. Didn't I tell you? I can always tell. Call it a mother's sixth sense for men who are interested in their daughters. Plus, you stink of his cigarettes.

I thought we were meeting back at the car, I said.

It was raining so hard and you were taking so long, I thought I'd come and get you.

In the dark, it was hard to read the expression on her face, staring straight ahead as she steered the car back towards the beach.

Are you going to tell me about him, then? Does he have any animals? Or kids, for that matter? I mean, he must be a fair bit older than you. My age, maybe.

He's only forty-two, I said.

Only forty-two, she repeated. He's not married, is he? I hope I raised you better than that.

Of course he's not.

Well, you've always seemed old for your age, even when you were little. And I get it, you know, from his perspective. Younger girls demand less—or at least, they demand different sorts of things. It's like how you might get a puppy, to keep an old dog young.

Gee, thanks, I said. That's hardly a flattering comparison, is it?

But what's in it for you?

I thought of the day after the ruins, when I'd stood on Jude's back porch, lorikeets alighting on my shoulders. Blue and green and red underwing, the sharp flash of them like the snap of a brightly coloured flag.

He's steady, I said.

Steady is good.

We were silent as we left the lights of the town behind us, blurry in the wet dark, like tiny wavering fires. Trees in shadow leering forward, flashing by. Branches in the headlights lit up white. I was thinking of Jude's parting words, *next time*. What would he have done if I hadn't found him in the pub that night? I would have tracked you down eventually, he told me when I asked, months later.

But how?

I had your number.

You wouldn't have called.

Sure, I would've. I did.

Driving back to the beach, I thought of our first meeting in the water, the way he'd warned me about going out too deep, swimming at dusk and dawn. The thing about sharks, he'd said, is that at heart they're ambivalent. Put yourself in their way and they'll bite, but it's not about hunger, or need. What we might be tempted to call fate is really just a matter of convenience.

The road into Sailors Beach has been replaced now. A new highway, smooth paved road, fresh tarmac unfurling across the hills like a long black ribbon, tugging the cars and eighteen-wheelers away from the city, bypassing the small coastal towns that nestle in the valley. It's no longer the same route I remember from when I was a child travelling with my mother up and down the coast between Victoria and New South Wales, on the Princes Highway. *The Princess Highway*, I'd thought it was called, because it seemed to belong to my mother and me.

We build new roads, rename the towns, reclaim and return the land here in Australia, the country I grew up in. As if it were possible to circumnavigate memory.

TWO

I once asked my mother why she'd loved my father and, if she'd truly loved him, why she had left. He was my twin, she said. As if that were all the explanation needed to answer both questions.

Jude was not my twin. We were not two mirrors. We did not dress alike, could not be easily confused for brother and sister—though we got looks sometimes, in restaurants. Waitresses trying to guess the dynamic. Father and daughter? Lovers? A student and professor with an inappropriate relationship?

After I got back to Sydney, Jude called me up at night. Hello, love, he'd say. It was always late, after he'd finished work for the day and returned home. I was learning his routines, trying to carve out a space for myself to fit in. Knowing that when his voice grew faint he'd be rolling another cigarette, phone pressed between his shoulder and ear, muffled by flannel. Talking on the landline because there was little service down south, in parts of the house the signal got lost. Sailors Beach was a sheltered place back then, and it felt sometimes like we had gone back in time, or were protected from it. Jude always did his best not to live in the modern world, and in a way we had this in common—both of us out of step with the present, longing for some other time, some other place.

For Jude it was the world as he'd known it—a place of pay phones and answering machines—and he remained faithful to ways of living that seemed to me absurd and romantic. The mobile he kept *for emergencies only*, a flip phone that looked like the one I'd had when I was thirteen. What was that, ten years ago? he'd said. Eleven, I corrected him, because every year separating me from my childhood counted. I imagined the pictures of my naked breasts I sent to him loading on his screen in pixelated bars, a slow reveal, peep-show nudes. He never reacted to these photos in the way that I wanted, or sent me any in return—it was not a ritual he was used to. Call me old-fashioned, love, he said, but I prefer the real thing. He belonged to a more tactile place, where photographs were pictures you held in your hand and maps were made of paper and glue. The dog-eared Sydways ageing in the back seat of his car, state lines in pink and blue. He still lived in the world I'd known as a child, and this felt comforting, familiar. It was how I'd imagined adulthood would be, growing up in the 1990s.

Each morning I left early for work, travelling across town to the east side of the city, where people wanted books on self-improvement or finding love with vaguely accusatory titles. Selling copies of *Women Who Love Too Much*, picking at the coffee grinds beneath my fingernails. I was touched by the earnestness of the people who bought these books. On my break I sat out the back by the flattened cardboard cartons and sacks of espresso beans reading *Henry and June*, and maybe I did think of us then, in some grandiose way, like lovers from another time.

Back home at night, I'd close the door to my room, shutting out the noise from downstairs, the girls drinking, laughing, the pulse of music like a heavy heartbeat, vibrating through the wooden floors, and their voices rising together in the chorus, singing 'I Wanna Be Adored'. Music bleeding through the lines. Pressing my phone against my ear.

The Stone Roses, said Jude. God, I remember when that was on the radio.

I think I remember it from the womb, I said. My mother used to listen to it when she was pregnant with me.

There was a kind of thrill or novelty for me at first in the difference between our ages. It was new, and I wanted to dwell in it, this way of living that might provoke curiosity or judgement from other people. With Jude, I was visible in a way I never had been before. I didn't feel shame around this but I sensed or feared that he did, and so I teased. Quick to make those jokes before anyone else could.

Over the phone, his voice was deeper and more resonant, like he was talking right inside my head. I sat on my bed on those nights on top of the quilt my grandmother made, wearing a woollen cardigan over my pyjamas even though it was February, the last month of summer, because that old brick house absorbed no heat. It was surrounded by highways, smokestacks crowning the hills of the nearby park. Grit from the street blew into my room beneath the wooden doors of the balcony. Afterwards, I'd sit out there and smoke beside the fake flowers and fairy lights

I'd wound around the iron railing when I first moved in—my early version of homemaking. Counting down the days until we might see each other again. Conversations ending, When can I see you? and How soon? I fell asleep at night listening to the sound of traffic on the Princes Highway one street over. Last exit from the city, my house perched at the edge of the road that would lead back down south, to Sailors Beach, to Jude.

Quiet on the CountryLink from Central Station on a Monday morning, hours after the commuter rush. In an empty carriage, I found a seat by the window. Two weeks had passed since I'd returned to Sydney from Sailors Beach, and for the first time I was taking the train down from the city to spend the day with Jude. I could have borrowed a car, but I wasn't yet confident at navigating the highways alone. Also, I liked the anticipation of it, the sweetness of delay. The slow train winding through the outer city suburbs that would lead me back to him, passing through Hurstville, Helensburgh, Thirroul, waiting to catch sight of the ocean. The taste of it first—salt in the air as we arrived at the last stop on the line. And then, stepping onto the platform, there above the gabled wooden station—a swathe of blue.

Jude's red truck was parked out the front. Don't mind the mess, he said, as I climbed in. There were mud-clogged work boots in the back, sawdust and tobacco caught in the grey woollen seat covers. A metal toolbox rattled somewhere each time we rounded a corner. I thanked him for picking me up, he asked me about the trip.

It was nice, I said. I read, looked out the window.

Still *The Lover*? he said.

No, now it's *Voyage in the Dark*.

If we spoke much more than that on the way to his house, I don't recall it now. I was nervous and conscious of the fact that we hadn't yet touched. One of Jude's hands on the wheel and one on the shift, mine in my lap. Worrying a frayed cuticle until it bled. It seemed to me that we'd grown so used to the distance between our bodies during those weeks of late-night phone calls that without it we lapsed into silence, both of us staring out ahead. Country song on the radio tuning in and out of static, a woman's voice wavering—it was 'The Captain', a song my mother used to listen to when I was small.

At last, we pulled up in front of his house. He cut the engine and I followed him up the front steps to the porch.

Here we are, he said, his key in the door.

And then, with the turning of that single gold key, we were released. Unlocking and kissing on the threshold. As he opened the door, I pushed him up against the jamb. He pulled me inside into the cool dark rooms, brushing the hair back from my face with his warm dry hands. His lips on my eyelids and ears and down my neck. Lifting my dress up over my head, my nervous fingers catching on his belt loops, wondering if this unbuckling is for women what the hooks of an underwire are for men until he said, Here, I got it, and removed the belt in one slick motion, silver buckle clattering against the floor. The shame of seeing myself as if from above—backed against the kitchen table, naked and bucking in the afternoon light—and Jude towering above me, mostly dressed, shirt undone and sleeves rolled to his elbows.

I closed my eyes as he pushed his way inside me but my body resisted, wouldn't cooperate, and I remembered a girl in high school, the first in my year to lose her virginity, saying, Want to know what it feels like? and taking my wrist in her two hands, twisting the skin to make a burn. I stood on the hard courts holding my arm and watching it redden, fourteen and terrified, wondering why you'd ever let anybody—

I'm hurting you, said Jude.

It's fine.

No, it's not fine.

I'm sorry, I said, covering my face with my hands. I'm sorry I'm sorry I'm sorry.

Tell me what to do, he said. Tell me what you want.

It's just a thing that happens to me sometimes. I start thinking and then I—can't. It's not because I don't want to.

Eyes watering, pressing them with the base of my palms. With my fingers still covering my face, he kissed my body, starting with my hands, gently prying them away to kiss each wrist, then holding them both in one of his. Moving on to the pulse points behind my ears, the crook of my neck, making circles around each breast, kissing his way down rib by rib, lifting my hips, and then, with his mouth, opening me up like a fruit. Twitching with it, my body made electric. Senses lighting up beyond thought. And deep within, a shift, like ice cracking in a sudden spring. First thaw. Warm waters rushing through. His palm flat on my stomach, holding me steady. I'm falling and the feeling is bottomless, holding on to him to brace myself, clutching the collar of his shirt in my hand. *Cresting*, like a sea. Until the feeling breaks, rolls over and floods through me. Wave after wave after wave.

In the downstairs bathroom, which was little more than a toilet and two rusty taps beneath the stairs in a space the size of a closet, I studied my face in the mirror on the back of the door. Eyes bright blue and reddened in the blurry glass, like when I was drunk. Face flushed in a rash of pink across my nose and cheeks. Ugly after, I now knew. Not dew-skinned, like girls in the movies. Dry-mouthed, drinking from the tap, spilling water down my chin, wetting the ends of my hair: it seemed impossible to believe that anyone could want me the way that he wanted me. I looked down at my thighs, blue veins and broken capillaries and pale skin, and felt an old fear that my body was transparent, making a map of every pleasure, pain and injury for anyone to see.

Back in the kitchen, Jude had dressed. Shirt linen crumpled but buttoned, jeans zipped and belt buckled, feet bare. Washing his face in the sink.

Tea? he said. I'm putting the kettle on.

Our abrupt intimacy was over, broken by his pottering, fixing the mugs and scooping tea leaves into a pot, whistling a tune, kettle coming to a boil. Crossing my arms over my chest, trying not to hunch. I stood beside the bathroom door, unsure if I should crawl around the table to find my clothes, or sit through tea boldly in the nude, unwilling to let the moment go. I did not know how to reach him then, his back turned to me, distracted now, and I realised it didn't matter—my body was just a body again, human and ordinary. The mood had passed. I found my dress, slipped it over my head.

Sitting opposite Jude at the table, with the tea brewing between us, I felt like we'd promised to tell each other a secret and after I'd revealed mine, he'd changed his mind. Though maybe it was a female thing, I thought later, to feel vulnerability where a man might have felt power, but still I longed to see him cracked open under my hands in return, while I remained clothed and composed.

I wish I didn't have to go back tonight, I said. My voice the voice of a sly beggar. I had nothing urgent calling me home to the city. The bookstore closed on the first two days of the week, so I didn't have to work until Wednesday. What I wanted was to be asked to stay.

I don't need you to be here, Jude would tell me in time, but I want you to be. And that's how it should be. It's better that way. Love, he would tell me, is all about choice. Free will. Need is about dependency.

Jude thought we should be like a gift to each other, but I longed to be essential. That was love, I decided, as our intimacy changed and deepened over the course of the year. Not being able to do without. Wanting—that was just desire, fluid and changeable as the tide. Need was real love, the truest kind I'd known, born as it is out of what we lack, and that was how I felt about Jude back then—that he completed me, we completed each other, as in the old myth about the origin of love. And if I was essential, the other half of whatever he was, then he could never abandon me.

Across from me at the table that afternoon, he shrugged.

So stay, he said, as if it were an easy thing.

I don't have any of my things.

I have things. A whole house full of things.

I shouldn't.

He was offering me what I'd wanted, but I was plagued by the feeling that the invitation wasn't genuine, that it was only because I'd prompted him that he suggested I stay. This cheapened it in my mind, and I felt graceless and worse than if he hadn't asked at all.

So don't. Forget it.

His tone had turned sharp, abrupt.

What? he said. Don't look at me like that.

Like what?

So *wounded*. Like a kicked dog. If you can't stay, that's too bad, but don't demur because you like to hear me asking. I won't be a beggar.

Okay, I said quietly.

Okay you'll stay, or okay you'll stop sulking?

Both? I said, hating the way my voice lilted upward, so unsure, like I was asking for permission.

Good. I'll cook dinner.

Okay. Thank you.

The storm over. Back to humming his tune.

My first night in the house. All of its doors were open to me, and I was free to roam as I liked, eyes lingering on objects and art and furniture, while Jude baked a fish in salt and chopped vegetables to roast for dinner. Steady rhythm of the knife on the chopping block. You're in charge of the music, he told me. Go and pick something out.

In the living room off the kitchen, I looked through the albums lined up on a long, low bookshelf made to fit a twelve-inch sleeve. Taking my time running my fingers along the dusty slips, as if they contained clues to the different chapters of his life.

Jude liked the Talking Heads *Speaking in Tongues* Nina Simone *I Put a Spell on You* Townes Van Zandt *Live at the Old Quarter* Karen Dalton *In My Own Time* Miles Davis *Bitches Brew* Lee Hazlewood *Cowboy in Sweden* Nick Cave and the Bad Seeds *The Boatman's Call* Dirty Three *She Has No Strings Apollo* The Band *The Last Waltz* Bob Dylan *Pat Garrett and Billy the Kid* Harry Nilsson *Aerial Ballet* Tom Waits *Closing Time* Patti Smith *Horses* Neil Young *Tonight's the Night* Bruce Springsteen *Nebraska* Lou Reed *The Blue Mask* Tom Petty and the Heartbreakers *Damn the Torpedoes* the Rolling Stones *Tattoo You* Roy Orbison *In Dreams* the Beach Boys *Surf's Up* Suicide *Dream Baby Dream* Captain Beefheart and His Magic Band *Safe as Milk* John and Yoko *Double Fantasy* the Flying Burrito Brothers *The Gilded Palace of Sin* Leonard Cohen *Death of a Ladies' Man* Frank Sinatra *Watertown*.

All unalphabetised, but that was Jude—careful only up to a point.

There were other records, too, by artists whose names and faces were less recognisable. Forgotten albums, compilations, brought home from the two-dollar bin at the shop. *Songs for Banjo. Songs for Christmas. Songs of Redemption.*

You know you've got two copies of *Blood on the Tracks*? I said.

Oh. One's probably Helena's.

Helena. It surprised me how easily he said that name, how well worn it was on his tongue. He'd been saying that name for a long time.

Who's that?

Bob Dylan?

No, of course I know who Bob Dylan is. Who's Helena?

My ex. Thought I would have mentioned her before. She's a big Dylan fan. We lived together when I first moved down here, so there's probably a few doubles in there.

How long were you with her?

He was by the oven, rotating a silver tray, tea towel wrapped around the soft part of his palm, the fish buried now, entombed in a thick crust of salt. I couldn't see the expression on his face.

Eleven years, he said.

Eleven years. It was hard for me to imagine a relationship so enduring—my parents separated four years after they married. My mother twenty-three in the wedding dress that had belonged to her great-grandmother, pearl buttons up to her throat, black leather boots peeping out beneath the hem in pictures because she didn't have the money to buy new shoes for the occasion, a crown of baby's breath around her long dark hair. Still a few months shy of showing. Fortunately, she'd carried small. Married years are like dog years, my mother was fond of saying. They count for more.

I dropped the needle on the record that was already in place, the speakers humming and vinyl cracking, jumping with its touch. The warmth in that old sound, like a fire starting.

I'd learn in time that in that house there were traces of her everywhere. *Helena.* I'd open up a drawer or put on one of Jude's large oilskin coats to walk the dog in bad weather and find something she'd left behind, like a sketch in charcoal on the back of an envelope, or a tissue marked with lipstick. Bloodstains on the mattress gone the colour of rust.

But that night, listening to the swell of music, Patsy Cline's voice strained with sorrow, I thought, She's got these little things, I've got you. Wrapping my arms around Jude's waist. In that moment, I felt so lucky I thought I might die. The only way I can understand this now is that what I was feeling, standing in his kitchen all those years ago, was a presentiment of loss.

When I woke in the morning—birds. The murderous, curdling cries of them. Jude was standing by the window in the early light. I'd never seen a man naked like that before. Modesty kept my few former lovers sheltered, touching beneath blankets or in the dark. Kissing with eyes squeezed closed, shut tight. And even then, they had been boys. Slim-shouldered and thin. Remembering the one I had a crush on for years at university. His hair was almost as long as mine and instead of taking his face in my hands or telling him my feelings, I used to braid it at parties and roll him thin and perfect joints as a testament of my devotion.

I loved best in gestures, in metaphors, and I wanted to build a life out of what I loved. Metaphors are lies, one of my professors had said in a lecture during my first year of university. How then, I might argue with her now, in the absence of figurative language, are we supposed to talk about love? *Love*, we say, and expect the word to hold so many things.

That morning, I marvelled at the sight of Jude's broad back, the dark line of hairs that led down from his navel until they grew thick and wiry, like steel wool. Loving to look, to see him in the sunlight, the bedroom bright and airy, watching him walk downstairs without shame, move through the kitchen in the nude. Windows bare so anyone might see, passing by on the path that led to the beach.

I followed Jude into the kitchen, feeling the light on my naked body, pressing against his back where he stood looking out at the birds. He turned then, grabbed a shirt that was hanging on the back of a chair. What are you doing? he said. Put this on. What if somebody sees you?

Where have you been all night? Off with your mystery man? said Petra, back at our house in the city, trimming her black fringe over the sink with kitchen scissors and a handheld mirror.

What mystery man?

He of the late-night phone calls. Every time it rings you disappear on us, go all sly and quiet. And you've got that look.

What look?

The *afterglow*. Of nonstop fucking. Nothing better for the skin. See? You're blushing. I take it he's pretty good at it, then.

I laughed, shrugged. Feeling the heat on my face.

Tell me everything!

Oh no, I said, I couldn't.

Come on, she said. Don't be such a prude. It's not a big deal. It's just sex.

It's not just sex. I think it could be—

What? Love?

Laughing then, shaking her head. Fine snips of black hair sticking to her cheeks, her long nose.

Love? said Bonnie, padding down the stairs, still in her night-gown. Blonde hair glowing in the afternoon light. Who's in love?

She is, said Petra.

Oh, that's wonderful! said Bonnie. But with who?

When I told the girls that I'd been seeing an older man I met down at the beach, Petra said, Hot, and Bonnie asked, How old? She had grown up in the north of the state, on the coast, and I knew she was picturing a different kind of man. Burned-out and leathery, rolling joints on the sand with wet fingers. Quick fucks in the back of a van, and then off to surf at dawn. Leaving behind a stale fug of hemp and nag champa, skin mottled from too many years in the sun. Not at all like Jude, who polished his boots and pressed his linen shirts at night, had studied theatre, spent his twenties and thirties building and painting sets for plays before he moved down south. Jude, who would bring me rare editions of my favourite classics back from the tips and estate sales and country op shops he frequented for work. Clothbound copies of *Wuthering Heights* and *Rebecca*, pages gilded gold. But these books had been lived in and loved, not like the ones we kept on the first-edition shelves at work, locked in a glass case. The books Jude brought me had been handled, covers worn, spines showing through the threadbare binding like a skinned knee. I liked the way they felt haunted by other hands, the feeling that time didn't really keep us apart, wasn't an unbreachable gap. That I could touch the same objects as the ghosts of other times. I felt their presence in the parsed-over pages, the pencil marks, obscure annotations. You like things that are old and broken, Jude often teased, and so did he. But where he wanted to fix things up, repair and repurpose them, I liked to watch them wear down, go to ruin. Yes, I ruined my books, like he'd said on the day that we met. I turned the pages with wet hands, salt and sand dried in the margins, the edges warped in waves, I spilled coffee, crumbs, blood from a chewed fingernail. And in this way the books held my life, were my life—at least until Jude. Always the feeling, in those early days, that he had brought me back to the physical world.

Sometimes, in my last year of university, when my life had felt too chaotic—or, worse, too drab, too predictable, all those hours spent alone in the library—I would go into Bonnie's room and look at her clothes. All the thick, soft sweaters folded into pastel blocks of cashmere and mohair, like colour swatches: peach and blush, milk tooth, dove, quail-egg blue. A droopy, loose-knit jumper that slumped across the top of the pile like a fat grey cat. Her shoes were neatly lined up at the bottom of her wardrobe— patent Mary Janes, bleached white sneakers, chic burgundy loafers that looked like they had whiskers.

Bonnie took good care of her things because she had moved to the city to become someone different, neat and put together. Someone with boundaries. No more running barefoot through the paddocks of her parents' farm in Mullumbimby with mud up to her knees or driving home drunk, packed into the back of someone else's car, sitting on some boy's lap, rushing past the highway memorials left behind after other accidents—white crosses and fake flowers slick with rain, stuffed animals soaked through and heavy with water. Where I come from, she'd told me on our first day of university, when I sat next to her in the lecture hall for orientation, teenagers move to the city or else they tend to die. Which was eerie, coming from Bonnie, with her round angel's face and soft way of speaking, her pale brows and hair so blonde it was almost white. This contrast had surprised me, and I liked her immediately. Bonnie had the kind of practical experience I lacked, and I hoped that she could teach me—how to dress, how to wear my clothes. How to be the sort of woman I aspired to be.

I loved to pass my hands along her smooth skirts and dresses lined up on their hangers and see them move like they were breathing, living things, and watch the light play on the orange and cream and navy silk, but I knew that even if I slipped on her clothes I could never inhabit that kind of life. I tried to keep myself straitlaced and buttoned up tight, but whenever I was walking in the city and caught myself reflected in a mirror or a shop window, there was always something undone about me, unkempt. Hair knotted at the back where I'd tossed my scarf over my shoulder, a look as if I'd just woken up. Skirt askew, or loose-hemmed, a missed button on my blouse. In those moments, it came to me like a shock: I am my mother's daughter. It was her face, blinking back at me in surprise. Something wild about us, our frayed edges.

Jude, I would think sometimes, should be with someone like Bonnie. Composed. Someone who knew the value of things, invested in quality made to last, and took pride in what she'd earned and made her own—no dresses in a heap by the foot of her bed. But why would Bonnie want someone like Jude? No time to waste on lonely, broken old men—not her type. And was Jude broken? How raw was the wound left by the last woman? I wondered about Helena, and the other woman I'd seen him with on my last night at the beach—Maeve. *An old friend.* What kind of woman would I have to be to keep him?

That morning, Bonnie looped her soft arms around mine, pulled me close, kissed me on the cheek. Oh! I feel so happy for you, she said, resting her head on my shoulder. I felt such tenderness towards her then. For three years we had lived together in that house like three sisters. Sharing each other's clothes, dresses hanging from the picture rails instead of paintings, sleeping in each other's beds when we felt lonely. How quickly the boundaries between our bodies had dissolved. Simple to hold Bonnie's hand or link her arm in mine. I could love her easily, abundantly, where with Jude I had to be so careful to parcel out my affections in case I scared him away.

But things that year were already changing, our paths diverging. We had been close, Bonnie and Petra and I, when we had shared the same schedule of lectures and classes, but Petra was applying for doctoral programs, and Bonnie was searching for what we referred to as *a real job*—meaning nine-to-five, with benefits like sick leave and holiday pay, a new uniform of office clothes, silky blouses and knee-length skirts. All of us out of university for the first time and grasping for something to hold on to, whatever structure or security we could find. Up until that point, I'd moved through the same general milestones in tandem with my peers—high school graduation followed by a year off to work or travel, then the four years of my degree. But for the first time it was becoming obvious to me that there was no one way to live your life. Each of us had to make her own choices, and in that we were all on our own. In the kitchen, the girls' voices came together like a chorus rising, asking, But when do we get to meet him? Yes, when?

They couldn't know then how much things would continue to change in the coming months. Neither could I. That we should have held on to the sweetness of those days, the three of us, making coffee, talking, idling away hours because we had nowhere to be. We were home.

Dates in the city. Revivals at the Chauvel, kissing in the dark of the cinema like teenage lovers. Kissing through *Breathless*, *To Catch a Thief*, *Casablanca*. But outside afterwards, as I blinked into the still-light, Jude was already striding ahead, putting distance between us, hands shoved deep into his pockets while I struggled into my jacket. He walked this way in the city: furtive, head down, like a man afraid of running into someone he owed money. Wait! I called out. Two steps to his one. Running a little to keep up, chasing him through the zigzagging maze of Chinatown later that afternoon. I caught his sleeve, stamped my foot in the street. Slow down, you're walking too fast, you're leaving me behind!

You'd have me drag my feet! he said.

I held out my hand and he looked down at it, as if he didn't understand what I was offering. At last he said, I think I'm a little old for that, love. But I stood there, stubborn, my empty palm open and outstretched. Don't give me that look, he said, and then he sighed, relented. I felt happy then, proud, as if I had won something. Walking side by side with his hand in mine.

I would learn that things I perceived as abandonment were Jude's acts of trust, like the way he always walked ahead without looking behind him, trusting me to keep pace, to follow. But I was the kind who always looked back, glancing over my shoulder whenever I turned a corner, as if I were a woman descended from the line of Lot's wife in the old parable. When I licked my lips, I tasted salt.

The sounds of the city grated on Jude—the sirens and car alarms that blared outside my bedroom window, the shaking steel of freight trains that ran on the railway line at the back of my house. Didn't you live in the city a long time? I reminded him, lying in my bed one night.

Yeah, and I hated it.

Close your eyes, I said to him. Don't you think the traffic on the highway sounds a little like the ocean? If you try hard enough to imagine, you can hear it. You can pretend.

He hardly ever stayed with me in Sydney. Memories of him there are few. Going to meet him when his train pulled into Central Station. Watching him step onto the platform in his brown, broad-brimmed hat, or standing out the front of Paddy's Markets, cradling some obscure fruit in his arms. He was always bringing me fruit—persimmons and pomelos, sweetsop and once, a durian. What? I'd joked. Afraid I'm going to get scurvy? Though it was true that at home there was only stale cereal, soy milk, soft dimpled oranges. A package of chocolate biscuits in the fridge, edges frilled like a postage stamp. Week-old leftovers Petra brought back from the restaurant gathering grease and congealing in plastic and Styrofoam containers. The girls worked most nights and I was there less and less.

The first time he came to my house, I had been nervous. Jude, standing tall in the doorway with the light behind him, casting his long shadow down the hall. Heavy boot tread on the floorboards. In the kitchen I began a series of apologies. Sorry we don't have any Scotch, sorry there's not enough chairs, sorry the record player's broken, sorry the light's out in the bathroom, sorry about the bras soaking in the sink. Leading him around the house in a grand tour of deficiencies, until he took me by the shoulders, looked down into my face, and said, Stop saying sorry. Really. It's fine. I lived in share houses once too. And I can fix that light for you.

But my heart dropped as I watched him sink into the low couch and prop his feet up on the coffee table beside the stacks of literary journals and magazines I subscribed to and the unreturned books from the university library I'd had on loan since the year before because there were his boots still on his feet. He left them on all afternoon, as if he might get up and walk out at any moment. As if he hadn't made up his mind whether or not to stay.

The steadiness I had taken to be ingrained at the core of him—did I realise then that it was not in him but in the Old House itself? His home by the sea. The only place where he was anchored, could settle. Outside of it he was easily set off course, batted about by the winds, irritated by the sounds of the city.

At my place, Jude was unsure where to sit or what to do without work to tinker with or records to turn, fish to salt, birds to feed.

Something about him was never quite at ease there. In our house of girls' things, he was like a man trying to shrink to fit inside a dollhouse.

That night, we sat on the sofa and broke the bread and drank the wine and ate the fruit that Jude had brought, watching *The Big Sleep*, Bogart and Bacall. Whenever Petra passed through the living room, seeing us curled up together in the dark, she winked and called us *lovebirds*, raising her eyebrows suggestively. You always did like a man you could climb, like a ladder, like a tree, she said to me slyly in the kitchen, while I was making tea and Jude was in the bathroom.

Not me, she said. Give me a lover I can look in the eye. Don't want someone always looking over me, looking ahead, looking out for someone new.

Bonnie tried to make small talk with Jude when she got home, but she had a tendency to speak more softly than usual around strangers. Her attempts at conversation came out in a near whisper.

Your housemate, Jude said later, when we were alone in my room. The dark-haired one. Hair like Cleopatra.

Petra?

She's always staring at me. It's unnerving.

Petra's just curious, that's all, I said. She doesn't believe in—

Catching the word on my tongue.

Doesn't believe in what? Love?

No, um. In monogamy. As a construct.

I never saw the point in open relationships, said Jude.

Don't you think that's a little old-fashioned?

I *am* old-fashioned, he said. Isn't that what you like about me?
Or are you telling me you'd rather have it this new way? Sleeping
around, seeing other people, like Cleopatra.

Of course not, I said. You know I only want you.

Guess that makes you old-fashioned too, he said. What about
the other one? The blonde.

Bonnie.

I can never hear a word she's saying.

Maybe you should get your hearing checked, I said. Anyway,
I only have two housemates. You should probably learn their names.

I thought of Bonnie, soft and fair, her quiet and husky voice,
and Petra with her frank way of speaking and slightly regal
bearing. How could Jude fail to remember them? Were all young
women interchangeable to him? Did he look at Bonnie and Petra
and see only that? *Young. Woman.*

Bonnie and Petra mean well, I told Jude. You're just different
from the other boys I've brought home.

Different in what way?

Well, you're not exactly a *boy*.

I'm old, you mean?

No, not old. But you're, you know, a *man*.

I hate that there've been others, said Jude, and I was so surprised
at the fact of his jealousy that I apologised. Why would he be
jealous, I thought, when I had never loved or been loved this
way before?

It wasn't like this, I said. It wasn't ever like this.

Tell me that you've never had anyone else. I want you to pretend.

Okay, I said, laughing. I've never been with anyone else. Happy?

Tell me I'm your first, he said, his voice low and his hands moving across my blouse. Tell me that you've never been touched.

I'm untouched. Chaste, a clean slate.

But you want it.

I nodded. The energy between us had shifted. My breath caught in my throat.

I want to hear you say it, said Jude.

I do, I said. I want you.

Ask nicely, he said, his fingers in my mouth so I had to move around them to talk.

Please, I said to him. Please.

Passing Petra by the stairs in the night on my way to the bathroom, I hissed, *Stop staring*. You're making him uncomfortable.

What? She shrugged. I'm just trying to picture how he fucks.

And I couldn't again after that. The feeling that the girls were right outside my room, ears pressed against the door. Every time Jude rolled over and his body made the bed creak, I cringed, thinking of the wall I shared with Bonnie, and Petra's room below with the TV turned up tactfully high, theme music for *Law and Order* carrying through the floorboards. Missing the privacy of the Old House, the big empty rooms.

Much better were the quiet afternoons in the dim light, Petra studying at the library, Bonnie at the cinema, my legs hanging from the end of the bed while he kneeled before my body as if in supplication. I was a greedy lover, he teased, and I was, I was, this desire, this pleasure, unknown and new.

Light streamed into my bedroom early in the autumn through the thin lace curtains. The morning after Jude spent the night at my house for the first time, I turned to look at him beside me. His face creased by troubled sleep, feet sticking out between the white cast-iron posts at the end of the bed. A doll's bed for a doll's house. It had been my grandmother's. And how did he look to me, sleeping beneath the floral patchwork blanket she had sewn long ago from scraps of the Liberty fabric she used to make my mother's dresses?

He looked old. Not older, old.

Later that day, we walked to a farmers' market in a converted train yard. I watched his careful process as he moved through the stands, squeezing the avocados and other stone fruit to test for their ripeness. A peach, he taught me, should have the firmness of an earlobe. He chose tomatoes that were thick and red and would look meaty when we cut into them, like a heart. Berries that stained our mouths and fingers, the last for the season. Walking around the stalls, picking up brown eggs and bunches of flowering gum, I had the sudden thought—This is what it would be like if we were married—and it gave me pleasure to picture it.

Jude wasn't wealthy, but what he had seemed bountiful to me after years as a student paying rent in the city, which cost more than half of what I earned at the bookstore. He wasn't frivolous or decadent, the way my father had been at first with my mother, but he spent money on things he cared about. Small pleasures—fine food and other delicacies. Jude bought the twenty-dollar bottle of wine, instead of the cheap cleanskins the girls and I carried in our bags to warehouse parties on Saturday nights, drinking from plastic cups or straight from the bottle. The wine I drank with Jude was like a whole meal—you could taste the fruit and the soil. At home he had a liquor cabinet with whiskey imported from Japan, and a gin that was so sweet and clear you could drink it straight, with an ice cube and a single orange peel. Learning that one experience could contain so many things, that all the senses are associative. When the wine landed full on my palate, it seemed that he'd brought depth to my world. A single glass of white could recall oysters and brine and lovers' spit and citrus fruits and sunburn, a glass of red grass and dirt and *blackberry, blackberry, blackberry*. Like the line from the poem Jude read aloud to me that afternoon in my concrete backyard, the pavement cracked with weeds, while we sat on the chipped garden furniture eating prosciutto with pearls of melon, smoked salmon with crème fraîche, cheese layered on thick crusts of bread, truffle honey, strong black coffee. How elegant he looked, long legs crossed, one elbow leaning on the table, those flashes of poise in the way he held his body—an actor's training. I want to do everything right this time, he said. His strange mood from the night before had passed. And although I'd never been in a serious relationship, I felt like I knew how to do this too. Yes, I nodded. I'd been waiting my whole life to love and be loved like that.

Tell me your greatest loves, the things you've loved the most, he said one afternoon, lying in his big brass bed at the Old House. Our hair wet from swimming, grit of sand between the sheets. We always brought the beach home with us, stumbling barefoot up the path that cut through the bush to his yard.

Out the window, I watched lightning soundlessly strike the horizon, waiting for the storm that would roll in off the bay. Down south, there was always the feeling of water in the air, even when there was no rain.

That's easy, I said. My mother, my younger brother. And the ocean. Though does it count if what you love can't love you back?

Unrequited love is still love, he said. But it's never a great love. Can't be. It's one-sided. Except in the case of the ocean. For the ocean, we can make an exception.

How about you? I said. Big, real, soul-splitting loves. How many?

Real love? he said. Just the one time.

And I couldn't decide if that was better or worse than all the other loves I might have imagined for him.

How did you know? What made it so different from all the other times?

Oh, it's just one of those things. You know it when you see it.

With Helena?

He nodded. *Volatile*, he called their love, *but true*. Once when they'd fought, he said, she'd painted her condemnation in angry red letters across the kitchen wall. He'd painted over them now, but in a certain light, part of the message showed through. *You don't* . . . Like a clue.

I didn't know how to love like that, in bold gestures. My expressions were small: a folded love note buried in a jacket pocket, a drafted email addressed and sent to no one. Could a quiet love like mine be just as true?

Helena was a painter, a sculptor, a dancer. Every time he mentioned her, she was a different kind of artist, and in my mind she was all the women I'd ever admired. She practised ikebana, made animal shapes out of paper and wire, cast their shadows on gallery walls. She'd travelled to Mexico, Morocco, Paris, Berlin, Santa Fe. I pictured her with paint on her jeans, stretching canvas over a wooden frame that Jude had built.

Anything decorative in the house, I was learning, had come from Helena. Pieces of pottery from the American desert, the series of tiny lead animals that lined the kitchen windowsill, a tin cowboy with a big silver key in his back that you turned to make his toy horse buck and spin—a wind-up rodeo star, his mechanical arm twirling a plastic lasso.

So much of the man I loved had been shaped and influenced by her tastes, and at first I was jealous of all her gifts and worldly offerings, collected from her travels and artist residencies in other countries—all things I never would have thought to buy a grown man. She'd known the child at the heart of him, a part of Jude I'd never seen. She'd glimpsed what was there before that heart hardened over, grew a thicker skin.

Now I understand that those relics were part of what had first attracted me to Jude—the poetry of them, and the mystery of his life before me. In the years since, I have often thought that those traces of her—that's what taught me how to love a man. As if she'd left them behind on purpose, to show me the ways of women more sophisticated than I could have hoped to be at the age of twenty-four. Maybe it was unusual how I felt mothered by the women in Jude's life—by Helena and, later, by Maeve—not in the sense that they nurtured me, but they showed me the ways of being the kind of woman I wanted to be. It was a similar impulse that had drawn me, in my first year of university, to Bonnie, and would become a pattern in my friendships with other women. Always looking to them to guide, to instruct, to teach by example. How to dress and wear my clothes, how to love a man, how to make a life out of art, how to make a family.

But when I spoke that afternoon, my voice sounded sulky, my face hidden in the crook of his neck.

You've kept a lot of the things she gave you, I said. For there were her records on the shelf, the ceramics she'd made and left behind, like the terracotta bowl handpainted with blue flowers that I'd fill with King's water that winter, though it was far too nice for a dog.

Well, I can't just throw them away, love, said Jude, patiently. It would be like throwing away a decade of my life. They're mine now, part of the house. When you live with someone a long time, you can't help but merge.

Jude closed his eyes, rolled onto his side, and I had the feeling—not for the first time—that everything that felt new to me was commonplace to him. Completely unremarkable to be lying in his bed together.

Don't go to sleep yet, I begged. Isn't it strange to see lightning with no thunder? When I was little, my mother told me this story so I wouldn't be afraid. She said it was just angels taking photographs of all the little people down on Earth, so they'd know what it was like to be human. The lightning was their cameras flashing. It meant we must be doing something special.

And why would the angels want a picture of us two?

Because we're lovers, I said. And they can't imagine what it means to be lovers.

I think the angels would have seen it all before.

And what about you?

What about me?

Rolling back over with a sigh. If you could, you'd follow me into dreams, he said, and I hated that he saw me that way, as someone always trailing behind, like a little sister, where I wanted us to be equals—like my mother had said about herself and my father, *twins*.

Sometimes I think you must have seen it all before. That I can't show you anything new.

You show me things I've forgotten, he said. Which is almost the same. Maybe even better. And anyway, don't forget I was young once too.

I don't believe you've ever been any other age than you are now, I said. I think you must have been born at forty-two. Do you still talk? You and Helena.

You don't have anything to worry about with Helena, said Jude. She's married to some doctor now, living out in the country. Had twin girls a couple of years ago. Blonde hair, curls, green eyes. Exactly like her. What matters now is this, he said. He pulled me close, kissed the top of my head. Here, with you.

I was so eager to be loved by him, to be held in his arms and reassured, to shut out the ghosts of other girlfriends from the room like a cold draught, I said nothing more. Climbing on top of him, my hand on his chest, an animal warmth. I bent to kiss him and let the damp ropes of my hair drag across his face, his chest. He reached up and moved his hands through it, as if it were light or water.

I can see it all over your face, he said. Such naked wanting.

I told him that I'd always been afraid of wanting anything so badly that it becomes visible. For years I'd tried to compress my desires, to burn them away, like waste. I had this theory, I said, that that was why I would never be graceful. My body jarred from the fight of trying to keep it all inside me, it made me clumsy. Desires would rise up and I'd knock an elbow into something, or my hand would give out on the glass I was holding and I would watch it as it slipped through my fingers, shattered. I hoped so badly, I told him, to one day be the kind of woman who could wear white.

I like you as you are, he said. Even if you're going to wear me out.

Are other women not like this?

No, he said, but then seemed to change his mind. Well, yes—but it fades. That openness, eagerness.

So you mean I look young.

You say that—*young*—as if it is a bad thing.

I don't want to be young, I said. I've never *felt* young.

Well, you're lucky, said Jude, because one day you won't be. Trouble is that it doesn't work in reverse.

I closed his eyes with the palm of my hand and kissed him deeply as the first sounds of thunder rolled in and broke across the bay. I was learning to love that at-sea feeling—how it felt sometimes like we were two shipwrecked lovers rocking together, his room at the top of the A-frame house with its rough wooden beams our lifeboat. Surrounded by water, far from anyone who might try to call me home.

Years later, at a gallery with my mother in New York, I would come across a drawing by one of her favourite Australian painters. A naked man and woman beneath a dark sky, holding each other among the black inky peaks of waves. I thought of those afternoons with Jude, lying side by side in his bed as if on the ocean floor. The title of the painting, like a poem: *Two Sunken Lovers Bodies Lay*. The expressions on the lovers' faces are ambiguous, heads bent together in what could be tenderness or grief.

I lay awake for a while that afternoon, listening to the waves, the rain, the drag of his breath as he fell asleep. I'd chosen to anchor myself here, in this watery place. I wanted to believe, back then, that we'd grow old together—or rather that I'd grow old and he'd grow older, for there was no way to bridge that gap in time. But maybe we could hope for a sanding down of those rough edges, the way time wears away at all of us, until we reached a state of greater equilibrium.

Even so, I caught myself imagining a distant future, telling this story to another man, in another bed. Stories I'd trade in for other intimacies to show the kind of woman I was. But I must have fallen asleep because sometime later, when the rain had stopped, when there was only the light music of water dripping off the leaves, the sky dark, Jude woke me by talking in his sleep.

I love you, he murmured, into my hair.

Are you awake?

I love you, he said again.

I love you too.

Thanks, he said. Thanks very much.

And then he was asleep again.

I wondered if it was a dream and who or what he was dreaming of, if he'd remember his sleep talk in the morning, and if he didn't, whether it still counted.

※

Still now there are things that haunt:

   What kind of women did you like before me, Jude?

   Any.

   And what kind of woman am I?

   Young.

Asking again, How many women? At twenty-four, I could count
my former lovers on one hand.

   Sweetheart, he said, I couldn't tell you if I wanted to.

You could feel it coming off the water, autumn in the air. Down south, the days that looked bright and clear were often the coldest. The wind made the ocean bristle, cut through our clothes as we walked along the shore. Sleeping nude and waking for the first time to the morning chill. Arms and shoulders cooled. Breakfast in bed, kissing jammy fingers. Toast crumbs sticking to bare skin, coffee spilled on the sheets. Jude dressed for work on a Sunday morning, kissing me on the forehead, his hair wet from the shower brushing against my cheek. Can't I come with you? I said. Unbearable, to be apart.

You won't be bored, watching me fix things?

I can amuse myself, maybe help a customer or two.

You'd want to do that?

I nodded.

I could never be bored, I thought, if he was nearby. It was that stage of love, where even the most mundane activity seemed like an adventure. Sitting in the front of the shop, drinking tea and reading with a heater by my feet for warmth, while Jude fixed up new pieces to sell in his workshop out the back. Listening to the drifting static of his radio in the next room—a familiar, childhood sound, between the high-pitched hum of the circular saw. Flipping the sign on the door, taking long lunches, fish and chips in our coats by the bay. The warmth of those parcels in our laps. Vinegar on our fingers and two brown glass bottles of beer. When I looked out across the water and saw Sailors Beach on the other side, it looked like home.

I had started leaving more of my things at the Old House, splitting my time between the beach and the city. Swapping my shifts to cluster them together so I could spend half the week with Jude. Taking the train on Saturday afternoons when I finished work and knowing he would be there to meet me at the station— that was love. I would stay until Tuesday, when I had to return to the city in order to open the bookstore the following day, but more than once I missed the last train, both of us slow to dress, to find keys and shoes, lingering until it was too late to leave. Calling in sick, calling in favours.

One morning I woke up with my eyes red and watering, a scratch in my throat.

You're burning up, said Jude, his hand on my head. You can't take the train back today. Stay. Sleep. Bringing the covers back up over me.

For five days I lived in his bed and he cared for me. Hack-coughing nights. Shivers and fevers. Sweating through the sheets. Even then, we wanted each other. The cold made me husky and low-voiced, and Jude said I sounded sexy, *older*, that I looked pretty even with a cold. Wiping my nose on the sleeve of one of his old work flannels. Sweating garlic, which I swallowed raw with honey from a spoon. Home cures.

At the end of that week, I had missed calls from my mother, from work. My mother wanted to know when I was coming to visit, whether I'd forgotten about her and Henry, whether I was *still alive*. It's like you're walking around with blinders on, her voicemail said. There was also a message from my manager at the bookstore, letting me know that though I'd been promised full-time when I was hired, they'd had to bring on someone else. I'd missed too many shifts—my hours were being cut.

Ladies and gentlemen, the amazing invisible housemate! exclaimed Petra, when I finally arrived home, and though I knocked on Bonnie's door many times in the days that followed, it seemed like she was never there. Notes I left on the bathroom mirror went unreturned.

Is Bonnie avoiding me? I asked Petra.

Why would she be avoiding you? She doesn't need to, you're never here.

I'm still paying rent, aren't I?

And under her breath, pushing past me where I stood with my bags in the hall—already I was on my way south again—she said, Don't know why you bother.

While my relationship with Jude seemed only to be getting stronger, I was aware that in other ways I was failing—as a daughter, as a housemate, as an employee. But for the first time, none of that mattered much to me. If I worried about money, I had the savings put aside for my trip—no longer spending my nights dreaming of being elsewhere, looking up flights or searching for sublets in Paris or Rome. I had so few real responsibilities at that point in my life and yet I was ready to abandon all of them. Forgetting, back then, that I still had to eat, to pay rent, that a world existed outside his bedroom door and that there might come a time when once again I had to live in it. I could not survive on love alone. Forgetting, most of all, that we had been together only four months and we were delicate and untested.

One evening, making dinner together at the Old House. Eyes weeping onion tears until Jude took the knife from my hand and said, Here, let me, while I tore off bits of bread from a loaf and packed them into my mouth—an old trick he'd taught me, that stops the stinging.

Have to go away this weekend, love, he said. Annual trip to see my mum. Her birthday on Sunday, you know how it is.

Your mother?

Without knowing it, I'd come to think of Jude like some orphan boy, blood ties to no one. Like my mother had said, *a stray*.

You know, I've never once heard you talk about your family, I said.

It's just my mum out in Parramatta, and a sister down in Adelaide who I hardly speak to anymore. Old man died when we were kids.

Oh Jude, I'm so sorry. I didn't know.

My hand on his arm, though he didn't turn to me or acknowledge the gesture, and continued to move the knife through the onion. What else could I say? A loss like that would run so deep, language couldn't touch it. That kind of grief, it changes the shape and colour of everything.

It was a long time ago now, he said. Can't really imagine it being any other way.

Do you want me to come with you? You could stay at mine. We could make a trip of it, go see my mum in the Mountains afterwards. She keeps asking when we're going to come visit.

No, he said, gentle but firm, kissing me on the forehead. I'd rather not subject you to all that.

But I'd love to meet your mother.

Some other time, he said.

She does know about me, doesn't she?

We're not close, like you and your mother, he said. It's been a long time since I introduced her to anybody. I'll be leaving pretty early Sunday morning, but why don't you come down and stay anyway? Don't feel like you can't be here just because I'm not. You could get some writing done, work on those stories you never let me read. Besides, it would be nice to have you here when I get back. Naked, preferably.

Stooping to kiss below my ear, pulling me close from behind. Running his hands over my body, soft in a black sweater, holding my breasts, slipping his fingers into my tights. How quickly his moods changed, pivoting like someone turning sharply on a boot heel. Vague thought before I closed my eyes, leaned into his hands—how many other women had he reached towards as a distraction?

I wish I'd known that, I said later, in his bed. About your dad. I don't ask enough questions, do I?

It's not your fault, he said. I'm not very forthcoming. Been told that before. Trying to do better now though, with you.

I love that you're trying with me.

A silent thanking in the dark of all the women who had come before me and broken him in. Thinking of what my mother said, *like horses.*

This is his place, you know, said Jude. Knocking on the wooden beams above. He grew up here, my old man—not in this house, but in a little fibro house a few towns north, in Shoalhaven. Moved up to the city to do his apprenticeship and find work, lived in rooming houses until he met my mother. He thought she was real sophisticated because she'd grown up in Sydney—never mind that she lived at home in the suburbs with her mother and father and grandparents all together under one roof, and had to share a room with her sister. He bought this land when he asked her to marry him, thinking they'd build a house here and live in it together one day, raise a family by the sea. It was a kit home, built bit by bit from instalments in a weekly magazine. It has siblings—you know, sister houses, up and down the coast. All with different extensions and additions. This town, it wasn't much back then. Still cheap, but it had the beach, and to my dad, that was paradise.

But my mother was young, said Jude, and she didn't want to give up life in the city. And then us kids were born, and my mother's mother got sick, and I don't know how time works but we never did move down here. Holidays, sometimes, but it was always half camping. Tarp over the windows and sawdust on the floors, no hot water. Ten years he spent, trying to finish it and make it good enough for her, to convince her. It started to cost them more money, having the house but not living in it. They used to fight about it. Mum often threatened to sell it after he died, but I think she felt too guilty. The house—the dream of it—that's what we were raised on. The idea that one day we'd move here, and everything would be better. The struggle would be worth it for this place by the sea. All those long hours at work all week and then driving down south on the weekends with his brothers, building it beam by beam, for her.

You should have seen it when I got my hands on it, he said. Abandoned for close to twenty years. In no state to sell, but too expensive to just tear it down. Birds nesting in the eaves, spiderwebs clotting up the windows. Attic full of pigeon shit. Had to redo the whole porch, where it had rotted away. My sister wasn't too keen on it though, she could never understand it. Why I felt like I owed it to him, somehow. I think she hated the idea of me living out Dad's dream, like it wasn't fair. And it isn't, I guess. But what is? My mother didn't mind, as long as she didn't have to deal with it or hear about it anymore.

He fell silent. I said that the fact that the house had remained standing all that time and had been owned by his family for so many years was remarkable to me. No one in my family had ever managed to hold on to anything that long. We'd moved around so often when I was a girl, never settling. Even after my grandmother died and there was some money, my mother would buy a house only to sell it on again. She changed them so much that by the time we left, they never resembled the place we'd moved into.

How did he— I began, trying to find the words. Your dad. What happened to him?

Heart attack, at work, said Jude. His heart gave out, and he fell from a ladder. Then Mum took up with this new man, a real asshole, a hawker. Turned up on our doorstep right after the funeral selling subscriptions, as if he could smell the grief, and basically moved right in. Even made us call him Dad. Took Mum's engagement ring off while she was sleeping, pawned it for cash. Came home with a bunch of flowers for her, saying she couldn't be mad about it. They needed money, and what did she need some dead guy's ring for? And then he just took off one day. Got in his car with its expired plates and never came back. We found out later he had another family up in Queensland. A wife and kids and everything.

There were worse stories, things Jude would tell me only later. Like how his mother's boyfriend came home drunk one night, stumbled into Jude's room, and pissed on his bed. He thought the man must have been sleepwalking and got lost on the way to the bathroom, but when Jude switched on the light, the man looked him right in the eye, and laughed. How I wished I could reach back in time when he told me that and pluck him out of that bedroom, that lonely childhood. Longing to have known him as a boy, that somehow I could have taken care of him like a mother and also grown up to be his lover—a strange but true feeling—and maybe that's when it started, the desire to have a baby that would be ours together. It seemed as close as I could come to meeting him as a child.

What was your dad like? I asked then. Do you remember him?

Kind, good with his hands. Skinny, but strong, especially in the water. He loved the sea, always wanted to live on a boat, but this was as close as he could get. I always thought they made a funny couple, my mum and dad, because she was tall, broad-shouldered. Not really beautiful, but a handsome woman. In pictures she seemed to tower over him. Dad was gentle, quiet. He probably could have been a poet, if his life had been different. He had that way about him, though he wasn't much of a reader. I guess that's all pretty generic though, isn't it? Truth is there isn't a lot I remember anymore, or maybe I've tried to forget. All I know is that when I was a kid, we were happy. Then he died when I was eleven, and that was it. I was grown.

What about you? said Jude. Your old man's not in the picture, I take it?

After my parents separated, we sort of drifted away from each other, I said, and I was grateful when he nodded and did not ask me to explain it more because I did not know how, did not understand it still. I had the tendency to think of the three of us like survivors of some terrible storm. My mother and I had clung to each other in the wreckage—she had chosen me, or we had chosen each other. We did what we had to do in order to be saved.

I used to visit him, I said, up until I was a teenager. Knocking on the doors of these sad bachelors' quarters or other women's houses while my mother waited in the car. And then one day, I just stopped going. When I think of him now, the memories are from a much earlier time, when I was really little. Memory's funny like that—the way it distorts distance. It's his voice, mainly, that comes back, and the old songs he used to listen to because they reminded him of his own mother. 'I'll Be Seeing You', 'The Way You Look Tonight', things like that. When I was small he would sing me to sleep, but they were so sad, those songs! They all seemed to be about saying goodbye. And the shape of him— sitting on his shoulders, feeling like the queen of the world. Teaching me to swim here at Sailors. It was the only holiday we ever went on as a family, the three of us together—or the only one I remember, anyway, and they split up not long after. Mainly, I remember what it felt like to be held like that. Lifted from the water, up over the waves. Trusting him. Safe. Haven't felt that way since.

Not even here, with me? said Jude.

Oh no, I said, burying my face in his neck. You're not safe.

What am I then?

You? You're the shark.

He seized my waist to make me shriek, kissing my belly while I laughed, sucking the skin below my hip to leave a mark. I want you, I said. Reaching into the bedside drawer, finding an empty box. Not a single silver-foiled condom, only the discarded wrappers from some other afternoon or night. It didn't matter. I trust you, I said, and it sounded like a vow.

Is this what his father pictured? I wondered, as I fell asleep that night. A love nest made of his family home. I put my hand on Jude's chest while he slept, pressed lightly. Felt the pulse of his heart beating beneath my fingertips. Good heart, I prayed. Strong. Faithful.

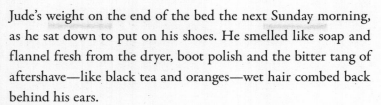

Jude's weight on the end of the bed the next Sunday morning, as he sat down to put on his shoes. He smelled like soap and flannel fresh from the dryer, boot polish and the bitter tang of aftershave—like black tea and oranges—wet hair combed back behind his ears.

Are you sure you don't want me to come with you? I said. Half rising, eyes adjusting to the lamplight. It must have been early, the sky outside was pale.

It's okay, he said, bringing the covers back over me, kissing me goodbye. I rolled over into the warm hollow his body had made and when I woke again some time later, he was gone.

In his absence, I filled the hours with small acts of care, stretching them out luxuriously. Drawing a long bath in the middle of the afternoon, smoking in the tub and reading *What We Talk About When We Talk About Love*, a copy I found on Jude's shelf. I could enjoy this time alone in a way I never did those nights in the city when both the girls were out, because I knew it was only a pause—soon, Jude would return to me. I could feel safe in this knowledge because there I was in his house, his things all around me. I spent the day dressed in tights and one of his jumpers, just to feel him close, to have the scent of him near.

In the evening, I made a simple meal from cans and packages I found in the cupboard, boiling water for spaghetti, frying garlic and anchovies with black olives and tomatoes, and ate standing up at the kitchen bench, picking the olives out with my fingers. Steam fogged the windows, like breath. Afterwards, I sat in the living room at the desk that Jude had set up for me by the window, looking out at the trees and the side of the porch. It was a mismatched thing, the top from an old drafting board and the base from some other table, legs painted teal green. He had spent the week fixing it up for me and I was touched by this—by the way he was making a place in the house, not only for me but for my work.

My writing habits, even then, were nocturnal, and I worked well for a while, absorbed in the notes I'd made on the lighthouse keepers' daughters that day at the ruins. Cutting the draft of the story into fragments with kitchen scissors. I liked to work this way, to shuffle the pieces around with my hands, like some kind of divination. Weighing them down with various items I found around the house so the wind wouldn't pick up their edges—a hammer, a reel of thread, a grey pockmarked stone that looked like the surface of the moon.

Around ten, there was a message from Jude saying he'd been late leaving and he was just passing through Wollongong. He was halfway home.

It would be at least another hour until he got back, but I wanted to stay awake so I could greet him—maybe we'd have a drink together or a cup of tea and talk and then make love, a respite from what I imagined was a long and difficult day. Taking my time getting ready for bed, making a ritual of it. Washing my face with warm water, applying creams and oils, brushing all the tangles out of my hair, which had grown long and unruly after a summer of salt water. I counted the strokes the way Bonnie did, and then braided it all into a crown on top of my head. Thinking how happy he'd be to find me that way—clean and soft, with sweet jasmine perfume that smelled like spring rain on each of my pulse points. A feeling, then, of wanting to be devoured, pulled apart limb by limb, or swallowed whole. I made myself up that way, like a young bride for the night, but I fell asleep in bed while I was reading, and sometime later, I woke up to find the house still and bright. Jude had not yet come home, though it was after midnight. There were no more calls or messages from him, and when I dialled his number, an automated woman's voice informed me that he was currently unavailable. His phone was dead, or he was out of range, or he'd switched it off.

I tried not to worry—to trust, like he was always asking me to do—but I couldn't fall asleep again. Wide awake and listening for the familiar faithful humming of the truck making its way up the hill. Strange country noises were magnified in the empty house, and there was no one to answer if I asked, *What's that sound?* Thinking of the things Jude would say, the list he cycled through: the wind, the house settling, a bird's cry.

It wasn't the usual, everyday perils I feared then—that he was with another woman, or that there might be times when it was easier for him to be alone than to be with me. My imagination skewed towards the tragic and sudden—car wrecks on slick freeways, crushed metal and flames. Fear turned me superstitious, and I wagered promises with some force I had no name for, made bargains with myself in the dark—prayers of the unfaithful. In bed I lay still, holding my breath at times to hear better. I would not move, I decided, until he returned. I'd had these kinds of habits as a child—waiting for my mother to come back from the shops, sitting on the edge of the couch stiff and unblinking as the clock in the hall moved past the hour she said she'd be home, as if I could give my body the power to freeze time. And maybe what I wanted—my oldest wish—was for no time to pass while the ones I loved were gone.

But my fear, and my patience, wore away as it got later. There was nothing special about this, I thought. I was just another woman waiting for a man to come home. I hated him then for putting me in that position, which seemed deeply embarrassing. Feeling foolish with my braids, my perfumed wrists. I pulled my hair loose, changed into an old T-shirt, switched off the lights.

I'm not sure how long I lay there for—I was angry and tired and afraid, and in that state five minutes can seem as long as an hour. But finally, there was the sound of his key in the door, his boots on the stairs, and then, at last, his body falling into bed beside mine.

You smell like the pub, I said. Have you been drinking?

Stopped for one on the way home. Ended up being in a lock-in for someone's birthday.

It's been hours. I waited up for you. I was worried something happened.

Sorrylove, he said, the words rolling around in his mouth, colliding.

Please tell me you didn't drive home like this.

Maeve drove, he said.

Maeve?

Remembering then the woman from the pub back in the summer. Her long dark hair and silver rings on her fingers. The way she walked through the crowd of men. In all the months since then, he hadn't once mentioned her name.

Ran into her and Willy. We had a few, lost track of time, they gave me a lift. That's all. Thought you'd be asleep. But I'm here now, aren't I?

I think now that Jude kept me waiting that night to prove to me, and to himself, that he could. You want a dog, not a man, he said to me on another occasion, when I was angry at him for coming home late or not answering his phone. Someone to come whenever you whistle, whenever you call. He wanted to feel free, and to Jude that meant belonging to no one. Maybe he liked women who played along with those kinds of games, pushing him away only to pull him back again. To behave badly and be reprimanded in order to be forgiven—somewhere along the course of his life, Jude had learned this as a kind of love. And while I was slow to trust, to let people in, I loved without reservation once I did, and in this way I was stronger than him. Although

I did not feel strong then, when out of relief, rage, frustration, I began to cry.

I was so worried, I said.

I'm here now, he said again, but more gently this time, and because I felt so grateful for that, I said nothing more. I let him pull me close, curled up against his warmth, and listened to the ragged rhythm of his breath. Already, he was sleeping.

In the end I never did meet his mother, although once, he showed me a picture. Dated on the back in a looping, cursive hand— *Julian + Valerie, 197–?* A woman standing in a scrubby suburban front yard, a small boy with short-cropped hair, freckled and fair, barefoot, shirt half tucked into his shorts, holding on to her hand. The house a white rectangle behind them like a blank slate with a screen door. Gnarled eucalypt out the front, his mother's hair a pale cloud, Farrah Fawcett curls. Suntanned shoulders, long legs, pale pink sundress. Looking elsewhere, her chin pointed upward, as if in defiance, her body angled away from the boy, towards the cigarette she held in her other hand, ash poised at the tip. The camera caught it, the moment before it fell. Neither one of them was smiling. But that boy—large watery eyes, Cupid's bow lips. Impossible to imagine he was ever that young. *Julian.* A compromise, he told me. His father wanted Jude, because he'd read somewhere that it was the name of the patron saint of sailors, but his mother insisted that no son of hers would be given a woman's name.

She's beautiful, I said. Like a movie star from the seventies. Thinking, Would anything illustrate the gap between our ages more clearly than comparing pictures of our mothers in their youth?

That generation got too much sun, said Jude. But I suppose she was once. It was a different time. And I didn't know if he meant another era, or time in their lives.

When I asked again about going to see his mother or visiting his sister and his nieces, Jude said, with an air of tired patience, I've tried all that before, love. Merging families. It never turns into the pretty picture everybody hopes it will be.

I hate it when you talk like that, I said. Makes you sound old, and hopeless. Like everything that could possibly happen has happened already. What if we get married one day?

Well, that's easy, he said, because I don't believe in marriage. Even if I did, I wouldn't invite them.

You wouldn't invite your own mother to your wedding?

She didn't invite me to hers, second time around—or the third, for that matter. Maybe that's why I've never been keen on the whole idea. Kind of ruined the concept for me.

What if we had children? Wouldn't you want your children to know their grandmother?

If he ever had a family, Jude said, he wanted to start anew, as the man he was now, a prisoner to no past. Could I accept that or—?

And so I fell back to thinking of him as a boy-orphan, or a man made at the age of forty-two, and maybe sometimes I dreamed of a child, began to long for one. A girl with my dark brows and thin lips, Jude's changeable eyes. Often, when I was younger, I pictured myself with a big family. Three children, four, five. How they would weigh me down, like sinkers on a sounding line, dangling from my arms, hanging from my skirts, anchoring me. Never letting each other drift away on life's loose tides. A family was a tether, and there was safety in numbers. In larger families, I'd always thought, you were less exposed. It was harder to see the absences, the wounds.

In the days before my period I often dreamed I was pregnant, waking up to my flat stomach and a hollow, empty feeling. Counting off the days on my fingers, thinking, What if? Relief and disappointment when the blood did come—this feeling a secret I kept from Jude. Feeling loss when I should have felt lucky.

I went through phases of trying to be good, measuring my temperature every morning and following the rhythm method outlined in a book I'd found in the shop, *Loving the Natural Way*. A faded cover, Adam and Eve with long hair flowing, holding hands in the garden below a pear tree in full bloom. Prescriptions of juniper berries and stoneseed tea. We didn't wish for it, didn't will it, but what if we found ourselves there?

Love child. That's how I thought of it back then.

Holing up by the beach together that winter, it was just the two of us—until we found King, and then we were three.

I may have dreamed of a child that winter but we were given a dog, as if he had been delivered to us. Instead of a baby in a basket, there was King on the shore one evening, sitting up on one of the wooden benches overlooking the water and staring out at the sea, like a human. He was so big that from a distance he looked like an old man in a coat.

When we got closer, he hopped up and began to wag his tail, as if he'd been waiting for us. His fur was a mix of colours that matched the landscape of the bay—sand, chalk, mud, dust and bark—but his muzzle was pure white.

An older gentleman, said Jude. A little like myself.

I reached my hand out to the dog and he pushed his wet nose into my palm, then sat in front of me and gave me his paw, as if to say, *Pleased to meet you.* Beautiful, giant paws that made my hand look small.

Look, Jude, I said, he knows how to shake.

He's very well mannered. A king among dogs, said Jude, and there was, I agreed, a great sadness and nobility in the way he held his large head, as if he were the last of his kind. A gentle giant, a king without a kingdom.

I scratched behind his ears and asked him the useless questions people ask of animals. What's your name? Aren't you beautiful? Who do you belong to? Neither of us had seen him before. He was not a local, Jude was sure. How could anyone forget the sight of him? When we walked him through town that winter, we turned heads.

There was no collar buried in the thick scruff of fur around his neck, and the beach had emptied out now the wind was picking up. The sky was darkening, the tide drawing up to the bush like a blanket. Soon there would be no more than a frill of sand around the shore.

I'd lived with dogs as a child, grown up around them—sleeping next to them, riding side by side with them in cars. My mother's Rhodesian ridgeback from my childhood, Lola, who liked to ride shotgun, and the boyfriend she had at one point who bred dogs as big as small horses, Great Danes and cane corsos. I was five years old—it was right after we moved to Sydney—and she let me feed them by hand, convinced that fear, like love, was a learned thing, and that animals could sense it, smell it on you. Like Jude had told me, with the birds. *If you trust them, they'll trust you.*

He does remind me of you, I said, all long-limbed and grey and shaggy. The dog was nuzzling at my knees, leaning his weight against my legs. He was so tall I could rest my hand on his back without bending down.

I hope you mean that as a compliment, Jude said, and I nodded. I did. Back then, I had only good intentions. I meant everything in the best way.

At home that night, blasting 'I Wanna Be Your Dog' by Iggy Pop on the record player because nobody shared any walls with us—a benefit of country living. We danced, the three of us, and he was already King—named and claimed by us, the ones who had found him and taken him in. The dog with his paws up on Jude's shoulders so they were almost eye to eye, barking in time to the music.

Jude turned to me with a look I didn't recognise.

Can we keep him? he said.

I remember he said it that way—*we*. For so long I'd felt like a beggar for his love, and now, for the first time, he was asking something of me. To share with him something that would be ours together, a partnership of sorts, a kind of parenthood, and I could never bring myself to snuff out the hope in his eyes whenever I caught it there. The way he looked at me sometimes, on waking: as if I were a surprise, a gift, my appearance in his life miraculous. He called me Love, as if it were my name. As if I could be the very thing itself.

Tomorrow, we had said, walking back along the track from the beach towards home, the dog leading as if he knew the way, could smell it, nosing through the bush and up the street as if on the scent of something he'd lost and was seeking to recover. Tomorrow, we'd take him to the vet in town—it would be too late at six o'clock on a wintery Sunday evening, and his people wouldn't be out looking for him in the dark. Not the shelter, we agreed, we couldn't do that, talking it over after we went to bed—because what if instead of being lost he'd been, you know. Lowering our voices, in case he could hear, *abandoned*.

There we were, at the top of the A-frame, King sleeping on the rug at the foot of the bed that had already become his. Three strays—together, we made a family.

Love—great love, as Jude would say—has a way of seeming both miraculous and inevitable. After my brother was born, all the years I'd been without him seemed impossible. I felt like he'd always been a part of me, had always been there, waiting in the wings to make his appearance. That kind of love, it alters the past as well as the future.

And so it was with King. Forgetting so quickly who we'd been before him, how silent the house without the clip of his paws on the floorboards, trailing us from room to room, or the yowls and low growls he made while he was sleeping, toes twitching and flexing in some imaginary pursuit. Tawny dog hairs we picked from each other's coats and jumpers and the seat of Jude's truck. Although the shock, that first morning, of opening my eyes to find his face staring into mine, his long whiskery snout. A wolf in the house.

You've got yourself a real fixer-upper, said the vet, when we finally took King in for an appointment. We'd been avoiding it, hiding out like bandits, afraid that he was a wanted dog and we'd have to turn him in, ducking our heads when we walked through town. Though we weren't exactly an inconspicuous trio—Jude striding down the street, tall in his wide-brimmed hat and black heeled boots, flanked by the long-legged dog on one side and me on the other, dressed in my long black skirt and lace blouse, eighteen years younger and a girl from the city.

The vet spoke about King as if he were a bad investment, like a sinking house or a broken-down car, listing his faults on his fingers. Cataracts, arthritis, weak heart. All of it costly to treat.

You could put up signs and posters around the town, he said. Someone might come forward. Could be that he was spooked by something. You'd never believe how far a dog can run when he's frightened. Even one in his condition. But of course, he said, there's always the chance with a dog of his size, not to mention his age, that he was dumped.

Who would do something like that? I said.

Oh, I see all kinds of things, the vet said. Cruelty, abandonment, neglect—you name it. Nothing surprises me anymore. Luckily, I'm not in the business of trying to understand people.

King was a mutt, he said, a dog of *doubtful pedigree*. Rough coat, whiskery around his chin and brows, with the long face of a wolfhound but a little squarer around the snout. Skinny legs, ears a little too large, and soft, which made him look melancholy. He was not quite as tall as if he were purebred—though if he stood on his hind legs, he was the same height as Jude.

So, we can keep him? I said. If there's no microchip, and nobody comes forward.

The vet shrugged. I'd say he's as good as yours, he said.

Afterwards, we walked across the car park to the small arcade and chose a name tag from the key cutters outside the super-market. Four letters engraved into a red metal heart and attached to the collar Jude had fashioned from an old belt, extra holes hammered in with a nail.

And while we're here, he said, taking two house keys, one silver, one gold, from his leather chain. When he pressed the duplicates into my palm, they were sharp at the edges and still warm.

A few days later my mother called. Where have you been? she said. I've been trying to reach you. When are you coming to see us?

It was early in the evening, though from the sound of it, she had been drinking. Her voice lush with drink and emotion in a way that recalled my childhood, the years before Henry was born.

What a week she'd had, she said, just awful. A fox in the henhouse, the yard full of blood and feathers. It's the cruellest thing, you know? They only eat one but they kill them all. All my lovely hens. And I had to clean up the whole bloody mess of it myself. Oh, it was terrible! *It's truly terrible*, to be a woman alone sometimes.

Over the phone, bright, cold sounds. Ice against glass, bracelets sliding up and down her wrists, my mother gesticulating, I imagined, the way she did when she was gin-drunk or agitated, waving one hand about while she talked.

You're not alone, Mum, I said. You have me, and Henry.

Henry's still a little boy! And he loved those chickens. Raised them himself in a box with one of those lamps. He would have been traumatised.

From across the kitchen Jude raised his eyebrows at me. Conscious of my mother's voice rising on the other end of the line, I motioned that I was going outside, patting my leg to get the dog to follow.

And you, my mother said, as I paced the hill outside the Old House trying to get a clear signal, you weren't around. You're always with *him* whenever I need you, and I heard it in her voice then, the tone of a jealous lover. Noted, too, some role reversal in that. Hadn't I once been the greedy one? Tugging on her skirts, pulling her by the hand away from the men who approached us at parks or birthday parties or in supermarkets. My stern child's voice scolding her, Do not talk to that strange man. Her then-red hair drew them like a flame, and I batted them all away. Freezing out her suitors by refusing to talk to them and once, when I was very young, kicking a potential boyfriend in the shins in the foyer of a movie theatre. I think now that this is something that happens in small families—roles get confused, relationships do double duty. So a daughter might play the part of an overprotective parent, or a mother might rely on the daughter like a partner. Mother as runaway child, daughter as mother, daughter as husband.

Over the phone, I told her about the dog. Thinking that my mother, great lover of animals, would appreciate the tale of how we'd seen him on the beach from a distance and mistaken him for an old man in a winter coat. Watching while I spoke as King sniffed, off-leash, at a neighbour's lawn and lifted one elegant leg to wet the trunk of a paperbark tree. I was, it's true, enamoured with him, convinced of his superiority over all other creatures, like the parent who believes her child to be the most advanced and gifted.

A dog? she said. What on earth did you do that for?

I was surprised. Hadn't she always said that it was best to date men who had pets, because it proved they knew how to look after something? Hadn't she furrowed her brow when I told her that Jude lived alone with no animals? *But oh*, I'd wanted to say to her then, *you should see him feed the birds.*

My mother went on to tell me we were crazy, that wolfhound meant half-wild for a reason, that big dogs cost more money to run and didn't last as long in the end.

It's just a heartbreak waiting to happen, she said. Why don't you get a puppy? Train it young. With an old dog, you never know what they've been through. All of a sudden, they can just snap. There's no shortage of strays out there. You don't have to take whatever one washes up on the beach. Why don't you go to the pound, take your pick?

We didn't choose King, I told my mother. He chose us. Or we chose each other. Or maybe it wasn't even a choice at all. Like love.

Still, it was true that once I was walking King through the playground overlooking the cliff in town after driving Jude to work and a woman had shrieked, swooped to gather up her toddler, and pointed, accusingly, at the dog. He's a monster! she cried, while King stood placidly, panting, saliva dripping from his tongue. How was it possible, I thought, that others didn't see the great beauty in him? And hadn't my own mother told me that when it came to dogs and horses, the bigger they were, the more gentle, and steady? That was why, she'd said, children were taught how to ride on Clydesdales.

It had reminded me of when Bonnie had said to me one afternoon, sprawled out on the couch in our house in the city: You know, Jude's not especially handsome.

What would she know? I thought. Her latest crush looked sixteen years old. Perfect olive skin, black hair combed and parted to one side, soft hands like a girl's, emerald eyes. Not all of us want to date someone prettier than we are, I'd said, and Bonnie pouted. I knew she never doubted her beauty—I'd sat in her room at night while she brushed smooth her pale hair with one hundred strokes, rubbed cream into her legs and hands, and applied oils to her face with a brown glass dropper, cupping her chin in her palm while she looked in the mirror. Bonnie and her crush would have made an attractive couple, with their neatly knotted scarves, cashmere coats, polished loafers. But me, I loved a mutt, a stray, and from the beginning I'd always thought Jude was handsome.

Like trying to unravel a lover's past, I wondered sometimes about King's other lives, his adventures before our time. I made a game of trying to guess his other names. Beckett, I suggested, since he was part Irish wolfhound, and because the serious expression he assumed when he was denied the food we were eating, laying his head down on his paws, reminded me of a portrait I'd seen of the writer. Existentially weary.

Who cares who he was before, what his other names were, said Jude, always firmly rooted in the present. He's King now. Was always meant to be.

Do you think he's happy here, with us? I wonder sometimes if he misses his old family.

Of course he's happy. Whatever was before doesn't matter now. He probably doesn't even remember it.

But I longed for the puppy he would have been in the same way I missed the little boy Jude I'd never know. Wishing that I could bend time, so we might meet as children. I liked to imagine King as a young dog, it made me laugh to picture how awkward he would have been, breaking in those long legs, with his giant paws and too-big ears. I felt both angry at the cruelty of whoever had let him go, and grateful that we were the ones to have found him. I watched carefully in those first few weeks for changes in his moods and behaviour. What was he thinking about when he crossed his paws, and sighed? A sound so deep, it was almost human. Was he missing someone? Those wistful eyes, so full of pathos. I believed he'd seen things, known things, I did not yet understand. He was, after all, older than both of us. Nine, in the vet's estimate—sixty-three, in dog years. *Past his prime.*

I was sure dogs had a long memory, and King was emotional, vocal about what moved him, prone to howl whenever one of us left the house, the way some people are prone to weep. We referred to these fits as *singing his sad ballads*, but that howl, it did have a mournful quality.

There's an old sadness there, I said to Jude, I'm sure of it. When I look into his eyes sometimes, it's like they're brimming. I think he has more feelings than you do. When was the last time you cried?

Oh, I don't know, said Jude. Probably in a movie. Probably one about a dog.

Anyone who has spent time with dogs can understand the argument that they are smarter than people. Or, at least, that they seem to know what we want before we recognise that we want it—before we have even dared to long for it, let alone figured out how to ask. King's welcoming bark when I arrived at Jude's at the end of the week, the sound of his paws on the wooden floorboards as he ran down the hall, his salutes like joyous cries. *At last! At last!*

Take it easy, mate, you're embarrassing yourself, said Jude, loitering in the kitchen, keeping his distance at first, pretending that he hadn't missed me at all while the dog howled at my feet, rolled onto his back, belly up, in surrender.

Never had my place seemed so silent when I returned to the city. Calling down the empty hallways, Hello? Bonnie? Hello? Petra? House dark and clothes in piles on the couch and kitchen table, dirty dishes in the sink, all of it abandoned in a hurry. My first night back for the week I spent alone, as if the girls had conspired to stay out all night in order to teach me a lesson.

And so, I wondered what I was coming back for. My three shifts a week at the bookstore hardly seemed like enough of a reason and neither did this husk of my old life, my room full of girls' things where I felt so lonely without the dog down the end of the bed and Jude's weight beside me and the sea singing outside our window.

Do you think a dog can get depressed? Jude asked me one night over the phone. King's miserable when you're gone. Gets all mopey and pathetic. Doesn't want to leave the house, in case you come back while we're gone. Stops every couple of paces to look back over his shoulder. Think he goes a bit mad, barking at animals or ghosts in the bushes. Things that aren't really there. You should see him. The way he sleeps by the door as if you might walk in at any moment, it'd break your heart.

He gets like that sometimes, I said. I don't think he likes us to be apart.

On mornings when we drove Jude to work and left him at the shop, King couldn't forget about him right away, and became stubborn. More than once we'd stood on the street corner at the end of the block in a tug-of-war, me pulling at his leash while he stood stoic, waiting for Jude to catch up with us. Sitting out the front with an unbroken eyeline view of the door, like a monument to canine loyalty, he was as tall as my waist and immovable. I had to bribe him, coat pockets filled with biscuits and leathery strips of dehydrated meat, leading him away with a closed fist. It was as if it were his task to make sure we never drifted apart or left one another behind, and I sympathised with that feeling.

I knew what it was to love like that—to want everyone you love to be within sight, within reach.

I think you should move in, said Jude. Not for me, but for King. I mean, I'm fine on my own. Used to the bachelor life, but it's a bit hard on an old dog like him.

And how do you know all this? I said, teasing.

Oh, he told me, said Jude. Me and him, we have these long conversations when you're not around. Guy stuff, you know. Shooting the shit over a beer and some kibble. He's got this idea that you're a real heartbreaker, a tease—a *treat 'em mean, keep 'em keen* kind of woman. I defended you, of course, tried to set him straight. But it wasn't easy, he'd even got to thinking you had another *dog* up there, some young pup in the city you like to run around with.

Tell him it isn't true! I said. Tell him he's my true love, the only one for me. Are you serious, though? About me moving in?

I know it's a lot to think about, he said, and maybe you're not ready to leave the city. You've got your housemates, a job, a whole life up there.

Petra and Bonnie aren't even here, I said. I'm by myself. I think they're mad at me.

You'd save money, and have more time to write—if that's what you want to do. In any case, you'd be able to take a minute to figure it out. Or is it too much? said Jude. Too soon? The idea of you and me together, every night. It's hard to come back from that, you know, if things go south.

It's not too much, I said.

Nothing, I wanted to say, *nothing you could give me would ever be too much.*

Well then, he said. Take some time. Think about it.

Looking back, it seems that was how Jude always was with me: keeping his distance, never asking for anything I might not want to give. That steadiness that I took to be a strength—his consistency—I realise now was a kind of boundary, a way of drawing a line in the sand. Like a sprinkling of salt at the threshold, it was a kind of spell to keep himself safe, unchanged. What he needed more than anything was to believe he needed nothing, that if I should ever leave, he'd remain the same man. But I had his key in my coat pocket and I was happy then, because it seemed like he was letting me in.

King had a murmur in his heart and was prone to fainting spells. Like a Victorian lady, we joked, though the first time we had been afraid. Up in the Blue Mountains at my mother's house, the whole town dressed up for Christmas in July—tinsel wrapped around the streetlights, a tree in the main square, snow from an aerosol can stencilled on the shop windows. Jude meeting Henry for the first time, strangely stiff and formal with children, extending his hand and Henry accepting it shyly, his skinny arm sticking out of a Guns N' Roses T-shirt. But then Jude showed him his pocket-knife, unfolding the tiny tools one by one, explaining what they were and how they worked, and they were friends.

As we'd walked through the bush early the next morning, King had seen water and gone running. The shock of the cold, the winter lake. It stopped his heart. Jude went wading in, wet up to his knees, dragging him out. He lifted him—dog dripping in his arms and Jude buckling beneath, stiff-legged in wet denim, jeans pasted to his thighs. The weight heavy and human. Jude wrapped the dog in his coat, pumped on his heart with his hands. I watched while he breathed air from his lungs between the dog's jaws until King rolled back over, staggered up, spewed water. A miracle! we said to my mother and Henry, back at the house, when we told them the story. King resurrected, running out to the garden to greet them, wagging his long tail and shaking water, trampling down the flowers, pansies flattened beneath paws. My mother didn't seem to mind. She'd quickly come to adore the dog despite her earlier reservations and would have forgiven him anything—which was more than I could say for her feelings towards Jude. Throughout our relationship, she continued to treat him with reservation, shaking his hand instead of embracing him or kissing his cheek. Playing the part of the overprotective patriarch. Aware of the strain of it in those moments—the way she felt she had to step in to fill my father's role.

I didn't know you could give a dog mouth-to-mouth, she said, but it was true, we'd seen it. A Christmas-in-July miracle, we insisted, elated with our magic dog who'd come back from the dead when we'd called his name. At dinner that night, Henry made King wear a paper crown from an old Christmas cracker, and we all fed him chicken at the table with our fingers, letting him lick clean my grandmother's best china plates.

It's his heart, the vet in the Mountains explained when we took him in the following day for a checkup. A dog of his size doesn't need much exercise, especially not at his age. He's not a young pup anymore.

Well, neither am I, joked Jude, but she was a serious young woman who used terms like *geriatric canine*, unimpressed by Jude's usual charm, and so he became unusually deferential, nodding and saying, Yes ma'am, though she could have been only a few years older than me, not even thirty. Neat black hair, dark eyes behind clear frameless glasses, white manicured hands and a long, slender neck I noticed Jude's eyes linger on as she bent down over the dog with her stethoscope before they quickly skittered up and away to admire her certificate for a PhD in veterinary medicine framed in gold on the wall.

You say you found him this year? she said. Some dogs run away from home when they approach their time. We don't know why. Privacy, maybe. Or to spare their families.

We were given a list of new rules: no dog parks, no games that required running, and most importantly, no swimming in cold water. Think of him like an elderly man, she said. Nothing that could shock or strain the heart. I left her office feeling scolded, defensive, like a bad mother, or the young mistress of an octogenarian. He might not have needed to run, but you should have seen him. On the beach with me in those early days, both of us returned to childhood, galloping while I threw a stick that sailed high in an arc in the air, and King jumping up, yelping. Pure joy. Who were we to deny an old dog a good time, I thought, especially if what she said was true, that this might be the winter of his life.

My mother suggested we all go out for dinner at the old hotel in town for our last night, but I said we should stay in, keep an eye on King. In truth, I didn't want to go anywhere that weekend, conscious of the unusual shape our family would take, strangers trying to slot us into the traditional roles. Afraid that, with my mother and Henry with us, people would mistake Jude for my mother's partner, not mine. So, I said I did not want to go to the doll museum, or on a hike around the Mountains to see the Three Sisters, and Jude said, No worries, I've seen all that before anyway, and I knew it must have been with some other woman. A lovers' long-weekend getaway before my time.

That night, washing up after dinner while Jude slipped out to smoke a cigarette and Henry fell asleep in front of the TV, his head resting on the dog's back, I told my mother that Jude had asked me to move in with him. She frowned, passing me a plate to dry.

Wouldn't you miss the girls? she said.

I think they'd rather someone who was home more often, I said. And it's a waste of money, paying rent when I'm only there half the time.

I can help you out a bit more, if that's what this is about.

I'm not asking you to do that.

So what's your plan, then? Quit your job and let him support you?

God, I said, you make it sound like I'm going to be a kept woman or something. You don't have to worry, I'll figure it out. The bookstore was only supposed to be temporary, anyway. And aren't you always saying they don't pay me enough?

Listen, she said. You can move in with him. Just don't have a baby. He's a lot older than you, and he's a man, so he's going to want one. They all do, in the end. No matter what they say.

I thought you'd be happy for me, I said, because though I knew that technically I was an adult and no longer needed my mother's permission for anything, I still wanted it, or at least, in its place, some kind of blessing.

Oh, I am, I am, she said. It's just, isn't it a bit soon to be moving in together? Isn't this all happening a little too fast?

Well, it's too late now anyway. I already told him I would.

It's okay to change your mind.

But I don't want to change my mind!

My mother hushed me, pointing into the next room where my brother was sleeping.

I took a breath and looked around the small kitchen, onion skins and carrot tops and eggshells overflowing from the small compost pot onto the black-and-white linoleum floor. All this, she had shown me earlier in a series of sketches, would soon be gutted and gone, the adjoining wall knocked down to make one large open room with a wide and glassy porch.

You're not pregnant, are you? she said then.

Of course not, I said, though once again I was struck by her uncanny ability to intuit what, in some secret part of myself, I wanted. My mother, a divining rod for my desires. *Anyway*, I wanted to add, *would it be so bad if I was?* Jude owned a house, we were in love, we took good care of the dog. Back then, I thought that was enough to make a life, and hadn't my mother once thought the same? Why couldn't I want the same things she had wanted at my age? Why did I have to be different? Why did she have to expect more of me? The urge I felt sometimes to lean back into the mould of her life and let it hold me, like something being set into place.

Conversations with my mother: *Don't make the choices I made*, she always seemed to be saying, and though I understood that my mother loved me, and believed that given the chance she would not go back in time and do things differently, I also sensed that she might regret, among other things, the timing of it all—my unexpected arrival in the middle of her twenties. And while intellectually I knew that both things could be true—that the love and regret did not necessarily cancel each other out—it was difficult for me to contemplate because a function of that love meant wanting me to make different choices, and might this not also imply that she considered them mistakes?

Well, I hope you're being careful, she said. This is only the honeymoon time. You think it's the real thing, but it's not. I mean, for heaven's sake, you're only twenty-four.

Yes, the same age you were when I was born.

Exactly, she said. Twenty-four years *young*.

My mother may have only been trying to issue a warning in her way, but when I went to sleep that night in the spare room beside Jude—one of the only spaces in the house that has remained unchanged—I found myself thinking of the words *honeymoon time, honeymoon time*, repeating them to myself, liking the ring of it. How it sounded in my head like an old sweet song.

One week later, I moved down south.

Jude in the kitchen in the weak winter light, peeling a red apple with a paring knife into a perfect unbroken coil, the way his father had taught him when he was a boy. King watching, sad-eyed and hopeful, head tilted to one side. Taking the blade in my own hand, digging too deep into the skin and slipping on the juice, nicking the tender fold between my thumb and forefinger. Jude took the knife from my hand, sucked the blood, and that was love: mouthfuls of juice and blood and spit, sweet and metallic. We picked fruit at farms on the weekends and it went bad when we forgot to use it. Kitchen table lined with spoiled apples, figs grown soft and rotten, persimmons with cracked skins.

It seemed, at first, that the house rejected my tenancy. I bumped into furniture in the night, bruised shins and stubbed toes on side tables and dressers that emerged suddenly from shadow, as if they had moved around in the dark. The rough floorboards left splinters in my feet. Jude sterilising a needle over a flame on the kitchen burner, digging out the tiny slivers beneath the lamplight, holding my foot in his lap.

I'd left the city with a suitcase full of dresses, my favourite novels, a framed photograph of my mother and father, as if I were going travelling, or were a child running away from home. And in that same spirit my departure had been hasty, leaving the girls with a month's rent and an empty room to fill. Jude's house was already set up with more furniture than he could use—antique dressers and desks with missing tops or broken legs and bookcases made of old floorboards lined the hall and the walls of the living room—and most of what I'd had in the city had come from Petra's parents, hand-me-down sofas and second-hand appliances we received whenever they upgraded. Everything else—the white doll's bed that had belonged to my grandmother, my collection of childhood books—I drove to my mother's house, as if we had broken up and I was returning the possessions that belonged to her.

In those first few days I drifted around the house while Jude was at work, trying to learn the space through touch, memory. King sniffing at my boxes of books and old perfume bottles, nosing at the dresses I hung up in the closet, sleeping with his head on my shoes like he was worried I might leave again. Following at my heels as I moved from room to room.

Most of Jude's furnishings had come from the shop, or from his own hands, and that gave everything a worn-in look, aged, like it all belonged together. Dark wood and faded rugs in rich earthy colours. I had always lived in houses of women, spaces of communal female living, apart from brief spells when a boyfriend of my mother's stayed with us and in those cases, it was always clear that they were in feminine territory, guests in a space where we made the rules. Even Grant, Henry's father, had never properly moved in. Before that winter at Sailors Beach, I hadn't shared a home with a man in any consistent way since we'd left my father twenty years earlier. All that time, like a long extended girlhood. An absence of men's things I hadn't noticed until I moved in with Jude. How I'd missed them without realising. The short clippings that stuck to the sink on days that he shaved, his closet full of blue plaid and red flannel and oilskin jackets. Three pairs of the same kind of boots lined up by the door—two black, one scuffed and brown. How out of place my long silk dresses looked, the bright vintage patterns, Liberty fabric, hanging beside his checked shirts. Blue and brown, maroon and green and grey. The thin white and soft peach ones he'd worn last summer folded up and put away for the season to make room for me.

I learned to wash my things by hand, not trusting the ancient washing machine that gnawed at my pearl buttons, ripped lace, shrank the delicates and twisted my stockings into knots. On warm days I hung them out on the back porch, where they looked sheer in the light. I found a peace in these rituals. Listening to the sound of the water filling the bucket, watching it darken the cloth like a growing stain, and swirling soap through in gentle motions with my hands made my mind go blank, as if the smell of lavender and vinegar might be an opiate—but I also felt ashamed at my new embrace of domesticity. Once, I'd pictured a life of travelling between foreign cities, black turtlenecks and books and eyeliner and cigarettes, disastrous love affairs I would mine later for material in celebrated autobiographical novels—not this daily, everyday kind of love. I should want more than this,

I thought—but then, I was happy, and the world outside Sailors Beach receded. When I woke in the mornings, I saw his boots kicked off by the foot of the bed, and that looked like love. All around me, I could smell the sea.

Although at Jude's I was surrounded by trees and nature, the bush was grey and resilient and I missed colour, softness, delicate and fragile things—my pink tasselled lamp, the floral quilts and linens stitched by my grandmother's hand. These I had traded in to sleep in his sparse room at the top of the A-frame, the black brass bed that creaked when we fucked, the faulty brace beneath that gave way sometimes so we sank and rolled together in the night, colliding in our sleep. Waking up with crooked necks.

In the early evenings, I harvested flowers from my new neighbours' yards with the kitchen scissors. *Little thief,* Jude called me when I returned home with a pink hibiscus behind my ear, clippings of camellia and red flowering gum, hands stained red and yellow with pollen. Walk around like that, he said, and you'll bring the birds.

And I did leave our rotten fruit out for them in the feeders, collected rainwater for the lorikeets. I soaked the labels off our empty liquor bottles and rinsed them—whiskey green, clear blue gin, thick brown longnecks—we had so many ways of keeping ourselves warm. I repurposed them, turning them into vases for my stolen blooms. An old habit—to save everything. I'd had that kind of childhood. Thinking of my father's coat, those large pockets from which he could produce a can of tomatoes or a bag of mandarins or a movie on a video cassette on a rainy day, as if pulling a rabbit from a hat. One of his magic tricks. My father the magician, gambler, thief.

We were learning each other's strange habits: Jude drinking beer in the tub, dripping pale ale into the soapy water. Condensation running down the brown bottles, labels softening beneath damp hands. You and your bachelor ways, I teased. We lived in each other's pockets then, as if we were joined by an invisible thread, the way Jude had said the moon was bound to the tide. Trailing his wet fingers across my collarbones while I sat beside the bath reading, reciting certain passages out loud, King's head resting on my knees. Boiling hot water in the kettle when the taps ran cool.

And my own bad habits: writing in bed, ink stains on the sheets. Water rings on his wooden table from my cups and glasses, Jude wiping them off with the edge of his sleeve. Plucking my half-smoked cigarettes from the ashtrays still burning, stubbing them out with a sigh. Picking up the teabags I left on the side of the sink and tossing them into the bin.

Sometimes I forget that you've never lived with anyone before.

I lived with Bonnie and Petra, I said. Are they not people?

That's different.

Maybe you got too used to living alone.

Well, lucky you came along then to save me from myself, he said. Kissing me on the head where I sat on the couch, curled in a corner with the dog.

The darkness of those nights, thick black dark like nothing I'd ever known before in the city, where my street and the park behind my house had glowed brightly with artificial light. At Sailors Beach we had to feel our way home up the hill in the dark, like we were swimming through it. No streetlamps there at the end of the road where it sloped up to the cliffs and the houses dropped away, giving way to bush. Jude pointed up at the stars one night when it was clear. Fool's cross, he said. Like the Southern Cross, but inverted, leading in the wrong direction. Thinking of the lighthouse I'd been to visit with my mother, the false beacons that did more harm than good.

From my first night living there, I came to think of the house as a shelter, though the wind came in through the cracks between the floorboards and shook the windows, swept sand beneath the doors. We were warm, the three of us—Jude beside me, King on his rug down by the end of the bed. And always, the waves outside our window, hushing us to sleep like a gentle mother saying, *Shh, go to sleep, it's all right now. You've come home.*

That winter when I was living with Jude, I was walking on the beach one morning when a woman waved me over, calling to the dog by his name. You're Jude's girl, she said, and I recognised her as Maeve, the woman from the pub back in the summer. Up close, her eyes were green, like my mother's.

Maeve lived alone in an apartment in Sydney, but she drove south on her days off, she said, to visit one of our neighbours, a man she had loved a long time ago. I nodded. I knew she was speaking of Jude's friend Willy. He lived in a weatherboard house on the other side of the hill, closer to town. A quiet man, with all grey hair, though he was in his early forties, like Jude. I remembered that he'd come to the beach from the Blue Mountains, further north than my mother's house, leaving behind a wife and young daughter. Trading in one kind of isolation for another, in Jude's words.

Do you know him? she said. You must.

Only to say hello. We see him sometimes, out on the pier, fishing or painting and drinking beer. But Jude's funny, he keeps to himself. I've never really met his friends.

Well, we'll have to change that, said Maeve, and as she nudged her elbow against mine in a gesture of camaraderie I thought of how jealous I'd been all those months ago. I recalled it almost fondly—that insecurity of early love. It gains a sweetness once love has aged and deepened. We'd come so far since then, Jude and I, and though not much time had passed, I'd almost forgotten her.

You know I keep asking Jude, When are you going to invite us over to get to know your new girl? she said. But he's always been that way. Keeps to himself, as you say, especially when it comes to women. He's very private. Always liked the nesting phase best. I suppose it's a different story with me and Willy. We've known each other so long—too long, maybe. We're like an old married couple, nothing left to discover. Except, of course, we don't live together—and he's still married to someone else.

It was possible, Maeve told me that morning, matching her step to mine and taking turns to bend down and send pieces of driftwood sailing across the sand for King, that she was in love with Willy again now, for a second time—but it was also possible that she loved only the memory of the man she'd loved before, back when they were at university together.

The three of us have known each other a long time, she said. Back then they thought of me as the younger woman. We're five years apart, Willy and I. What a difference time makes. Strange how we've gravitated back together after all these years. With some people it's just magnetic, isn't it? Though I never thought we'd end up here, in this sad little beach town, of all places.

Back then I was in love with all of it—the gentle rhythms this life might offer. Getting up early to have coffee with Jude before driving him to work, smoking and reading on the couch while I waited for him to come home. Collecting driftwood from the beach in the evenings, the dog dragging the biggest pieces home in his mouth, catching the sides of the doorframe, scuffing the dirty white paint. Jude had practical skills I'd had no time or reason to learn, living in the city, like how to make a fire that would keep burning. I'd pictured a winter by the fireside, casting tall shadows on the walls. Watching our shapes come together, merge, become one. When I'd told all this to Petra before I moved down south, she'd chided me for what she called my *domestic fantasies*, and so I'd learned to keep such visions to myself. To Maeve I said simply, It's a different place in the summer.

At the entrance to the beach we parted ways. I'm so glad we finally got to meet, she said. Sometimes I think I spend too much of my time with lonely old men.

How come you've never introduced me to your friends? I asked Jude later that evening. We were sitting in the kitchen, chairs pulled up to the stove, drinking tea and whiskey with the burners on for warmth.

Because I don't have any.

Don't be all charming and wry. You get away with everything by being charming and wry. And anyway, you do. I met one of them today, Maeve. She went on and on about how she was dying to meet me. Like I was some big mystery, a secret you've been keeping from everybody. She even knew King.

You've met Maeve before, he said. At the pub that time.

That was hardly an introduction, I said. I don't think she remembered me, and I didn't exactly want to remind her. Things were different then. Don't you think we should invite them over? Maeve and Willy?

Why should we? said Jude.

Didn't you say they were your oldest friends? Willy lives down the road, and you never see him.

People from another time, love. I like it like this, the three of us. Don't you? You, me and King. What more does a man need?

You don't need friends?

At my age? Less and less.

It was hard to argue with him when he played the card of time—his winning hand, all those years he had over me.

I suppose we became friends, Maeve and I, because we were two women, both trying to edge our way into the lives of these solitary men and belong with them in a place that felt almost uninhabitable. Bordered by the bush on one side, the bay on the other. We had grown up in cities and to the locals that meant strangers, other men's women.

Also, there was a wildness about Maeve that I liked. She was older than me, and seemed to suit the landscape better—or at least know how to adapt to it more naturally than I did. Maybe Jude was right and I did think of myself back then, like my clothing, as *delicate*. And though I like to think I've since become a more practical woman, at least in terms of how I dress, when I first moved down south I wore the same clothes I had in the city— those long skirts and silky blouses with tiny buttons, and antique dresses I'd saved up for, layered with tights and cardigans. But the wind cut through them, the sleeves snagged on stray branches, the hems dragged in the dirt. Sand stuck to my stockings, kicked up by King's paws as he ran along the shore.

Maeve always dressed in brown boots, a black T-shirt, black jeans and a dark duffel coat. Only on the coldest days would she add a thick fisherman's sweater underneath and a red knitted beanie. I could spot her on the beach from a distance then, her hat like a lifeguard's flag. Together we would walk along the beach while I threw sticks I found in the sand for King—such a large dog, his loping gait always reminded me of the awkward lurch of a very tall man.

Despite her simple clothes, Maeve wore a lot of silver rings on her fingers and gestured freely with her hands while she talked. The way she spoke about her complicated situation with Willy—uninhibited, open—made me feel drawn to her. There was something familiar and comforting to me about how her long dark hair got whipped up and tangled by the wind. I think she reminded me of my mother, as she had been when I was small, though Maeve was thirty-seven—the same age I am now—and she had no children.

One morning not long after our first encounter, I ran into her on the beach again when I was walking King after driving Jude to work, the bed of the truck loaded up with antiques he'd repaired at home, others strapped to the roof. That was when we were waking up early, so he could close up in the afternoons and come home while it was light—winter hours, quiet streets in town. I can still remember the feeling of waking up in the dark, shuffling around his room, learning to navigate around the furniture, feeling my way down the hall while I was half-asleep to put coffee on the stove, wearing stockings and one of his woollen jumpers, sleeves spilling over my wrists, because the Old House was impossible to heat.

It was a Saturday, and on Saturdays, Maeve told me, Willy spent the day with his daughter. Every week, his wife drove down from the Mountains to deliver her, and then drove her back again a few hours later. They were still working out the arrangement, Maeve said, and though she was quite fond of the girl—her grey eyes just like Willy's, and her serious demeanour that did not seem childish at all, though she was only four and a half—children get attached, and her situation with Willy was uncertain. Everything still in a fragile state. She did not know if it would hold.

Sometimes I feel like I'm picking through the wreckage of their marriage, she said. Looking for survivors.

It was August, and as we walked the sky above us was slate and low, though the wind was unseasonably warm. Maeve complained about the smell of the ocean, that it smelled like something dead or rotting—plus wet dog, seaweed and brine. She told me she'd been sick—driving into town the day before, she'd had to pull over twice to throw up on the shoulder of the highway.

I said something about how it was that time of year, there were all kinds of viruses going around, and that I hoped she'd feel better soon.

Maeve shook her head. I'm not really sick, she said. I'm pregnant.

She told me she had been to the doctor that morning because she had suspected what the problem might be. She called it that—*the problem*. The only practice in town was a small wooden house. The waiting room was down a short hallway, in what was supposed to be a living room, and the doctors' offices were off to the side, where the bedrooms would have been. There were faded ads for vaccines peeling off the walls, and a poster on how to identify dangerous melanomas that was so old I remembered it from the school nurse's office when I was a child. All the magazines were from years ago, as if time stood still in there.

The doctor said there can be risks. You know, for a woman of *my age*, Maeve said, rolling her eyes. Even though he looked close to a hundred himself.

I knew the one she meant—an old man with thinning, pure white hair, liver spots staining his large hands. I'd been there with a fever that would not break, pain in my back, when I first moved to the beach. *Honeymoon cystitis*, the doctor had declared, as if a urinary tract infection could somehow be romantic. Tearing off a script for antibiotics with a wavering hand.

Doctors just say that stuff to scare women, I said, and that guy is ancient. Imagine how much would have changed since he went to medical school. My mother was thirty-six when my younger brother was born. It's not so uncommon anymore.

The thing is, she said, a part of me feels that he's right. I'm not getting any younger. The decision's not as easy as it would be if I were your age. It's become a now-or-never sort of thing, in my mind.

After the appointment, Maeve told me, she'd sat on a bench in the park down the road overlooking the ocean and remembered all her failures with other people's children. She'd dropped her younger brother once, when he was a baby. She was seven and had been trying to carry him outside into the backyard when he'd dived out of her hands, like he was trying to do a backflip, and knocked his head on the ground. Then, when she was sixteen, she had a part-time nannying gig, and her charge, a toddler, had started choking on a piece of dried fruit. She opened her tiny pink mouth and Maeve could see it there, a chewed-up apricot wedged down the back of the little girl's throat. For a moment, Maeve said, her whole body was stunned by panic—her knees went weak. Then, remembering what she'd seen her mother do with her younger sibling, she opened up the kid's jaw and stuck her hand in, the way you give medicine to a dog. Instead of pulling the fruit out, though, she pushed it further down by mistake.

It worked, she swallowed it, Maeve said. But afterwards, she wouldn't stop crying. I had to rock her for hours, until her mother came home, and for days after, my arms ached from the weight. Like I'd been carrying a sack of angry, screaming potatoes.

I'm sure it would be different with your own kid, I said.

You know, it's funny, in the city I work with teenagers, she said. Teenagers, I can manage. They're like us, except everything is dialled up. But if I'm honest, I think part of the reason I took that job, got into social work to begin with, was to have an excuse for not having my own children. I could say, Oh yeah, I love kids, but I already have a caseload of seven to worry about. So I'd seem selfless and giving, when I feared I was being the opposite.

Used to living among other itinerant, off-season people, I was surprised to hear about Maeve's work—that she lived a more conventional life than I had imagined for her, with all the silver rings on her fingers, her complicated love affair. She was an adult in a sense that even Jude was not. People depended on her in a real way, and I wondered if that alone made her qualified for motherhood—more qualified than me.

What did Willy say when you told him?

We had come to the wooden walkway that led from the beach, through the trees, to the main street. There, at the dip in the road, we split—she would turn right to walk up the slope towards Willy's house, and I would walk up the steeper side of the hill to Jude's.

I haven't yet, Maeve said. I came straight down here to clear my head. Don't even know why I'm telling you. I suppose I just wanted someone else to know. You know, to make it real.

I won't say anything, I said. Not even to Jude.

I don't want to make you keep secrets from him.

It's okay, I said. Some things should stay between women.

I reached out and squeezed her hand to reassure her. Her fingers were cold from the winter morning, and she looked surprised by the gesture. Maeve was open, I realised, but she was not easily affectionate. When we met on the beach, we never hugged or kissed cheeks, but nodded and fell into step with one another, like two men might. I was reminded in that moment that we did not know each other well, were only new friends, and though we were both women, we were not guaranteed to share an easy intimacy.

I walked back up the hill with King, cold air sharp in my lungs, both of us puffing out clouds of hot breath. Around us, the bush was dense and grey green, even in the middle of winter. The landscape doesn't shed seasons down south the way it does in other places, you have to track time in other ways. Silver spur quivering with water from last night's rain. Smell of tea tree and wet earth in the air. Calls of a kookaburra somewhere up high, waves in the distance, the pealing cries of butcherbirds. Then a sound like giant metal wings, a helicopter moving out towards the navy base.

Instead of going straight home, King and I kept walking, taking the track towards the top of the cliffs beyond the Old House, until all construction fell away and the bush took over, trees thickening at the edge of the national park. That far along, the beach changed—it became a sheltered, smaller cove, and once a house had stood proudly on the rise, at the highest point above the sea. There had been a fire, Jude had told me, a few years ago in the park. Cigarette tossed into the bush, and the eucalypts just burned, air thick with blue smoke. The wooden house had been destroyed, and everything that couldn't burn had slid away down the cliff, onto the beach below. You could still see parts of it there, the innards spilled out across the sand: a bathtub scarred with rust and filled with rain, plumbing pipes like organs. The bush had moved in to reclaim the land, but a few burned and blackened beams remained that looked no more stable than a child's fort of sticks. Tin roof in peels, rusted, melted metal. Trees grew from within, bark limbs reaching through empty rooms, embracing what remained.

I don't know why I was drawn back to that burned-down house, but I visited it often with King on our walks that winter. Jude thought there was something morbid in it, though I'd tried to explain to him about the lighthouse, the one I'd seen with my mother back in the summer. How we'd both been compelled by the ruins. And there was a beauty to it, the way colour was growing back into the land, the shock of green. It looked like hope, tender and new. But the bush was like the ocean, Jude had said. It's easy to get lost out there. If you go out too far, it starts to look the same in every direction. It becomes impossible to tell which way leads towards home, and which will take you further astray. I felt his love then like a rope around my waist. If I strayed too far, it seemed, or went out too deep, he'd pull me back, a tether to the known world. I felt both limited and also comforted by this. It was a new feeling. Not even my mother loved me that way. *I hope you're being careful* were her only warning words, her advice always slightly abstracted, leaving me to figure things out on my own from her clues and riddles, her cryptic lines about men and animals.

That morning, standing in front of the ruined house, I tried to imagine what it might feel like to bring something so small and vulnerable into this place. Never far from the unknown. Signs warning visitors about unstable ground—you had to tread carefully, pay attention to the changes in the wind and tides. Waves inching away at the coastline. In eighty years, I'd read in a report in the local paper, this town could be under water. I remembered it because of the unusually poetic language in the headline. With predicted rising sea levels over the next century, Sailors Beach could *slip beneath the waves*. How it sounded almost like a relief—to surrender like that. Back then, I often confused danger with beauty, drawn as I was to stories of other people's tragedies, tales of lighthouse keepers' daughters, lonely men and women living out on the edge, perched above those same wrecking waters. I thought of Maeve. The trust she had put in me made me feel protective of her secret—as if it were the baby itself, and I could help her keep it sheltered, safe, as long as I didn't say a word.

That night, Jude sat on the edge of the tub and we played Samson and Delilah. Kitchen scissors in my hand, cutting the ends of his hair where it had grown out, grown too long, curling around his ears and down the back of his neck. Thinking of when Petra and I used to get drunk on cheap red wine and cut each other's hair into bobs and fringes when we were bored and broke and avoiding study. Fear and tenderness when I noticed Jude's thinning crown, as if I'd seen through to the bone.

Hey, I said, standing behind him in the tub, watching snips of hair fall. Gold in the sunlight but dull beneath the bathroom's bare waning bulb. What would we do if I got pregnant?

From that angle, I couldn't see his face, but I could feel the shift in his posture. Sitting up a little straighter, his shoulders back, clearing his throat.

Whatever you wanted to do, he said.

Do you really mean that, or are you just being gentlemanly?

Either way, he said, we'd figure it out.

Though later I'd decide this was noncommittal, evasive, at the time it struck me as generous, a swelling in my chest, another unfamiliar feeling—assurance, or security, or trust. We were in this together, *we'd figure it out*, and that made our love seem durable.

I kissed his cheek then, my hands resting on his shoulders. Feeling the soft-worn fabric of his flannel shirt beneath my fingertips.

Listen, he said, feeling the back of his hair. If you ever write about me, don't mention my bald spot.

Time slipped away from its usual tethers of days, weeks, months. At Sailors Beach, we thought in the broader terms of seasons—off-season, wet season, whale season, fire season.

I'd quit my job as a bookseller when I moved in with Jude, and in the absence of shifts and semesters, I found grounding in the rituals of those days. There was always something to be done—plants to water, birds to feed, dead leaves to sweep from the porch. Stoking the fire at the end of the day, breaking up sticks and twigs for kindling, tearing up newspapers. The satisfying rush when the flame caught the balled-up pages and the wood snapped, shifted, settled. Predictable and tactile, where the time I spent at writing on my computer was not.

Winter, Jude said, hurt his bones.

Like an old man, I teased, thinking he'd laugh and feeling sorry when he didn't. Running Radox baths that turned the water green and smelled like my childhood fevers, my father's cure for aches and pains. I threw out the box and bought Epsom salts instead, scented them in jars with dried lavender and rosemary from the window boxes in the kitchen.

Mostly, we were happy then. Hands in each other's fleece-lined pockets, cheeks reddened by the wind when we walked King along the beach in the evenings. Dressing beneath the bedcovers in the mornings in the still-dark. So much wool that when I think back to that time, the memories have a muffled quality. All those jumpers and stockings and the itchy checked camp blankets with the satin stripe along the hem that Jude brought home from the shop. At night we piled the bed with them, so we could sleep skin to skin. My hands got so cracked and dry that the skin snagged on the sleeves of my sweaters. Small wounds reopened, paper cuts never seemed to heal.

With winter came a new tenderness between us. Gentle with each other. And I took this as a deepening, not a waning, of passion. This is real love, I told myself. It wasn't the stuff of the summer. It was reading in bed, falling asleep with the light on.

Do I remember the first week we went without making love? Jude pulling his boots off on his side of the bed at the end of the day. No ceremony to this undressing. Jeans in a pile and coins scattering on the floor, shirt smelling of sweat and stuck with sawdust. Slipping beneath the sheets. Picking up my roaming hand and placing it on his chest.

Tired, love.

Tired with what? Tired with work, or tired with me?

Crying dreams, sometimes, where he told me there was another woman. Or worse—he just didn't love me anymore, and no words of mine could bring him back.

Do you love me? Do you love me? I asked, shaking him awake in the dark.

His rotation of answers:

You know I do.

Don't make me say it all the time or it will lose its meaning.

If I didn't, would I still be here, in bed with you?

I needed to hear it, the reassurance of those words. Repeating it to him over and over that winter, *IloveyouIloveyouIloveyou*, like a prayer. Sometimes I would keep myself awake after Jude had fallen asleep to look at his face, missing him even in sleep. So sure, in these moments, that if he ever tried to leave me, I wouldn't let him. Undignified, the scene I'd make. Not too proud to beg. I'd wrap myself around his legs the way I used to hang from my father's when I was a child and he would come to visit—remembering the way he used to play along, swinging me from his boot with each heavy stride. I wanted us to be like rocks or anchors, keeping each other in place. Love, I'd read, was supposed to be a light and weightless feeling, but I had always longed for gravity.

It was King who gave us weight. When I woke and saw Jude's shape in the dark—the bump on the bridge of his nose, long elegant feet sticking out from the covers—and the dog on his rug at the foot of the bed, giant head resting on his paws, I looked at them both and it seemed like I'd been given everything I ever wanted.

The trouble is that our dreams, like our memories, are not immune to revision. How often had I seen my mother fall in love with a ruined house, only to grow tired of it once the work of renovation was done? There's no mystery left, she would say, nothing left to discover. It had been this way with Grant, Henry's father, who, much to her delight, was an architect. He met my mother when he was working on a house down the road from one of our old places in Sydney, by the Cooks River, and saw her digging through the skip bin in her overalls to salvage the original timber floorboards ripped out by his clients, while I kept a nervous watch. When he saw us trying to drag these planks back home down the street, he offered to give us a hand. He looked around our dark brick Federation bungalow, with its overgrown and untended yard and potential view of the bend in the river, the sloping kitchen at the back that filled with water when it rained, and said he'd be happy to sketch some plans up for my mother over dinner. This was how he won her over: by tracing on a paper napkin over candlelight the kind of life they might share. A painting studio overlooking the garden, a vegetable plot fed on rainwater runoff—the full urban-bucolic dream. The attic could be converted into an extra bedroom, he said, because maybe my mother thought about having another child? He saw that it was only the two of us, that we were lacking in husbands and fathers and brothers and sons, and visualised all the ways our small home might be extended.

Henry's father was not a drinker, or a gambler, or a thief. He was what my grandmother, Sylvia, would have called *a good man*. Too good, she likely would have added, for a woman like my mother, who, at thirty-five, was still fast and flighty. A week after that dinner, Grant, true to his word, walked back into our house with a roll of drawings under one arm.

Aren't you going to take your boots off? my mother asked that morning, and I saw the look that passed between them, a look that contained the germ of my little brother, who at that moment must have been readying himself to make his appearance, gathering himself together in my mother's womb. She was looking at Grant, and asking him to stay.

My mother and Grant would never live together in that house at the bend of the river. By the time the work was done, Henry was two and their romance was over.

It was useless, she said. I kept feeling I'd lived out the whole thing already, in the blueprints. What would be the point?

Later, she explained it to me like this: You were getting older, and I knew it couldn't be just the two of us forever. I thought I wanted Grant, but once I was pregnant I realised that I didn't want a man after all, I wanted another baby.

By the time we had this conversation I was old enough to understand what talking about the future with a certain kind of man, in a certain kind of light, might cause you to do.

I suppose I was going through a phase, that winter at Sailors Beach, of wanting a baby. Instead of a girl, I now pictured a boy with an angel's face—long blond hair, pale blue eyes, lips like a thin red ribbon. In other words, I imagined he would look like my brother, who looked like me because we both looked like our mother. We were made in her image, her genes muscling out the influence of our different fathers—no more than a hint of their different jawlines, the angle of their profiles. The slight dimple in Henry's chin, where mine was pointed. We had in common our mother's heart-shaped face, small lips, large eyes, the stubborn gap between her two front teeth that grew back in all of us despite corrective braces. Growing up, Henry used to call himself my twin, my double, though he was twelve years younger and another man's son, and he was fair-haired where we women were pale and dark. In any case, I was tired of thinking in terms of mothers and daughters. I wanted a son.

Maybe because Jude was older than me, a baby actually seemed like a possibility—never mind that we didn't have much money, that I was between jobs and wanted to be a writer, had a degree in literature and art history, of all things. I was still young enough to have a romantic picture of how our life might be: writing through the day while Jude went to work, cooking together in the evenings, long nights reading by the fire. I could carry the baby on my chest while King and I walked on the beach, collecting firewood. Jude was the kind of man who knew the right names for things, he could teach our son about the stars, the rhythms of the moon and tides, the habits of migratory birds.

Or maybe it was because I was in love, and I wanted to create a tangible testament to that, the way people in love always want to document it somehow. What I longed for was a guarantee that if this love ever ended, at least there'd be a record of it, outside of the two of us and our two bodies. Though part of me knew, of course, that it could never work like that—what a burden to put on a child. Had I not seen my own father's eyes fill when he looked at me when I was a girl, any time an expression crossed my face that resembled my mother's?

Years later, when I spoke of this time to a friend, she said, How did you expect to survive? Sustaining yourselves on sex and cigarettes alone? We were both in our early thirties, living in New York, and none of our friends felt they could afford to have a baby, whether or not they wanted one, but it hadn't seemed so crazy to me back when I was twenty-four. In many ways, I lived with Jude as I'd been raised—a cobbled-together life. Taking piecemeal work where I could get it—transcribing documentary footage and interviews for a friend of my mother's who worked at the ABC, writing papers for undergraduate students. Hardly anything would have to change, I'd thought, though sometimes I heard my mother's voice in my head: *That kind of love? It's terrifying. You think you're ready for it, but you're not.*

Talking with Maeve also made me feel close to the possibility of motherhood, and I was pleased whenever I ran into her on my walks with King. Spending time with her was a way of trying it on, like wearing a friend's clothes—a way of stepping briefly into that life, imagining myself into it, seeing if it might suit. Although I didn't admit this to Jude, or even to myself at first.

It's good for me to have female company down here, I said, when I told him I planned to meet Maeve on the beach one Saturday morning while he went to work and Willy spent the day with his daughter. And anyway, I want to get to know your friends.

A few weeks had passed since we'd last seen each other, and when I asked how she was when we met on the beach that morning, she replied, Still pregnant. It's not too late, though. You know, if I change my mind.

How are things with Willy? Have you told him yet?

She shook her head. That's bad, isn't it? It's just that things are complicated between us right now. We were supposed to be taking it slow. He already has a kid, you know? So I worry the decision won't be weighted for him, the same way it is for me. His daughter's only four, and he didn't split up with his wife that long ago. As soon as one of us is on the loose, we're back together again.

Kicking at the sand with her boot.

It's so easy for a man to think of a woman as a trap, Maeve said then. I never wanted to be that for him. I wanted us both to be free. But maybe that's naive. If I'm honest, I think what I'm waiting for is some sign that he wants to be with me first. It can't just be because of this, she said, pointing at her stomach, though her figure had not yet changed. Still dressed in the same black jeans, loose-fitting T-shirt. They measured the growth of a fetus in comparison to fruits, she told me. Right now, it was only the size of a plum.

What if this is the sign, though? I said. Even if it's not the one you were looking for.

She smiled then and I thought that she did look happier that day—full, in the way I wanted to be, warm colour in her face, though she said that she felt rotten.

Maybe you're right, she said. You know, in all my life, in thirty-seven years, I've never once been pregnant. No accidents, not even a scare. It just never happened, so I never felt like I had to make my mind up about it, one way or another. A woman at work said it was the body's *last-ditch effort*, the closer you get to forty—which I didn't find particularly flattering. But it did make me think, maybe this one really wanted to make it. Maybe it *is* meant to be, and that's why he and I have come back together all these times over the years. For this.

She thanked me for being a good listener and said she had resolved to tell Willy that day.

Then the secret will be out, she said, and you can tell Jude. I'm sure he's curious about why we suddenly have so much to talk about.

He has been asking, I said. Think it makes him nervous, like we're conspiring.

Jude's always liked keeping the parts of his life separate. Not mixing crowds, compartmentalising.

Why is that?

Oh, I don't know. I think deep down, he's always seen himself as a loner. You know, because of his family. No matter how many women have tried to love him.

I had to fight the sudden impulse then to grab her arm. *How many?* I wanted to shake her and say. *How many women? And what number am I?*

Tell me, Maeve said. How did you get so wise for someone so young? Do you think about all this stuff? Having kids?

I don't know, I lied. Feeling my pulse quicken and the heat rush to my face at the thought of my dream-baby. That was something private. I didn't want to share it with anybody, not even Jude. I think that on some level it embarrassed me—that I wanted what women have always been supposed to want.

What a silly question, Maeve said. Of course you don't. You're only twenty-something. That would be like babies having babies. You still have so much time, so much living to do. You should get out there while you can. Leave the sad old men to me.

That night, I sat in the kitchen while Jude worked on a piece for a client—an antique cabinet with angels painted on the doors, wood split and cracked in places. The figures reminded me of my mother's early paintings that had hovered over us from the walls of my childhood homes—women suspended over landscapes of hills and smokestacks and red-roofed houses, lifted by some unseen force. They had no wings, her women, and yet, sad and serene, they floated.

I loved those nights, watching him work, the care and concentration he gave to each stage of the process—stripping back the paint to reveal the original grain, sanding it down, finishing it with glossy varnish. Jude, illuminated by a circle of strong lamplight. It must be satisfying, I thought, to make something with your hands. To feel its smoothed and solid edges.

We often spent our evenings that way in the big kitchen, though the living room was warmer, with rugs and a fireplace and the worn leather couch. I would read or play records—old blues, jazz, and country albums borrowed from the two-dollar bin. Jude was always bringing home things he collected from the side of the road to fix up. Even King was like that—an old, lost dog we found on the beach, milky-eyed and half-blind, fur matted with sand, too skinny for his size. I still thought of Jude, back then, as someone who could save things from ruin.

A storm was coming in that night, and we had the radio on for the weather. Trees throwing branches against the windows, sweeps of water and air smacking at the glass. House heaving, as if it had come alive, the doors swinging and slamming and sucking in and out against their frames. All afternoon, the anxious clipping back and forth of King's paws as he scratched at the floorboards and paced the perimeter of the kitchen with a low whine that reached its crescendo in one long, unrestrained howl before the first rain fell. It's said that dogs can smell lightning before it strikes, sense the electricity in the air.

A voice spoke of wind in terms of knots, warned of squalls and swells and surges—but I wasn't listening. I was thinking about my conversation with Maeve.

Hey, I said to Jude. Reaching out to brush his leg with the tip of my stocking foot. You know what I asked you the other day?

About what? he said, without looking up from his work.

About the baby.

What baby?

I asked you, remember? About what we'd do if I got pregnant? You said it would be my decision. Well, what if I wanted to keep it?

I'd tell you to quit smoking for a start, he said. A point of tension at the time. At the start of winter Jude had vowed to quit, throwing his pouches of tobacco in the bin. *Cold turkey.* Stubbing out my just-lit cigarettes, or snatching them from my fingers still burning. Finding butts in my coat pockets ringed with lipstick, though I'd promised to stop too.

I'm serious, I said. Have you ever thought about it? Having kids?

He frowned, squinting across at me through the lamplight.

At one time, maybe.

I think you'd be a good dad, I said. You're very paternal.

Oh dear, he said. Should I be concerned that my girlfriend finds me fatherly?

Not in a weird way. I can just see you with a child. Walking on the beach with a kid on your shoulders, or holding a small mittened hand. I think of it sometimes. How gentle you'd be with a baby. How little it would look in your arms.

That's sweet, he said. Although, I have to say, I definitely wasn't thinking about any of this when I was your age. Kids were the last thing on my mind back when I was twenty-four.

So, what about now?

What about now?

Well, you're not twenty-four anymore.

Yes, he said. And aren't I lucky I have you to remind me?

Turning the volume up on the weather report.

My God! Maeve exclaimed, the next time we met on the beach. Sometimes you really do look like a child. People must think that I'm your mother when we're out together.

I had my hair in two braids—I'd taught myself how, in the French style. And perhaps we did look alike, with our pale pointed faces, dark hair. Maeve's threaded with grey—she didn't dye it, the way my mother did—and I thought that was sophisticated, worldly. Her eyes green where mine were blue.

She'd told Willy about the baby and things between them were good, so much better than they'd ever been. He was getting sober again, she said. He'd quit drinking for the first time when his daughter was born and started up again during the mess of his separation, but this was his second chance, he'd said—at fatherhood, at everything.

So, she said, I guess you can tell Jude. No more secrets.

You should be the one to tell him, I said. You and Willy. His two oldest friends having a baby together—he'll want to hear it from you. You'll come over, we'll celebrate.

It was the only time we invited them around for dinner. A housewarming, that's how I pitched it to Jude, since we never had one after I moved in, and though he was resistant, stalling with various excuses, when they arrived on our doorstep on a Friday night a few weeks later, there was much laughter and backslapping and kissing on both cheeks in the European fashion. Jude looked genuinely happy to see them, I thought. I had done a good thing.

Did you hear the news? said Willy, Maeve's hand fluttering to her middle.

Jude clapped his hands—he was delighted for them, he said, *just delighted*—and swept Willy out to the porch to smoke cigars to fatherhood like two men in an old-fashioned movie.

Jude and I were the only ones drinking, but later, I joined the men outside beneath the bloodwood trees while Willy rolled a joint and passed it between us, Jude raising his eyebrows when I accepted. Didn't I tell you my best friend grew up in Mullumbimby? I said, thinking how different, those nights with Bonnie. Sitting in the cracked concrete yard, throwing love notes over the fence because for a while she had a crush on one of our neighbours—one of three brothers who lived next door. A house of boys beside a house of girls, making jokes about cults and communes. That was me: young and blush-cheeked, coughing on the exhale. Looking up at the stars, talking about the cosmos. Sky so black and clear that night you could see Venus with the naked eye.

This would turn out to be a different occasion from the kind that I was used to—those parties I'd followed Bonnie and Petra along to at other share houses across the inner city, with bathtubs full of ice and beer, pills crushed to powder with somebody's library card, plastic cups and fake flowers. All day I'd been nervous as I filled old bottles with the clippings I'd stolen from the neighbours' gardens and set the table with a sheet, lamenting our lack of tablecloth. Jude was a practised host—he remembered when to turn the fish and flip the record and refilled the glasses with sparkling water before they got low, where I sweated by the oven and burned my thumb on the edge of a tray of roast vegetables and had to make conversation while holding my hand under cold running water, turning my fingers numb and red, drinking my wine too quickly.

After dinner, when talk turned to their old university days, I slipped outside for air, a quiet cigarette, sitting beside King on the porch. Saw the stars hash together, double, blur. It had rained again, and in the wet night, it seemed that they were dripping, the whole sky hung out to dry. It was September, spring—not that you could tell. Down south the winter was long, and that year it lingered all the way through to November.

I smoked a cigarette, maybe two, but some time must have passed because when I came back in everyone was gone, the table emptied, red wine rings on the white sheet, candles—thin and tapered green, a gift from Maeve—burned down to stubs.

From the front of the house, I heard voices. Walking down the darkened hall, I saw the three of them on the doorstep, laughing. Willy punching Jude playfully on the shoulder, saying, You sly devil, you. Cradle robber. Maeve's voice in a low murmur, She's a lot more mature than either of you. Not that that would be hard.

Oh come off it, said Willy. I could drink and vote before she was born. We were graduating when she was starting kindergarten. It's barely legal. Any younger, and you'll get yourself arrested!

I remembered one time in the supermarket, kissing in front of the canned soup—Jude had made some joke to make me laugh—when a woman slammed her trolley into ours. Can't you find someone your own age? she shrieked. I didn't know which one of us she was talking to.

I never got used to the different reactions Jude and I provoked from other people. Often enough, I was congratulated for finding a mature man, as if this spoke highly of me and my intelligence, while Jude received looks that suggested he was too much of a child for women his own age—which was patronising to me also since, by then, I perceived us to be equals. Of course, I have lived enough years by now to have seen this kind of thing many times over: the husband who leaves his wife for a university girl or a teenager, the family abandoned. It happened to my grandmother, it has even happened to friends of mine. As my mother would say, it starts so much younger than you think. Still, the truth was that it worked both ways—that for whatever sense of youth I restored to Jude, I was attracted to the years of experience he had over me and the knowledge they might hold of things I hadn't yet had time to learn.

In this way we flattered each other, but our relationship divided other people—Jude getting the conspiratorial winks from other men, while women eyed him with suspicion, or even disgust. It was the oldest people who were the kindest—grandmothers, from a generation where such gulfs in age were common, if not recommended. And Jude knew how to be good to these women, holding doors open, carrying grocery bags up a set of stairs or out to the car. To these ladies we encountered at the shops and at the markets, he was nothing but a gentleman.

From my place in the hall, I heard his voice at the doorway, steady and even. A warning tone.

Careful, mate, he said. If I didn't know any better, I'd think that you were jealous.

Jude was right, I realised. I'd heard it too—excitement in Willy's voice. Are men always jealous of each other in that way, or was it merely a mutual curiosity? To want to know what the other man knows.

Still, I remember telling Jude that night as he fell into bed beside me that I thought they'd seemed happy. Now, I think what I was feeling then was our own happiness, brought into relief by the other couple, and a vision of what our own future could hold. Something Maeve confessed to me later: You two always seemed like you'd just finished fucking or were just about to, and I hated you for that. How obnoxious we must have seemed back then, parading our early love. I don't blame Maeve for that now, but I was surprised when Jude turned from me and said, almost to himself: Maeve and Willy, it's a huge mistake.

A few weeks later, driving back from town one Friday evening, we parked the truck out the front of the house and I spotted Maeve in her red hat pacing up and down in the car park by the entrance to the beach. Soft rain in the near dark. Beneath the light of the streetlamp, it seemed to make a veil around her, barely clinging to the wool of her hat and jacket.

Have you seen Willy? she called out, waving us over. He's not home and the house is all locked up, and now my phone has gone flat and I can't reach him. Can you believe it? I'm having a baby with someone who won't even give me a key to his house. And now it's getting late, and I'm stuck here. Pregnant and stranded—

She started to cry and Jude reached out, placed a hand on her shoulder as if to steady her. Come on, he said. You can call him from our house.

Yes, I said. Come and wait inside, where it's warm.

Thank you, she said, rubbing her eyes with the sleeve of her coat. I'm sorry about this. I cry when someone's rude to me, I cry when they're nice. I'm a fucking mess.

Inside, sitting opposite Jude at the big wooden table, Maeve told us what had happened while I put the kettle on for tea. They'd had a fight about the baby, she said, she and Willy. It started when they were talking about whether or not to move in together. Maeve hadn't expected anything would need to change—after all, they weren't really sure if they were back together again, or if they should be in a relationship at all. Willy hadn't split up with his wife that long ago, and Maeve had lived alone for a long time, valued her independence above all things. But Willy had insisted that if there was any chance they could make it work—even a slim one, he said—and they could raise the child in a proper home, mother and father together under one roof, they at least owed it to the kid to try.

He acts like he's an expert because he's had one already, she said. But I don't want to do things the way they did, him and his ex, getting married because they thought it was the right thing to do. I was there, I saw what it did to them—what they did to each other. He said I was being selfish because I didn't want to give up my life in the city, the apartment I've lived in for ten years. And he's right, I am afraid of how isolated I'd be down here. Then he said I was doing what I always did—keeping him at a distance. That all I did was reel him in, then throw him back out again. How could you say that? I said to him. And weren't you the one saying you wanted to take things slow? He said, Well, there's nothing slow about getting pregnant straight away, as if it was all my fault, like I'd planned it that way. Like it had nothing to do with him at all. So, I told him to forget it, I'll go it alone, raise the kid by myself. Why not? People do it all the time. Like your mother, she said, turning to me. And look at you, you turned out all right.

I nodded, though I'd never spoken to Maeve at length about my childhood and her reference to it made me uneasy. It was presumptuous, I thought. Yes, we had done all right, my mother and I, I felt defensive of us and yet I also felt something was being erased—some truth, the complexity of my experience. Given the choice—if such a thing were possible to choose—wouldn't I have wanted my family to stay together? Not if my parents were going to make each other miserable, of course. You had to be careful what you wished for, but wish for it as a child I often did—that they would fall in love again and remain that way forever, the three of us rejoined. At least until Henry was born and I either grew out of it or felt that I'd been compensated, given something different in exchange for what I'd lost—there was my brother's hand in mine.

Age, I realised, could not account for the depth of one's experience, and though Maeve was older than me and I knew, like all of us, she had her own damages, I was also sure she had never experienced that kind of loss, for she would not have spoken of it so lightly if she had.

But Maeve was no longer looking at me. She had turned her attention to Jude. She was telling him how she'd just had it, and instead of driving down the coast after work, as she did most Fridays, she went home, swearing to herself that this time with Willy would be the last. But when she opened the door, her apartment seemed changed—suddenly it felt too sparse and so quiet, without the sound of the wind and the waves.

At first, I thought I'd walked into someone else's place, she said. I didn't recognise it as my own. I looked around at all the things I'd collected—books, plants, records, my coffee machine, and yes, they were all mine. I'd invested in this solitary life, you know? And for a minute I thought, maybe I can have it both ways—move in with Willy, but keep my apartment in the city all set up, just in case.

Right, I said, so you'd always have a place to go back to.

The thing is, Maeve said, looking up at Jude, you can never go back, not really. It doesn't work like that. I stood in the hall and didn't even put my bag down. I turned around and drove straight here. I love Willy, I always have, and he's a good dad too, even if he is a lousy boyfriend a lot of the time. Seeing him with his daughter, I thought he'd changed. How patient he'd become. But now he's gone off and disappeared somewhere, won't return my calls, and it's just like it was ten years ago.

It's pretty irresponsible, said Jude, with such authority that his interjection shocked me, as if he'd spoken loudly, though his voice was level and even. Jude could be sharp at turns, and stern, but he was never one to raise his voice. To disappear like that on you. But he's always been like that. Never sticks around long enough to fix anything.

What about all your games of trust? I thought. The freedom to leave and return at will—that was true love, Jude had told me.

We should be a pleasure to each other, not a necessity. *A gift*. Or did those rules only apply to him and me?

Well, to be fair, he probably thought you weren't coming down, I said. Maybe he went out to clear his head. I'm sure he's home by now.

I really did think he'd changed, Maeve said. But none of us really do, do we? If anything, I think we tend to double down over time, become more stubbornly ourselves. People don't grow up after all, I'm sure of it. We just get more things, have children. You'd think I'd know better by now. It's right there in front of my face, all the mess he left behind with his ex-wife. I mean, on paper they're still married. Stupid to think it'd be any different with me. After all these years, you'd think I'd learn.

You've always seen the best in him, Jude said, reaching across the space between them and squeezing her hand. She nodded, her face charged with an emotion I didn't fully understand. A reference, I guessed, to other days in their shared history.

She reached into the pocket of her duffel coat then, and produced a blurry black-and-white picture that looked like a moonscape, or an aerial view of a distant planet. Something far-off and alien. The sonogram. She told us she had been to the obstetrician the day before and heard the baby's heartbeat for the first time. It sounded like the ocean, she said. Like when you're under water, and you can hear your pulse in your ears.

Would you look at that, said Jude, taking the picture from her, holding it up to the light.

I brought it to show Willy, she said. In the end, whatever happens between the two of us doesn't matter. I've made my choice.

She had a whole world inside of her it seemed, and in that moment, I felt empty. I hugged my teacup tight between my hands to keep them warm.

I can feel her, Maeve said then, wrapping her arms around her middle as if she was cold or had a pain there. Turning over, or something.

May I? said Jude.

Jude, I scolded. You can't ask that, it's rude. I'm sure Maeve gets sick of being touched by strangers all the time. Right, Maeve?

Actually, she said, it's been a while since I've been touched. And then she blushed. What I mean is, when Willy's not around, I worry that she won't get enough, I don't know, affection, or love, with just me to talk to her. I have these weird thoughts, like, what if it stops her growing? Like a plant that only gets sun in one spot.

I'm sorry, I said, because I could see it in her eyes, shining darkly in the low light.

You needn't worry, said Jude. She's got you, hasn't she? You've got more than enough love in you to give.

That's such a nice thing to say, said Maeve, smiling. Corners of her lips quivering, her cheeks wet.

I'll get you some tissues, I said, and walked to the bathroom to tear a reel of toilet paper from the roll.

When I returned to the kitchen, Jude was kneeling beside Maeve on the floor. His hand on the rise of her stomach, and hers on top of his, holding it in place. Laughing together. A look on his face I'd never seen before—though maybe a glimpse of it, the night we'd found King on the beach and taken him home. Dancing in the kitchen, the dog's paws up on his shoulders. The look when he'd turned to me and said, *Can we keep him?* Fear and awe, tenderness and wonder. Boyhood returned to him.

It's a beautiful thing you're doing, Jude was saying, emphatically. A pure and beautiful thing.

Thank you, Julian, said Maeve, and it struck me then, the way she called Jude by his full name. How much better it sounded, coming from her. It felt as if she had tried on my coat and it fit her the way it was supposed to, where on me it hung over my wrists, was too big in the shoulders.

I walked into the room, swinging the door closed behind me with a bang. Blaming it on the wild, wild wind, another coming storm. Jude returned to his chair at the table and I sat myself down on his lap, looped my arms around his neck, kissed him in the place below his ear that made him shiver. As if to say, *Mine.* The coat might suit you better, but it still belongs to me.

Maeve stayed with us for dinner, until Willy finally called and told her he was home, he'd only been out walking. His voice on the phone, she said, sounded lucid and clear. Jude offered to let her spend the night anyway, but she shook her head. Oh, I couldn't, she said. Then it would be too much like the old days. Remember how I'd show up at your old place in Darlinghurst looking for Willy, and the two of us would drive around the city together in circles?

Yes, said Jude, out all night hunting him down. Trying to smoke him out of some pub or gutter.

He really tried to ruin himself, back then. And I was so young, sleeping in his bed until he showed up again. I thought my love could save him.

You never know, Jude said. Maybe it did.

I rolled my eyes at the two of them and left them on the doorstep while they hugged goodbye, holding each other for what seemed like too long a time. *Saviours*, that's how they thought of themselves, rescuing the lonely and long-suffering with their love, and I had a sudden surge of empathy for Willy. Did Maeve love him as the person he was, or did she love the drama of him? Maybe it made her feel good about herself, to think she was cleaning up the mess of his life, while she remained neatly within the boundary of her apartment, with her books and her plants and her records. As she said, *picking through the wreckage*. Who was that serving more?

After she left, Jude opened another bottle of wine while I cleared away our plates, filled the sink with soap and water. A record was playing, a woman's voice singing '(I Can't Get No) Satisfaction'. I wanted a cigarette, but my hands were wet. I wanted to go outside, feel the cold air on my face and smoke in my lungs. My body was empty, it belonged only to me, and I could do with it what I wanted.

So, said Jude. Want to tell me why you're angry with me this time?

I'm not angry.

Yes, you are, he said. You only do the dishes when you're mad about something.

I said nothing, continued to scrub at the cast-iron pan with steel wool. My hands were deep in the hot, soapy water, and when I pulled them from the sink, they were red up to the wrist. Flecks of suds and water on my face and jumper. Watching the food scraps soften as they floated in the sink among islands of soap and grease. Pushing the hair from my face with the side of my palm.

Jude, I said. Do you think Maeve's pretty?

Where's this coming from?

I mean, she is a lot closer to your age. Whenever you're together, it's like I'm not in the room.

I think I know what's going on here, he said, wrapping his arms around me from behind, his lips at my ear. You're jealous.

I scrunched my shoulders up, turned my face away from his kiss.

No, I'm not.

Yes, you are. I think it's sweet.

Kissing my neck, moving his hands down my body, pulling me close. The fly of his jeans like a knot at the base of my spine.

Come to bed with me, he said.

I'm doing this, I said. Go on upstairs if you're tired. Lifting the glass he'd left by the sink and wiping away the ring it had left on the clean surface.

Come on, don't be like that, he said. You don't have anything to worry about with Maeve.

I know that, I said. We're better friends than you two are these days.

Oh, and here I was thinking this was all about me, said Jude. Dropping his hands, sulking off to bed with the bottle of wine, whistling for the dog to follow.

After I finished cleaning, I rolled a joint with the weed I'd started buying from a local at the surf beach. My blue cloud cigarettes. Their earthy taste, like dirt and dry grass. It relaxed me, helped me sleep, and reminded me of nights at my old place with Bonnie, when we would sit up late together talking. Sitting alone outside on the porch, I was surprised to realise that I was lonely. I'd thought Jude, his house by the beach, the dog would be the cure, and maybe that was where the dream of a child had come from—another way to fill the space I felt inside.

I expected Jude would be asleep by the time I came to bed, but he began pawing at me immediately, clumsily grabbing at me in the dark, lifting up my nightgown. I could taste the wine in his kiss, as if his mouth were full of sediment.

Make a baby with me, he said.

You're drunk, I said. Go to sleep.

Come on, he said. I know you want to. All those cute stories you were telling me the other day, about babies and mittens and playing in the sand.

Don't tease me about that, I said. It isn't nice.

What's the matter? You don't want to now? Aren't you in love with me anymore?

Of course I am. You know I love you.

So, what? You changed your mind?

I don't know, I said. Maybe it was just a phase.

I rolled away from him, towards the window. Moon shining bright and full through the open curtains like a searchlight. I closed my eyes and imagined I could feel its light on my face like the sun, except instead of warming my bones it was making me cold to the touch. Thinking again of Jude and Maeve in the kitchen, his hands on her body. Did Willy touch her that way?

Jude, I said. Did you and Maeve ever—?

Once, he said. A long time ago. One of us was on the rebound, can't remember who now. Doesn't matter, it was years ago. Maeve and Willy and I, the three of us have known each other—

I know, I said. A long time, a long time.

I hated the way they spoke like that. As if there could be no measurement of their past in years. As if I, so young, couldn't possibly understand the way time worked, and what it did to people.

Sorry about last night, love, said Jude, peeling an orange with his hands, tearing it into segments. Tossing the rinds into the sink while King sat by his feet. Smell of burned coffee and sage. Sure you'll be pleased to know I'm paying for it today.

His face creased with sleep, eyes dull and watery, whites reddened. Rubbing my face against his chest, his woollen jumper scratching my cheek. Feeling gentle towards him. Up close, he looked so tired.

You still going to your mum's for the weekend? he said.

I nodded. I don't want to leave you, I said. But it's her birthday and I promised Henry. Are you sure you don't want to come?

It's not a matter of want, he said. I have to open the shop, you know that. It's a long weekend, and things will start picking up now it's spring. Might do us some good, anyway, hey? Give us a chance to miss each other again.

I do miss you, I thought, though he was right there with me, standing in the morning light, and I was holding him.

My mother was out in the garden when I arrived, wearing what I referred to as her beekeeper's outfit—broad-brimmed hat tied to her chin with a red scarf, long sleeves tucked into gloves, and socks rolled over the legs of her overalls to protect herself from ticks and spiders and the sun while she sowed and planted. Cool air off the Mountains, hard October light. I stood for a moment at the back kitchen window, watching her work. She seemed grounded. Kneeling in the earth, pulling up weeds with her hands. Wiping dirt from the side of her face with her wrist.

I left lilies in the sink for her—pink, her favourite—and filled the basin with warm water, an old trick she'd taught me to get the buds to open. When I was growing up, my mother had always kept fresh-cut flowers in our rented rooms. Her one small extravagance in a life where nearly everything we had was second-hand or borrowed. It might have seemed to others that she didn't have her priorities right, spending her extra cash on sword lilies or birds of paradise, but over my life I've come to find comfort in her insistence on small glamours. The flowers had seemed like a promise that a different life was destined for us. Glamour, my mother knew, could be another temporary cure.

Hello stranger, she said brightly, coming inside. Beneath her gardening clothes, she wore sailor stripes—white and blue—and when we hugged, I felt the heat of the sun on her shirt.

The house is quiet, I said. Where's Henry?

Playing table tennis with the kids next door. Where's that boyfriend of yours? Or am I supposed to say partner? I guess he might feel a bit silly, being called a boyfriend at his age. Hope you haven't told him how old I'm turning.

Your secret's safe with me, I said. I left him at home with the dog. He has to work this weekend.

Perhaps my mother caught some edge in my voice because she raised her eyebrows and said, The honeymoon is over then, I take it. Sawing the stems off the lilies with a bread knife because she couldn't find the scissors or her garden shears. It was possible, she told me, that she'd buried them in the garden with the daffodil bulbs.

So, what was it, then? Drinking, or other women? In my experience, it tends to be one or the other. Or both.

Nothing like that, I said. We just need a bit of space, that's all. Couple of nights apart, he says it will do us good.

Strange, my mother said, and frowned. Whenever I've been in love with someone, really in love, I've never been able to keep away from them. You should have seen your father and me in the early days. Wearing each other's clothes, following each other from room to room. It was like one long conversation, those first few years.

Yes, I thought, remembering those first few weeks in the Old House with Jude, when he'd sat by the bath to keep me company. Getting up early, dressing under the covers in the dark, to have coffee with him before he left for work. This would be the first night we'd spent apart since I moved in, and it made me sad to think of it. That already, we needed each other a little less.

Though maybe you're right, my mother said. Maybe we burned each other out, carrying on like that. Or maybe it's my fault. I never really taught you how to live with a man. Never was much good at it myself. And you did move in with him rather quickly.

I suppose we have been drinking, I said. And there is this woman, but Jude says they're just old friends.

And you believe him?

I nodded. She's a friend of mine now too. And anyway, she's about to have a baby with someone else.

My mother shrugged. There's a certain type of man who loves to feel needed, *necessary*, she said. You know, to be of use. Playing the part of the protector, having someone to save. It's a bird-with-a-broken-wing sort of thing.

Not Jude, I said, although I'd had a similar thought the night before, watching him with Maeve. He wants us to be independent. To be able to spend a night apart and for it to be okay. He's always saying things like love is founded on trust—that it needs freedom, like a fire needs air. That we should be a gift to each other, not another burden.

My mother laughed, a short, sharp sound.

I love you, honey, she said, but don't you think if he truly valued independence he'd be with someone closer to his own age?

Not that there's anything wrong with your dynamic, it serves you both—and you've always been very grown-up. But we're not always so aware of what we want. Even when it's right in front of us.

Have you heard from your father lately? she said then.

No, I said. Have you?

He calls sometimes.

From where?

Oh, you know. Wherever he is. Ballarat, Lismore. Wherever there's work.

What kind of work?

Whatever he can get.

My father had lived this way for as long as I could remember. Seasonally. Fruit picking up north, or working on ships that went back and forth across the Indian Ocean. My father, the sundowner. And then on the side, trying to double his luck, double his money. His magic tricks. Turning a little into something grand. Turning a little into nothing at all. Horses, my mother had told people when they'd first met. We both love horses.

I didn't know you'd been in touch with him, I said. How did he find you up here?

I like to let him know where I am. I write, to wherever he was last, and someone always tracks him down. So he knows where to find me. Just in case.

In case of what?

Don't look at me like that, she said. What, you want your father to disappear off the map? One of us has to keep an eye out for him. It was your decision not to keep in touch. When you wanted to stop visiting, I respected that. Doesn't mean I have to do the same. Your father and I, we have our own relationship.

I don't think much of any of it was my decision at all, I said. When you left, I don't remember being given a choice in that.

My mother smacked the knife down against the counter. After living apart from her for some years, I was no longer accustomed to the swiftness of her anger. She closed her eyes, and when she spoke again, her voice was strained.

One day, she said, when you have a child, you'll understand. As a woman, there's certain things you learn to live with. Compromises you make, for love, or out of loneliness.

For sex, you mean.

She made a cluck of disapproval, *tsk*ing, the expression on her face one of distaste. For though she had often spoken to me frankly about her own desires, those flights of passion that had ended in the drama and violence of birth—my mother twice split apart and stitched back together, first with me, in the traditional fashion with the intervention of metal forceps, and then with Henry, from sternum to navel, because he was breech and carried high—she did not like it if I talked that way.

The point is, she said, I didn't want you to have to live that way. For you, I wanted better. You're not very forgiving of the people you love, you know that? My little girl with her heart of leather. Who taught you to be so tough?

I thought to myself, You did.

Whenever my mother talks about leaving my father, she uses the plural *we. We left*. And I think that's what she wanted—a partner in crime, a daughter riding shotgun like a right-hand man. But between us, largely unspoken, is the first time she left, when she did not take me with her. Only once has my mother told me the story of her absence, when, on my sixteenth birthday, she found herself unexpectedly drunk for the first time since Henry was born. Calls in the night and another man on the end of the line. Love songs played over the telephone. One time, she told me, it was me who answered to an American voice drawling her name over and over. I must have been no more than three and a half, but it was a summons I would eventually follow, so many years later, out of another kind of desire for a different kind of life from the one that had beckoned to my mother, one that would call me across the Pacific and all the way east, to New York.

What I remember is that one morning, she was gone. I'm not sure for how long, for time in the absence of someone you love cannot be measured in the same way as regular time. Three days, two weeks, a month or more—what difference does it make? It is all interminable. My father and I learned to depend on the kindness of strangers, by which I mean other women. They fed us, we slept on their couches and sometimes, depending on the woman, one of us was let into their bed. These women were different from my mother, closer to my father's age, houses thick with incense and music and purple cloths draped over the furniture. They took our hands in theirs and read our fortunes and said my father would be lucky, and with women, he always was, and yet still, he ended up a bachelor.

Then one day my mother returned, and I was passed from some other woman's arms back into hers. It was my grandmother,

Sylvia, who, believing families should stay together, had driven the twelve hours from Melbourne to Sydney, the sunnier city, where my mother lay with the American troubadour in a hotel overlooking the harbour. I don't know what words my grandmother spoke to her. Maybe the sight of her alone, clipping across the lobby in the suit she wore to my parents' wedding, was enough to throw cold water down my mother's back. My grandmother collected her daughter like an errant, runaway child and put her on the first plane home.

But Sylvia couldn't have known that when my mother did return, she would only leave again a few months later, this time taking me with her. My father let us both go then, and in that way, he was like Jude—he believed that if you loved something, you should never hold on to it too tightly, loving with a loose grip. Or maybe he knew he couldn't stop us, stop her. My mother, only eight years earlier riding bareback through the dirt trails on my grandmother's property. Still at heart that same girl. Easily spooked.

I was always going to come back for you, she said, her hand on my wrist as I was halfway out her door after putting her to bed on the night of my sixteenth birthday.

I never learned what happened with the American—if she rejected him or, as I suspected, he rejected me. A certain kind of man might think there is something noble in taking on the responsibility of raising another man's child—might even come to find joy in it, or at least a quiet dignity—but, as my mother would discover, not most. Though Henry's father, for a while, had tried.

Sitting at my mother's kitchen table that weekend all those years later, I recognised what I had always known—that my parents had loved each other. How much easier, I've often thought, to understand their separation if they hadn't. Whatever story I wrote for myself must always begin with the story of their love, and in comparison, no love of mine could ever be as terrible or as true. Across time, my father and mother still touching through telephone wires, letters in the mail, the bones in my face, the blood that moved in me. Love could endure more than I had allowed for, I realised. Some things last a long time, and maybe there's hope in that.

Back at the beach after my brief absence, we were in love again, like we had been at the start of the winter. My heart was not leather, I wanted to tell my mother. I could be forgiving. I could let love in.

Some time passed before I saw Maeve again. I hadn't spoken to her since the night she'd come to our house with the sonogram, or seen her on the beach or in town, and I wasn't sure if she was coming to Sailors Beach at all anymore. In any case, I made no effort to track her down. As quickly as she'd come into my life she disappeared, and by then I was beginning to agree that we were better off without anybody else. Returning to our quiet ways, just the three of us—Jude, the dog and I. As we read together by the fireside after dinner, I pictured us grown old, taciturn. It seemed then that our love might hold.

At the end of October we celebrated Jude's birthday. Forty-three candles sunk into a cake I'd made, which wasn't soft, as it should have been, but firm like a mattress, egg whites whipped stiff with all that I wanted to prove. Singing to him out on the porch. Trying to light each tiny flame as we gathered beneath the bloodwood trees, the wind knocking them down one by one until Jude said, Fuck it, forget it, and huffed them all out in one whiskey-wet breath.

You'll be a handsome old man, I said to Jude, pushing his hair back behind his ears to show where the grey was coming in.

Aren't I already? he said, returning to our old jokes, the familiar scripts, but I was picturing him at seventy, eighty, a weathered face and those same sad, changeable eyes, still sharply dressed in his pressed shirts and polished boots. If I'd made a wish that night, it would have been that I'd get to be the one to see it, that our love might be the kind that lasted decades.

Don't get me anything, love, he'd said, I have everything I need. And so I don't know what Jude wished for, if he wished for anything at all.

It was a cold, wet spring and mostly we stayed sheltered. In the first week of November, a series of storms felled a tree down the road and took out a powerline, so for days we went Victorian. Feeling our way through the house in the dark, touching by candlelight, heating canned soup over the fire. Still now, the taste of long-life milk, powdery and sweet, stirred into tea, recalls that time.

The squall also brought down a wreck of birds on Sailors Beach. They were seabirds—shearwaters, Jude said—with grey, greasy feathers and bloated, rubbery-looking bodies. King ran ahead of us, barking, as we picked our way between them on the shore. The dusk, and the heavy clouds, cast everything in a strange blue light.

It's these storms, said Jude. They break their necks when they try to fly against the wind. Stopping to push sand across their bodies with his boot.

Until that year I'd always lived in cities, and while I was used to birds flattened by cars or electrocuted by the wires of a telegraph pole, the remains of a feathered wing left behind and stuck to the road, the sight of them cast along the white sand made me uneasy. It looked like someone had shot them down.

Jude put his arm around me—he always stood on the ocean side to protect me from the wind that skimmed the water. As we walked I thought of Maeve, remembering the day she had complained about the smell of the ocean. How it reminded her, she said, of something dead and rotting. Wondering then if she had sensed it, in some animal way—as if prescience were another early sign of pregnancy. Though perhaps by then I wanted to see her as a harbinger of bad tides, as if she'd stirred up the winds and brought down the flock herself, with one swoop of her silver-ringed hands.

Love, I still believe, exists outside of time. Or it is its own time. It makes its own measures—not in minutes or hours or calendar days but in something closer to seasons, or tidal movements. All winter long we'd been suspended in it. Marking the weeks by watering the plants, marking the months by blood. But suddenly I became aware that time outside of Sailors Beach was passing in the regular fashion. I knew by then that love alone would not sustain us. We could not always stay that way, sitting by the fire, drinking whiskey for the extra warmth. It was spring, soon it would be summer—a year had passed since I finished university. What had I achieved in all that time? It made me nauseous to think about it.

Somehow, I had let myself come temporarily adrift. My abandoned poems, abandoned stories, I would fix them, finish them, spin them into something—print, gold—and when a story I wrote about the dog was published in a local magazine and awarded a small prize, I felt for the first time like the alchemy might work.

Three copies arrived in the post along with a cheque for five hundred dollars, and I told Jude I was thinking about going back to school to study writing, maybe applying to do a master's or a PhD. You *are* a writer, he said, tapping the cover of the publication, which displayed my name beneath the story's title. You don't need school for that.

Jude believed in learning through experience, building a life for yourself with your own hands. Institutions had let him down, he felt—his self-taught carpentry had got him further than all those long-ago years of acting training, from which he retained only a certain grace of movement, a way of inhabiting his body I've known in no other man since.

But I needed guidance, I told him, structure. In many ways, my life as a student was the most stable one I'd known, and over the years I would often feel the urge to return to it, whenever I was between jobs or between lives, feeling lost and purposeless. University arranged my time into a recognisable shape, gave value to my searching, my formlessness. This, of all the reasons to pursue an academic life—the longing for a vessel that would hold me.

It would only be a couple of days a week, I said. I could take the train up for my classes.

Plus, I told him, I might qualify for funding and that would help, since all winter, the shop had been slow. And if I got my PhD I could teach, which seemed more sustainable—not to mention ethical—than writing illegitimate papers for undergraduates. I was pleased with myself for arriving at such a sensible plan.

You've really made up your mind about this, then?

I still have to apply, see if I get in.

Well, good for you. My little Brontë, he said, and it seemed then that he was encouraging me. At the end of the week, Jude brought me home a copy of *Letters to a Young Poet* signed, *With love from King—your better muse. Woof woof!* We celebrated, toasting to the book I would write.

Later that night, after Jude had switched off the light, he mumbled something into the back of my neck, so softly I had to ask him to repeat it. My skin was damp with his breath. You don't need me anymore, he said.

I do, of course I do, I said. But isn't it better, like you said, to want each other instead? And I do want you. Turning him onto his back, kissing his chest in the divot of his breastbone. Let me show you how. He rolled away from me onto his side with his same old words. He was tired. It had been more than a week since we'd made love.

You never touch me anymore, I said.

Sex is not all there is, you know.

You wouldn't have said that six months ago.

Well, maybe you taught me something, he said, and I cried about this later, in the shower, remembering what he'd said. I didn't want to be the one to teach him that, I wanted so much more to be the one who'd taught him desire, the way he'd taught it to me until I was fluent in it, this new language my body had learned.

Jude had turned forty-three, and in January I would turn twenty-five. No more symmetry between us.

Those, I know now, were the last of our good days. But if we had experienced in those weeks something of a brief renewal—our love reborn from spring rain—King was failing. Around this time, one of his eyes completely clouded over. He went blind on his left side. Not long afterwards, he lost all interest in food. He ate slowly, and even this required a tender, patient coaxing. Each night, I sat with him, feeding him kibble by kibble, straight from the palm. Cooking him boiled chicken and sweet potato on the stove to inspire his appetite. Lying on the floor with his head on my belly, his paws around my waist—an embrace. We were more gentle with King than we were with each other. At night we let him sleep on the bed with his head on the pillow, filling all the space between us. Dogs dream, researchers believe, for the same reasons we do. As a way of cataloguing their memories, processing the important experiences of their day—moments of anxiety or joy. Sorting out what will be stored and what left to drift down into the silt of the mind. King had reached the age where, if he were a human, he might be inclined to reflect, to look back on a life lived, and it did seem in those days that he slept more and more. Busy with this task of sorting out, of letting go.

During the day I went walking, up and down the hills towards the national park, past the ruined house or along the cliffs on the long path that led into town. Often, I went alone. King's back legs had grown stiff with arthritis, and I worried over his weak heart. Other days I spent researching graduate programs at the local library, which was not a large, glassy space like the one I'd loved on my old university campus but a squat, red-brick building with an only slightly more reliable internet connection than we had at Jude's. I had no intention of leaving him, which meant I was limited to applying to places I could reach by train, but sometimes I looked at the courses at grand and gothic-looking institutions overseas and felt something like regret. My world had narrowed over the last year, as if any dreams or ambitions I might've had for my life beyond Sailors Beach had slipped away beneath the waves. I had a sudden urge to call Bonnie, to get in touch with her again. Though I wasn't surprised when, standing in the little car park behind the building, where I watched a teenage boy and girl in sloppy crimson uniforms share a cigarette, I got no answer.

The next time King and I walked to the beach that spring, all the birds were gone. The work was too quick and too thorough to have been done by any natural process. Someone must have come and cleared them away—preparing, perhaps, for the high season—though I don't know who is tasked with such a thing, or if anyone would choose to take it upon themselves. In the weeks before I left Sailors Beach, not a single feather remained from all that plumed carnage. Nothing that I might collect in my coat pocket, or keep in the drawers of my desk. No relics I might leave behind. *Remember me here.*

One evening, I returned home from the library and was surprised to see Jude's truck out the front, parked beneath the fig tree, since he often complained about the birds that dropped fruit on the windscreen from above. He rarely got home before me, and from across the street I could see that the house was dark. Stumbling inside, feeling for the light in the hall, I remembered the way it had appeared to me that day in the summer when I'd come around to find him gone without warning. That air of abandonment around the eaves.

But I was no longer a stranger, this place was my home now. I moved through the rooms flicking switches, filling the house with the warmth of dull yellow bulbs. But in the kitchen, I caught it again—the buzz of a room only recently departed, not yet settled into silence. A record was spinning though the album had finished, the needle bumping in an empty groove.

Jude must have come home early and taken King for a walk while it was still light, I thought, but I heard his paws on the back door then, followed by the sound of that familiar lonesome yowl, the dog's wet nose pushed up against the glass. I opened the door and he licked my knees, grateful, and leaned his body against my legs, brown eyes looking up at me from beneath the shelf of his shaggy brow. Sometimes he did look like a mythical beast, the last of his kind, some ancient and slow-moving creature—except, of course, when he went running after a rabbit. But he was getting too old for that, poor King, his fur now the greasy, threadbare coat of an older dog. When I stroked his back, I could feel the bony ridge of his spine.

Where's Jude? Where's Jude? I said to the dog. Thick-dark night beyond, a blue so deep you could drown in it, and lit up, brilliantly, by the moon. So large and round I felt I could stretch my fingers out to it, the kind of light that made an impossible distance seem, miraculously, within reach. Drawing me out onto the porch. The moon was cold but generous, I thought. No one ever went blind from looking at the moon.

The day after I'd been with Jude for the first time, we'd stood out here, I remembered, in this same spot, watching the galahs and lorikeets that feasted from the trees in the summertime. Playing his game of trust. He'd pressed a piece of spoiled fruit into my hand and taught me how to feed the birds. Trust me, he'd said, holding me steady while they came and settled on my shoulders. I'd leaned back against him, felt his hands on my waist, my body growing light.

The porch overlooked dense bushland, sloping down to the beach. Scrubby eucalypts, tall trees, bottlebrush and paperbark. Pale stretch of sand illuminated, dark water beyond. On some nights you could hardly see it, you could walk straight out and think you were walking towards the horizon until your feet got wet if it wasn't for the sound. You could hear it, just beyond. Rushing, rushing. Oldest song I knew, the one I'd heard as a child when I was looking for my father in shells and in the bath when I held my head under. I'd thought we were all connected by water, then. The ocean was always there, moving in the dark. Sometimes violent, tossing with restless rhythms, as if in a bad dream. Sometimes gentle, like a mother soothing a child to sleep, or a lover's breath. There was something tidal, too, about love. Each day, rushing forward or receding, growing closer or further apart.

Down on the beach, I saw a figure walking slowly across the sand. Moving in and out of shadow, patches of bush. I could tell it was Jude by his long-legged stride, his overcoat. My heart rose with recognition the way it always did when I spotted him in the distance on a busy street or coming towards me across a crowded room.

Where's Jude? Where's Jude? I said to King again, in the voice we used to get him excited for a walk. He lifted his paws up to the wooden railing, and from his perch he barked twice, as if in warning.

My view was partly obscured by trees, but in the gaps between the leaves I caught a glimpse of red moving between the bushes, like a flag. It was Maeve, the top of her red hat. They had stopped walking and stood close together, facing each other. Maeve was tall for a woman, and Jude was on a slope or perhaps his boots had sunk into the sand, because it struck me that they were eye to eye. She had her back to me and Jude was standing on the ocean side, shielding her from the wind the way he always did for me when we walked together on the beach at night. That's Jude, I thought. Always the gentleman. And then I watched him lift his hand and touch her face. His lips were moving, saying words I couldn't hear. He was holding her face in his hands.

King barked again and they parted, glancing up in the direction of the porch. I sat down quickly to shield myself from view. It occurs to me now that the sharpest feeling I had in that moment was not one of betrayal but one of shame. It was the shame of witnessing a private moment, of seeing something I was not supposed to see. The intimacy of it, the tenderness of that touch, the way they broke apart—and yet it was I who felt indiscreet and indecent. It seemed clear I couldn't stay there, a trespasser where I didn't belong.

It's okay, it's okay, I said to the dog, to calm him, though I felt it—the world tilting off its axis—and when I stood, I wavered, blood rushing from my head. I heard my heartbeat in my ears, a sound like the beating of so many wings. I took Jude's keys from the hook by the door, cool metal growing warm in my palm, a comfort to trembling hands. I called to King, Let's go! Let's go!

When it came down to it, I was like my mother. I chose flight.

So many times since, I have returned to that scene on the beach in my mind. Two figures coming together briefly and then parting. It rises up through my memory whether I call to it or not and after everything that followed, it's become impossible to separate how I felt then from what I know now. I replay it, and watch the figures move together, slowed. From this distance, it's tempting to see that single moment as carrying within it all that the coming months would hold.

Looking back, I am certain only of this: the relief that night of the truck kicking into gear, of gripping the gearstick in my hand, the tension and release of my feet on the pedals. The shake and rattle of riding down the dirt road, two hands tight on the hard leather wheel.

It seemed essential to go back to a place from a time before Jude, and as I crunched the gears between second and third and steered the bulk of the truck onto the highway, I remembered the cabins a few towns over. Swan Lake. The inlet, with its flat disc of water and black-necked birds, was only half an hour away. We'd been happy there—my mother, Henry, Grant and I. Rearranging ourselves into a more recognisable shape of a family.

Why drive for more water when we have the ocean outside our door, whenever we want it? Jude had said when I'd suggested one day that we go visit the lake from my childhood. It was just like me to want to make up for lost time like that, to write him into my past, where Jude was firmly anchored in the present. Never thinking ahead or looking back.

Searching for Swan Lake on my phone, I found results for the ballet, season tickets to the opera house. The place didn't appear on any map. Perhaps it wasn't the true name of the lake—maybe it had been the name of the holiday site and it had since changed hands. Or maybe it had only ever been my mother's name for it, another one of her whimsies, wanting everything to be an adventure, to prove that our life without my father could still hold magic and beauty. I would have to navigate by memory, past the shuttered surf shops, empty supermarkets and drive-through bottle shops, towards the dunes.

As I steered the truck around the bay, images came back to me from long ago. Memories emerged out of the dark, briefly illuminated like the passing scenery before falling back into shadow. The year we left my father. The year of motels. Paper lampshades and salmon-pink curtains, alternating views of a car park or a swimming pool, green neon sign outside the window lighting up the room: *Vacancy*. Driving between New South Wales and Victoria, my mother at the wheel, along the Princes Highway, the Kings Highway and the Hume. Up the coast at first, and then inland—we had no real direction, no particular place to go. Sleeping stretched out on the back seat some nights, wrapped in the rabbit-fur coat that had belonged to my mother when she was a girl. My grandmother had prepared her for a different kind of life, the boot of our car full of wedding silver and lace tablecloths and other heirlooms, hastily packed and no use in those months on the road when we lived, more or less, out of the car. Our leaving, like my own that night, had been haphazard. We were ill-equipped for the circumstances.

Oh, what are we going to do? I said to the dog, but when I looked in the rear-view mirror for his shape in the back seat, I found it empty. Only my own face blinked back. In my hurry to leave the house, I had forgotten him at home. I'd taken nothing with me, not even a change of clothes.

By that point, I had found my way to a road that ended in water. The trembling lip of the lake, sucking at the shoreline in the dark. I parked by a set of picnic benches and got out of the car, wrapping my arms around myself, the collar of my too-thin city coat turned up against the wind. Here, I'd once swung from the low branches at high tide. Walking through the bush to the sand dunes, sliding down steep hills on flattened fruit boxes, Henry on my lap. I was rushing away from childhood back then, though I did not know it yet. I was trying to hold myself back for him, my brother, as if I could wait for him to catch up, hold out for a second childhood. But that summer the blood would come, and I would stay stranded on the shore, watching the other children swim because my body was a wound, I was a woman now.

The bush grew right up to the edge of the water, clustered around it, roots and trees wading, as if the land had been flooded.

From memory, it was a short walk down a sandy path to where the cabins stood in a clearing. But nothing was as I'd remembered—there were no lights in the distance, no murmuring hum around a campfire, no smoke rising above the branches, or the smell of propane and citronella, just thick-growing trees all the way to the dunes. All signs of the cabins were gone, as if the bush had finally devoured them, or they had never existed at all.

I thought of Maeve in our kitchen, the day she'd showed us the sonogram, saying, *You can never go back, not really.* Jude's hands on the rise of her belly. Jude's hands on her face. That night by the lake, everything felt tremulous, uncertain. I regretted the way I'd left without warning—no explanation, not even a note—for I knew abandonment to be an irredeemable act. Once you leave, there is never any guarantee you won't leave again.

My phone was ringing in the palm of my hand. Jude's name lighting up in the dark.

Maybe it wasn't too late to turn back after all. Jude, King, the Old House—that was the place that felt most like home. If I could forget, pretend I hadn't seen a thing, then nothing would have to change. And what had I seen, really? Two figures coming together briefly and then parting. I must have misunderstood.

What the hell is going on? he said when I answered. Where are you?

I told him I'd gone for a drive, that I'd been looking for Swan Lake.

Jesus, he said, I thought something terrible had happened. I thought we'd been robbed. I came home and all the lights were on, the door wide open. King gone, car gone.

King's gone?

He's not with you?

I thought I left him inside.

Well, he's not here. I've called him, looked everywhere in the house. If he's not with you, the dog's gone.

King must have followed me, I realised, down the hall and out the front door. I'd meant to take him with me, but in my distress I'd failed to put him in the car. I had left him behind.

Hold on, I said to Jude. I'm on my way. I'm coming home.

In the movies, all good dogs return home—a hopeful idea, that the things we love are never truly lost and can be returned to us, or find their own way back. Down on Sailors Beach I called his name. Voice breaking thin and high against the waves. Cold wind stinging my face, making my eyes water. My hands were numb, my throat ached. I sat on the sand and cried. Jude, his house by the beach, the dog—it wasn't that I had lost them, I thought. They'd never belonged to me at all.

Then, in the distance, I saw them: Jude striding along the shore with the dog by his side. Walking at his heel, the very image of a faithful companion. When King saw me, he came running too fast in my direction, swinging along with his odd seesawing gait, his long legs covering the great stretches of sand between us. Barrelling forward and barking as if to say, *I found you! I found you!*

I held King's head, breathing in his warm and familiar dusty smell, feeling the grit and knots in his fur. I love you, I love you,

I said to the dog, while he licked the salt from my face and hands. I'll never leave you again.

I wish, said Jude, you'd talk to me the way you talk to the dog.

He was calm. Now that King had been found, there was nothing in his mind to worry about. He seemed bemused by the drama, and this made me angry—the way he stood there looking down at us with his hands in his pockets, as if he were outside of it all. His composure struck me as cruel.

I got up, brushed off my coat, and wiped my face with my sleeve.

Jude, I said. Are you fucking Maeve?

What are you talking about? he said. What kind of question is that?

I saw you. Together on the beach tonight.

How many times do I have to tell you there's nothing going on there?

But I *saw* you!

King started to bark then, yelling back at us whenever we raised our voices, the sound ringing out across the trees, the empty beach.

Is that what all this was about? We almost lost the dog because you went running off into the night instead of waiting to have a reasonable conversation, like an adult?

Don't ask me to be reasonable! I saw you!

What did you see? Tell me. What did you see? I mean, for Christ's sake, what do you think is going on—I'm fucking around with Maeve behind your back while she's six months pregnant with my friend's kid? Is that what you really think of me? Is that what kind of man you think I am?

Jude told me that Maeve had come to Sailors Beach that night to break up with Willy—for good this time—and she was going back to the city to raise the baby alone.

She needed someone, he said. That was all. It was nothing to do with me at all.

Are you in love with her?

I'm not going to answer that, he said. King! Would you please shut up! Quiet, King!

Between us, the dog was baying with increasing distress, stooping low to the ground, hackles raised. When I reached my hand towards him, he backed away.

It was one old friend comforting another, that's how Jude put it. It was nothing, he said, I had to believe that it was nothing, or—

Or what?

Or there isn't anything left here.

He turned to leave and I called out after him. My voice, bullied about by the wind and waves. I yelled, stamping my foot like a child.

You always think you can fix everyone. Why can't you just love me? Isn't that enough?

When you're like this, he said, you make yourself real hard to love.

I waited for Jude to turn back and make sure we would follow as he walked away from us across the sand, but he didn't, he never did. He walked on ahead without looking behind him, and I watched his back, his winter coat, until the bush obscured him, and he was gone.

That awful night.

Do you love me? Do you love me?

And Jude, tired, stern: Go to sleep.

I hated when he treated me like a child, and I hated it more when I acted like one.

Act your age, he said.

And I yelled back, I am! I am!

Slamming the door to the bedroom so that the house shook. Making the dog bark, howl.

Voices tight in the dark. Fighting in tense whispers, as if we didn't want the dog to hear.

Where were you?

Out.

Out where?

Where do you think? Same place as always.

I've been calling you.

Didn't have my phone on me.

But you always keep it in your jacket pocket. You think, after all this time, I don't know how you wear your jacket?

I dripped water on the floor, brought the sand in with me, bled on his sheets, ground down the gears on his truck, left my clothes on the couch, scratched the records by leaving them out of their sleeves, left water rings on the wood, broke his antique crystal glasses. It's like living with a teenager, he said. I was clumsy, careless. *It's not my fault!* I wanted to say. I hadn't learned how to contain myself, to be easy, gentle, to hold on to anything without breaking it. With the pressure you put on things, love, Jude said, they'll never last.

Tired, love.

Tired love.

I made him so very tired.

THREE

In the weeks that followed, we lived together in the humbled quiet of two people who are no longer lovers. Careful not to touch or linger, the house full of evidence. Here is the kitchen where he took off my clothes, here is the porch where I spread my arms for the birds. Polite, after all the months we'd been so reckless. Saying *please* and *thank you*. Asking in the evenings, Would you like tea? Is it okay if I leave my light on?

But at night our bodies betrayed us. We fell together in the dark, finding the shape of each other as if easing into well-worn clothes. Grabbing at wrists, handfuls of hair, trying to find something to hold on to. Waking curled around one another like two animals sleeping together for warmth. It was sad to greet the morning that way, in such old, familiar intimacy, and remember the distance with which we now conducted our lives. Was this intimacy too? Strained and cautious. Slowly building back up all the barriers we'd broken through. Falling in love in reverse.

That was the summer it would get so hot the roads up north would start to buckle. In my last days down south I could watch a piece of fruit ripen on the windowsill over the course of a single day and begin to bruise by night. Soft plums and dimpled peaches, skin mottled with a faint fuzz of mould by morning, Jude muttering about the waste and tossing them outside for the birds.

There were bushfires in Victoria. When the eucalypts caught fire, the smoke burned blue. Ash travelled north to Sailors Beach, capped the white dunes, flakes of black debris skirting the shore-line, the ocean's dirty hem. The heat came in waves of wind from out west, sweeping sand beneath the doorframes. It accumulated nightly, grain by grain, until one day we came downstairs to find a series of tiny dunes cropped up on the kitchen floor. A haze of grit and dust in the air, eyes red and watery. My hands left fingerprints on every surface I touched. I noticed for the first time how dirty the house could get—as if we'd lived all winter in the dark.

When I told Jude I thought I should move out, or at least go stay with my mother for a while, he held up his hands and said, Hey, I'm no captor. He seemed to take it so lightly, as if I'd hardly made a mark.

In all our time together, I never once saw him cry. Saw his face go pale, ashen, eyes redden but never brim. His heart was a dry country. In those moments I'd sat beside him and hooked my fingers through his, stroked his arm, while he stared straight ahead, unblinking. As if he were afraid of all the water that might spill over from within.

So that's it? I said. You're just going to let me leave?

I wanted smashed plates, doors slamming. To stand back and see the damage we'd done. I wanted to dig my nails into his skin.

I want you to be happy, he said.

How dare he want what was best for me, I thought. How dare he think he always knew exactly what that was.

Whenever we fought, I was reminded of the brown bird that had once been trapped inside our kitchen. It rallied, throwing itself against the walls, beating wings against windows, as though feathers so light could possibly break glass. I felt like that—like something winged and frantic, coming up against the limits of flight, while Jude stood stoic in the middle of it all, watching, immovable. He'd remained still, then reached out and caught the bird with a tea towel, covering it with both of his hands. Opening the door, setting it free.

All his rules for butterflies and birds. He treated me like a light thing. Loving things loosely and then letting them go.

You don't have to do this, he said, but he had a box of my clothes in his arms, and continued to load them carefully into the car.

On my last night we went for a drive, crossing the bridge leading into town, where kids jumped from the railing to swim at high tide, when the lake spilled over below. Silty waters. Silky rays lying across the sandy floor. But that day it had run dry, as if the water had soaked into the land, patches of sand marooned in tiny islands. You could have walked right across the bed of it.

We parked on the hill, past the caravan park, overlooking the ocean below, the truck sheltered by the thin and towering bodies of the angophora trees. I saw one like a hand, thick branches spread like five fingers reaching upwards.

It smells like dog in here, I said. Wet dog.

That's because you always let him ride in the front, rather than tying him up in the back, said Jude, and rubbed his eyes with his fists.

Well, he's getting old, I said, and I remember that on that particular day we'd left King at home, since it was no longer easy for him to lift himself into the back seat or jump up into the bed of the truck.

I reached my hand across the seat.

I'm tired, love, said Jude, but I still felt him rise and harden as I moved my palm across the fly of his jeans.

Then let me, I said, unbuckling.

My mouth on his mouth, searching. Thinking, This could be the last time. Leaning across the gearstick into his lap. Remembering the afternoon last summer when he came to get me on a whim, and we drove from my rented room in the city back to the Old House, itching to touch. Prickle of sweat on the back of my neck, thighs sticking to the leather seat beneath my dress. We took the long way back, along the old highway, past the rolling hills and apple orchards, and parked the truck along a quiet stretch of the Hume, making love with the windows down and the radio tuned to an old country station, smell of bushfire in the air—backburning season. This is not real, I'd thought back then. He is a dream and I have dreamed him. It was a strange feeling, stepping into the life I'd always wanted and imagined for myself, like I'd cheated somehow. It was love the way love should be—a story I was telling myself and roping him in. A thread I tied around the two of us, binding him to me.

We are taught that love is not so different from hatred, that instead of opposites, the two extremes of the human heart might in fact be twins. But it's grief, really, that is love's twin, that knows no bounds of time or space. Wave after wave it keeps coming, whereas hatred cools, fades. So many times I swore that I loved Jude, that no one had ever loved or been loved this way before, and then something broke through, a new depth. Colder and darker moved the waters of my love.

Thinking, in those first few days in the Mountains after I moved back in with my mother, of something she'd once said: There is no end to grief, because there is no end to love.

I know that in the year before I was born, my parents moved into a small white house that my grandmother purchased for them as a wedding present—a gift, I am told, that made my father feel inadequate and added strain to their marriage, though it was not the final cause of their undoing. For a time we lived there, the three of us together. Of this place I have no memory, other than a photograph I saw on one of my few childhood visits to Sylvia's house. It was taken a few months after my birth, but my parents look semi-Edwardian, dressed like figures from another time. My mother in a white nightgown and black gumboots, dark hair to her waist in unruly waves, and my father, ten years older, in that same woollen overcoat, long hair combed back behind his ears. You can barely see my tiny round head among the bundles of beribboned blankets my mother holds in her arms. It is the only picture I have ever seen of my parents together, though it is lost to me now—the photographs long ago divided up between my mother and her brothers after my grandmother's death, along with the rest of her possessions, turned in her absence to artefact.

That summer in the Mountains I understood something about my parents and our transience, which began for us when my mother left the first time to follow the sound of an American's voice and my father and I went door to door looking for comfort in the arms of other women. We couldn't stay anymore in that little white house, where the three of us had lived, because what good is a home once the ones you love have left it? What good is a home that has failed to keep them all safe, contained, within reach? My mother's truancy from our household had revealed it for what it was—a flimsy construction, no more secure really than the shelters I used to build in the backyard as a child. Beds of leaves, sticks sunk into the dirt, circled with rocks and feathers and other things I had collected and deemed precious and dear. Such structures could not be expected to hold us all together, keep us all in place.

It seems now that we have always been drifters, my mother, my father, and I. We swayed, touching others only lightly, ebbing closer and away with the loose tide. I wondered if this was what it had been about with Jude—a tethering. How I'd thought of him as someone who could brace the weight of winds and tides, hold me against the drift, anchor me.

In the Mountains that summer I took a job babysitting the small daughter of a woman who lived down the road from my mother's house—a young PhD student who took the train to the university on the outskirts of the city three days a week. Another single mother my mother had befriended. I liked her apartment, above a corner coffee shop, and being in closer proximity to academic life again, which was something I missed. Her living room filled with anatomy books, antique medical slides in a glass case, framed posters of Georgia O'Keeffe paintings on the wall. The baby was eighteen months old and easy to love. Kissing her cheeks, lifting her high above my head to make her laugh. I could love a child, I realised. I had the capacity, the space inside, it was my brother who'd first taught me how.

Sometimes I felt sixteen again—living with my mother, babysitting, sleeping in the same bed I'd slept in as a girl—but my face in the mirror had changed, narrowed, and when I took the little girl to the park, people assumed she was mine. I didn't mind, it didn't embarrass me the way it did when I was younger, pushing Henry's stroller in the street, afraid of being painted as a teenage mother. The way people had looked at me back then—like a failure. Leering, it was almost lewd, when I was only once-kissed, a virgin.

It was different now, charged with new feeling, as the other parents smiled and nodded their approval, asking how old she was, if she was sleeping through the night. Another way of brushing hands with a life that might have been mine, through this temporary mothering.

Sometimes, while I was washing the dishes at my mother's house, or reading books with the neighbour's baby on my lap, images came back to me from the previous summer: Jude rolling my swimsuit down past my waist, red fabric stretching across my knees as I tried to open my legs until, with one final tug from his hand, it was gone, tossed in a wet heap on the floor. Telling me I tasted of the sea. And how afterwards I'd gathered up my things in a hurry, said, I have to go, my mother's waiting, and he'd laughed.

One evening, after coming home from the neighbour's, I asked my mother how she first suspected she was pregnant with me. We were sitting in the darkened living room, the lights turned off to keep the house cool, waiting for the nightly news. It was a week before Christmas, fires were burning around the country, and I was not bleeding.

I felt murderous, my mother said. I was so angry. Whenever your father tried to touch me, I wanted to cut off his hand. The smell of his sweat alone made me want to vomit. I lay awake at night worried I might smother him.

I asked her if it went away, that feeling, and she said yes, as soon as she found out the reason. All that rage transmuted into love. And then she paused and said, But I suppose you could say it came back.

In the country, my mother told me, my grandmother had developed a reputation—a single woman, the only divorcée for miles, and unafraid of blood, known for delivering horses on her property. In another time, she might have studied veterinary science, but instead she married into medicine and became a doctor's wife, and then, when my grandfather left her for one of his graduate students, a doctor's ex-wife. Women used to come knocking on Sylvia's door—young wives, teenagers, the other women of married men. Hushed conversations held out in the barn. Her prescriptions: a bath of boiling water, a glass of gin, the right kind of touch on the lower abdomen.

My grandmother had been pregnant when my grandfather left. She'd gone to a new doctor, since the old one was a friend of her husband's, and told him she didn't want another child. Three was enough of a handful, she couldn't manage four. He'd shrugged. Why not? he'd said. You're a married woman, aren't you? Too stubborn to tell him otherwise, the ring still tight on her finger. Swelling hands and ankles—these were her early signs, along with a metallic taste in the mouth.

The great irony, my mother said, was that the woman my father left us for, she couldn't conceive. It just didn't take. I felt sorry for her, in the end.

What happened to Sylvia's baby? The one she didn't want to have.

She always said *my body took care of it.* But it wasn't until years later—when I told her I was pregnant with you, actually—that she told me how. Gin-drunk and riding horses till she bled. Can you believe it? *Just in case you change your mind*, that's what she said. But of course, I didn't want to change my mind, and in any case, it was the eighties, not the sixties. I could have gotten an abortion if I'd wanted one. But she could be like that—

I know, I said. An unsentimental woman.

That night, we watched an aerial map on TV of the fires in Victoria travelling north, crossing the border of New South Wales. Footage of families wading waist-high in water. An image that stays with me still: a small child, hair androgynously long, alone in a tin boat, gripping the tiller in one hand beneath a red sky, respirator strapped to their face. In the light of the amber afterglow, the waves in the water looked like licks of flame. Even in the Mountains, I could smell fire in the air. We watched them on the screen, whole towns turned to tinder. Mallacoota, Eden, Merimbula, Cobargo. Names I'd learned on those days on the road with my mother, and it seemed that all the past would be burned away, erased by fire.

Back then, there hadn't been bushfires near Sailors Beach since I was a child, but I remembered driving through the aftermath on our way to Swan Lake, passing through forests of burned and blackened trees. Eucalypts stripped bare. The eerie silence of those stretches, without the kookaburras laughing or the currawong's cry. The bush shouldn't be that quiet. Ash covered the ground like snow. All the birds were gone.

We'd had no television at Jude's, listened to the news on the radio at the shop or in the truck. His house was surrounded by wilderness—the blue gums and bloodwoods seemed to cradle it in their branches. One road in and out of town.

No, no fires here, Jude said when I called him up after my mother had gone to bed.

How could I have explained it to her, had she heard me talking through the walls? *I am trying to leave a man I still love*, or *I am trying to stop loving a man I have left.* In one of these I had succeeded, but as I lay awake, listening to the sound of helicopters moving across the valley, it was hard to tell in which.

I was superstitious in those early days in the Mountains. Counting and recounting the days of the month on my fingers. Lying on my mother's couch reading *Play It as It Lays* with the curtains drawn against the heat, dressing all in white, like Maria. Frequent trips to the bathroom, thumbing the black cotton of my underwear to check for traces. Willing the blood to come.

It would also be true to say that I never learned how to make a clean break. I have no memory of the words my parents used to explain their separation to me—if they tried to explain it at all. Maybe, like me, they stood mute in the face of loss, were rendered inarticulate by it. Whenever in my life it has come time to have those conversations with someone, I have felt that I lacked the right language. I didn't know what I was supposed to say.

How's King? I said.

He misses you. But you know dogs. They forgive and forget.

Yes, I agreed, dogs are much better than people.

Late-night calls in the week before Christmas like the early days of our love. We talked about the dog or the weather, the unbreaking heat that made the air quiver. I didn't mention that I thought I might be pregnant. It was enough just to hear his voice, to know that he was out there. It was enough that when I called, he answered. I could reach him still.

Maybe, like Maeve, I was looking for a sign, but there were too many that summer to make sense of. Nothing seemed to cohere. The gaunt horses I saw on the news, running through smoke. Fish that turned up dead in the thousands on the riverbanks of the Murray–Darling Basin, bony bream and cod and silver perch. Each passing day was like turning over a new card representing an unreadable future. It was Jude who taught me to love that way. Looking for messages in the wings of birds, the patterns of the wind, longing for an omen, an augury. Positive or negative. He loves me, he loves me not.

I had one once, Bonnie said, when I told her I might be pregnant. An abortion, I mean. Not a baby, obviously.

It was Christmas Eve and we were lying on her bed beneath the slow revolving fan in the room that used to be mine, sweating through our summer dresses. After I'd left, she'd moved in for the bigger closet and the balcony where I used to sit and smoke, which she'd decorated with living plants—geraniums and ferns and ponytail palms—where I'd only ever had chains of fake flowers wrapped around the railing. She hadn't removed them, they were still there. Once-red roses bleached pale by the sun.

My period was six days late, and though we had hardly spoken since I'd moved to Sailors Beach, Bonnie was the only person with whom I'd shared this news. Bringing her a secret like a gift, as if that could make up for all that lost time when we'd fallen out of touch.

When did this happen? I said. Recently?

It was ages ago, before we knew each other, she said. But don't tell Petra. She'd never believe it, anyway. For some reason, she thinks of me as so pure.

Of the three of us, Bonnie had been the first to lose her virginity, at fourteen. The boy a friend of her brother's, out in the back paddock of her family's farm.

It was when I was in Germany, Bonnie said, at the end of my gap year. I was nineteen.

She didn't really know the guy, she said, it was a one-night thing, and she was about to go home and start university. The doctor spoke little English and Bonnie's German was more social than medical, so she'd had to mime—rocking an invisible baby in her arms, then making a sign like in the game show program *Deal or No Deal*, crossing her wrists to make an X. Then, made frantic by their lack of shared language, the struggle to communicate, she made an action like slitting her throat with her finger. The doctor had looked back, horrified, but she'd seemed to understand.

How come you never told me about this before? I said.

Bonnie shrugged. It wasn't like I ever considered keeping it. Guess I don't think of it much. You wouldn't keep it, would you?

I don't know, I said.

Do you still love Jude?

I think a part of me always will.

It always feels that way at first, she said. But it will stop. I promise.

And I didn't know then if that was better, if I even wanted it to. At the time, that seemed to me like the saddest thing.

I thought you were mad at me, you know, I said, because it had been a long time since we had talked this way, the two of us. For leaving.

I was, she said. But it's okay. I still love you.

Patting my hand.

I still love you, too.

There must be people out there who are not drawn to the shadow of what could have been, who feel no pull towards the other lives they could be living, but I certainly have never been one of them.

I had borrowed my mother's car to drive to Sydney to visit Bonnie, and on my way back to the Mountains, I pictured it—going home to Jude, raising a child together by the beach in the house his own father had built and once dreamed of filling with a family. Imagining the pleasures that that life might hold—the one that I'd clumsily abandoned. I saw the possibility that a baby might make him love me more, more than he ever had. Lying in bed naked in the Old House, the warmth of his palm on the small growing round of my belly. I remembered the way he had moved his hands across the rise of Maeve's stomach. *A pure and beautiful thing.* From one point of view, what I'd seen between them that night on the beach might come down to the simple equation: a woman with a baby and a man without a child.

Maybe he had been in love with her, or maybe he was in love with that feeling, and in that way, we weren't so unalike, and had been drawn to her for similar reasons. A way of trying on a life we weren't quite ready to inhabit ourselves. All along we'd danced on the edge of it—by the side of the highway with the windows rolled down, on the beach with the sand beneath us sounding like a violin being bowed at high pitch, out in the yard with the birds.

I had wanted us to exist as one body, four arms and four legs. It had become intuitive, the way I responded to his touch, his shifting moods, all the seasons of his day. I was physically attuned to the way he walked into a room. Sensing him before I could see him, through some vibration or sweet hum in the air. Even when we were not touching we were one, joined by an invisible thread, like Jude had said about the moon and tide. Two thin pink lines on a test I found in the back of my mother's bathroom drawer that afternoon confirmed it.

On Christmas Day, we sweltered—my mother, Henry and I—staying inside with the lights down and the fans on high, watching holiday movies set in colder climates. *Miracle on 34th Street*, *It's a Wonderful Life*. There must be something comforting about living in a place where the seasons changed as we were taught they should, I thought, neatly segmenting the year into quarters. Longing for snow while on our table the salad leaves wilted and the oysters began to sweat. Beside us, our tinselled tree dropped brittle brown needles onto the floor. By the end of every film my face was wet, tears leaking, and Henry teased me for crying but shuffled next to me on the couch to rest his head on my shoulder, and I was grateful that he had not yet grown out of showing his affection.

All day, I ate barely more than a few mouthfuls of trifle. The smoke in the air tasted like a morning after too many cigarettes, which I'd finally quit. I told my mother I had cramps—which was true, though there was still no blood—but she narrowed her eyes at me when I waved away a glass of wine, and I was sure that, in her prescient way, she knew.

I called Jude that night and for the first time, he didn't answer. Out with other women, the thought came so sudden and clear. I lay curled into a ball on my childhood bed that had once been my mother's when she was a girl. I'd have a daughter, I was sure. Women are born with all their eggs in their ovaries, like the seeds of a fruit. I'd been with my mother since she'd been in my grandmother's womb, and now I was sleeping in her bed and my mother was in the next room sleeping in her mother's. It made me think of us like Russian dolls. Women carried inside women carried inside women.

In the morning, I woke to an email from Jude. I was surprised. We almost never communicated in that way. His emails were like telegrams—brief and perfunctory, as if every word cost him something. There was nothing in the body of the message, just one line in the subject box. No pleasantries, no punctuation: *the dog died*

It was his heart, said Jude, when he finally returned my calls two days later. His voice was thick and low, and I could tell he'd been drinking. Too small for a dog so big. And you know, he was old, especially for his kind.

He told me he had King's ashes in a wooden box, that he was going to scatter them by the beach tomorrow.

When did this happen?

He'd gone downhill quickly, Jude said. King's breathing had grown slow and laboured, his heart beating with an irregular rhythm. He'd never kicked the cough he'd developed after that time in the lake in the Mountains, and it had gotten worse. Hacking, and retching. His smoker's cough, we used to call it. By the end, he was vomiting water, and that was when Jude had called the vet, who told him that because of King's weak heart and his poor circulation, his lungs would have most likely filled with fluid. It would have felt like he was drowning. And so the vet agreed to make a house call on Christmas Day, and administer an anaesthetic. A syrup of blue barbiturate solution injected into the vein while Jude held the dog's head on his lap. In a matter of minutes, he was gone.

Why didn't you call me?

I don't know, I suppose I should have. But there wasn't a lot of time, and I didn't want him to be in any more pain than he had to be. He always had a lot of dignity, you know. I can't really explain it now, but at the time, it felt like it was something that was happening just between him and me.

Instinctively I wrapped my arms around my middle. Yes, I thought, I could understand that feeling. Remembering the way Jude had told me last winter that if we got pregnant, it would be my decision to make. At the time, I'd thought that was generous. I didn't know then how lonely it would feel. To be alone with a choice like that.

Do you want me to be there tomorrow?

Over the phone I could hear the wet drag of his breath.

If you want to be, he said. Just thought you should know.

The following morning, I dressed for a funeral and drove south to Sailors Beach for the last time. Black buttons at my wrists and up to my throat, a loose, high-necked dress of my mother's I'd found in her closet, silk fabric dampening beneath my arms. My own scent unfamiliar to me then, an acrid smell, like souring milk. I wound the windows down on the Princes Highway, breathing in hot air and baking tarmac, smoke and salt in the breeze while the sun burned down the left side of my face.

All week I had both grieved the dog and nurtured the thought of the child that Jude and I might have. It was the only way I could make peace with King's death—to balance the ledger. Something lost, something gained. Something given, something taken away. The love child I'd longed for that winter had come too late, but that was nothing new to us, I thought. We'd always got the timing wrong.

We had agreed to meet at the far end of the beach by the bench where we had first found King. For once I was early, and while I waited, I watched the way the wind dimpled the water, waves peeling back, like ruffles beneath dancers' skirts. White foam petticoats. Still trying to see the beauty in it all, and gather it towards me, wanting to believe that Jude and I might be saved. I thought of taking off my shoes, wading in, black dress around my body blooming. Leading Jude by the hand to the water and washing him clean, so we might begin again in the same ocean, beneath the same sky, almost a year to the day that we first met. Blinking salt water from our eyes. As in my mother's favourite painting—a man and a woman among rough peaks, heads bowed together in ecstasy or grief.

Looking back down the beach, I saw him walking across the sand, slanted forward as if the wind were much stronger than it was. He raised one hand and I saw that it was wrapped in a bandage.

When he reached me, we didn't touch. He was holding King's ashes in a wooden jewellery box that seemed too small for such a large dog.

I feel like we should say something, I said, but I didn't know how to account for all those dog years, so many of which remained unknown to us. Guessing at his age. Forty-nine? Fifty-six? Sixty-three? Like my mother said, some things count for more.

To King, king among dogs, said Jude.

All good dogs return home, I said.

A handful of silver ashes tossed and caught in the wind. They stayed suspended for a moment, hovering in the air between us, before another current came and bore them on. I watched them settle on the surface of the water, and gradually get carried out to sea until, beneath the sun, they were indistinguishable from any other patch of light.

Afterwards, we walked along the beach at the edge of the water, sinking into the sand a little with every footstep.

What happened to your hand? I said. Wind blowing my mother's dress around my knees, lifting it full of air, a black balloon I had to smooth down with my hands. Hair in my mouth, ocean spray wet on my face. I licked my lips and tasted salt.

Come have a drink with me, he said. I have to tell you something.

I told him I wanted to talk to him too, but I'd rather go back to the house, where it was quiet and we could be alone.

I lost the house, is what he said. That was how he put it—as if it were something he'd misplaced and no longer knew how to find.

What do you mean, you lost it?

Thinking of the cabins I'd tried to go back to—how it seemed as if the bush had come forward to devour them, to reclaim the land. I asked if it was his family, if his mother and sister had finally convinced him to sell the place and move on.

There was a fire, he said. The whole place would have burned to the ground had it not been for the rain the night before.

I asked him how it started. Can't you fix it up again? I said. Like you did before?

He shook his head. I was never supposed to be there, he said. I should've known. It wasn't right.

What do you mean?

Everything is fucked, he said. It's all full of water. When they let me back inside, I had to wade my way through. There were records and pots and pans all floating around the place, glass everywhere. All of it good for nothing. It's roped off now. Nothing left there worth saving.

Were you there? I said. Was King?

No, said Jude.

So, you were away, then?

Yes.

Visiting your mother?

No. Someone else.

Right. Someone else.

My eyes were stinging, as if the smoke were still lingering.

I'm really glad you weren't there, I said.

Tears rolling down my face, I pictured them making clean wet tracks through pale ash, though of course, I reminded myself, the house was not still burning. The waves rushed towards us and the trees bent back against the wind, the way they always did. The sky above us was blue and clear.

My father was a teller of dog stories, and there was one I remembered from when I was a child about a wolfhound, a hunter and his baby. Out in the woods one night, the man leaves his son in a makeshift cradle under the watch of his dog while he goes hunting. But while he is gone, a snake enters the campsite—though in other versions of the story, I said to Jude, the animal changes. The snake in the cradle, the wolf at the door. The dog goes crazy, barking, knocking everything over, blankets in disarray, shaking the snake between his teeth. He's protecting the baby, see? But when the hunter returns, he sees the upended cradle, blood at the dog's mouth, sheets scuffed with dirt and mud. The dog, he is sure, has killed his son. He takes the dog by the collar, drags him into the woods and shoots him. Only when he returns does he see the limp body of the snake and the baby crawling out from beneath the pile of sheets unharmed, and realise what he has done. How he's misread everything.

I always hated that story, I said. We were sitting side by side at the bar at the pub in town. It frightened me. I never understood it. I mean, what's the point of a story like that? It just seemed cruel. What's the moral? Don't take your own mistakes out on your dog?

Fear blinds us to what we love, more like, said Jude.

Well, I suppose there's truth to that.

What are you drinking these days? he said. Still gin, is it?

I shouldn't, I said. Driving.

But he ordered me a gin and tonic anyway and I sat there watching the ice cubes melt, condensation sliding down the glass, playing with my straw, unsure of what it was I wanted.

I'd once said to Jude that if we ever broke up, we wouldn't be friends. Of course we would, he said, I'm friendly with all my exes. This was a point of pride for him, but I didn't see how I could sit beside him and forget what we had known, when we had been so naked with each other, and I felt the strain of it that afternoon. Angling away from each other, new distance between our bodies. Apologising if his elbow touched mine or my foot brushed against his leg. Whenever we lapsed into silence, I could hear the ocean outside.

He'd cut his hair short, I noticed, studying his face in profile. It made his neck look vulnerable, exposed. His ears stuck out. Up close, I could see how thick and tightly wound the bandage was on his left hand, fastened with a safety pin. Resting on the bar top beside his pint, it looked like a giant white paw. Sucking the foam from his upper lip, clean-shaven. Everything about him raw, in a way that hurt to look at.

Your hair, I said.

I know, I know, he said, feeling tenderly at the back of his neck with his good hand. It's too short. Had to find a new haircutter, didn't I? Doesn't quite have your touch.

Are you going to tell me now what happened to your hand?

Oh, it was stupid, it was nothing.

Tucking it away beneath his other arm, as if he was ashamed for me to see it.

I thought you might invite me back to your new place, I said. I want to see where you've been living.

Checking up on me, are you, love?

It's not like that, I said. Though I do care about you. You know that.

Would be easier if you didn't.

Tried. Can't.

I thought I saw him smile then, or maybe wince. It was difficult to tell, seeing only the side of his face. He didn't look me in the eye anymore, but he placed his bad hand in my lap then and let me nurse it in both of mine.

His new place was on the B side of a squat apartment building set a few blocks back from one of the busier surf beaches. It was small, neat and white. Standing in the cramped kitchen alcove, Jude had a stooped look about him. Too tall beneath the low, flat ceilings.

I sat on the floor while he fixed us drinks—ice and bitters. All he had in the way of liquor was a half-drunk bottle of Aperol, he said. Sugary and medicinal.

I thought you hated stuff like that, I said. Alcohol for children, you used to call it.

I do, but it's all that's here. And it's better than nothing. I would have picked something up, but I didn't know if you'd want to come back here.

He sat beside me and together we raised our glasses in salute to the dog.

Poor King, said Jude. I would have given him a proper backyard burial, you know, at the Old House. It's what he deserved.

The thing is, I'd been thinking of selling it anyway. Starting over somewhere new.

I nodded, but I was distracted. Something about the apartment had been bothering me since we'd arrived, and I realised then that it was the smell. No scent of salt or sandalwood, tobacco or wet dog. It smelled of paint and the plastic-coated wood of cheap cabinetry, but beneath that something powdery and floral. All the white doors and cupboards were conspicuously shut, and I was sure if I looked inside them, I'd find women's things.

But there in the hall was the antique sideboard with the painted angels on the doors that Jude had repaired in the winter, and draped across the back of the pale leather couch was King's rug—the red and brown one he'd scratched up and I'd come to think of as his, that used to lie by the foot of Jude's black brass bed. Dog hairs on the carpet beneath me, I picked them from the sleeve of my dress. Tawny and coarse and familiar. I had a feeling then that I could not get enough air into my lungs. Windows sealed shut, silencing the sound of the surf. I reached for my drink. I drank.

I closed my eyes and turned my face up towards his. Leaned in close enough to smell soap and shaving cream and the alcohol on his breath. All of it wrong, a stranger's scent, too sweet and clean. Another wave of nausea. Pushing my lips hard against his to swallow it down. His kiss was dry and papery. He had lost himself, I realised, and I wanted to bring him back, to make him remember the man he was when we had loved each other. There, in the living room, the weave of another woman's carpet pressing tracks into my knees. The body doesn't forget so easily, I knew. I tugged on the collar of his jacket, pulling him towards the floor, but when I reached for his belt, he took my wrist with his good hand.

What's the matter? I said.

We shouldn't.

Isn't this why you wanted me here?

I don't know what I wanted, he said. But it's probably not a good idea.

Oh, because suddenly you're too old to make mistakes? Whose apartment is this, Jude? How long have you been living here?

He looked away and said nothing. How I hated to see him like that. Slumped against the couch, head hanging low, long legs almost reaching to the wall opposite.

It's only been three weeks, I said. You can't be alone for three weeks?

I got up to leave, but when I reached the door, he called me back.

Wait, he said, from his position on the floor. We were supposed to talk. You wanted to tell me something.

This is what did it, I said. This place. Animals hate change and you never should have moved him into some woman's apartment.

Driving north to my mother's house, I swore that I had loved the dog more than I had ever loved Jude. But lying in bed later that night, I remembered what the vet had said last winter. *Nothing that could shock or strain the heart.* Like cold water, abandonment, grief.

When Henry was small and our ridgeback, Lola, had died, my mother told him that she had gone to dog heaven. In dog heaven, I thought, if there were such a place, we would still be asleep in the Old House, Jude and I, with King down the end of the bed dreaming and the waves outside our window.

At the clinic, I sat in a room full of mothers. That was how it seemed to me—regular women in their thirties and one lone husband scrolling on a screen the size of his hand, where I had imagined frightened teenagers. These other women, they probably had children at home already. I wondered if this made the decision easier, having had some prior experience of maternity. You had a sense of what you were capable of, what you could and couldn't handle. I watched them flick through the pages of magazines and look up at the overhead clock, shift in their seats, as if waiting for any other appointment. A dentist, a meeting at the bank. And if not for the grim-faced woman standing outside on the corner in her thick woollen skirt, holding a printed poster of a fetus in utero, glowing and membranous and alien, from the outside you might mistake it for another kind of building—a modelling agency, an orthodontist's surgery, an architectural design firm. There was no signage, just a heavy steel door, bushes and palms growing high around the entrance. You had to know what you were looking for.

Inside, the decor was modern and spare. Pale blue walls and a single orchid on the receptionist's desk. I tried to find comfort in this elegance—which seemed to aspire to the generic elegance of hotel lobbies, implying anonymity and discretion—and it did make me feel less queasy and sordid, as I supposed was the intention. I didn't belong to elegance, but like my mother, I was calmed by the presence of it. It seemed to suggest somebody was in control.

Jude would have come with me, I knew that. He would have wanted to do the good or noble thing, and he'd always said it would be my decision. But the thought of him in such a place—hulking in the plastic chairs beneath the low ceiling, large dry hands clasped together, staring absently at the fake potted plants, awkwardly adjusting his long legs to let the other women pass by in the small waiting area—it would undo me to see that. And the way he would have scowled at the dull-eyed pro-lifers out the front, pushing past the woman with the severe dark bob streaked with grey and the thin line of hairs above her upper lip with his arm around me, protective, while I ducked my head down. I don't think I could have gone through with it, had he been there, and I understood then why he had not called me on the night of King's death. Some things you have to do alone.

One by one, the women were called away. I waited, and then I heard my name.

Naked below the waist in a paper gown, legs open. A blush-coloured examination room. Roses and tissues on a side table, and the smell of iodine. The doctor was apologising about the temperature. The air-conditioning was broken, or the heater wasn't working. Something about it wasn't right—I don't remember anymore, or it never really registered. She was a young but matronly-looking woman with a round face and blonde hair pulled back into a low ponytail. I was looking up at her different-coloured eyes as she hovered above me, and nodding, to give the appearance that I was listening. So focused on seeming responsible and in control that I hardly heard what she was saying. Instead thinking, One blue eye and one green. Did that mean her mother's eyes were green and her father's blue? Or was it a flaw in the genes? Thinking back to the diagrams we drew in high school science. Thinking of Jude's changeable eyes, mine, what colour our baby's might have been.

A series of questions. Age. Date of last period. Number of sexual partners. Method of contraception.

Trust, I wanted to say.

I know at some point the doctor asked me if I'd considered all my options, if I was certain. I said, resolutely, Yes, because I understood this was necessary in order for the transaction to be completed. There was no space for ambivalence in that room.

She asked me to lift my feet into the metal brackets. White rubber gloves stretched over her wrists with a snapping sound. I felt the pressure of her fingers pushing down on my pelvis and then her hand inside me. Between my legs a metal coldness, like a spoon held against warm skin. Wincing. I knocked my knees together, bone against bone. She tapped them impatiently to remind me to keep them open. Such skinny legs, she said. Do you diet?

One foot slipped from its silver stirrup and I thought of horses, of my mother's body, her shattered clavicle the year she turned sixteen, and my grandmother before her, riding to make the blood come—and then a sharp pain, blackness.

I woke, dry-mouthed. Spots of light.

You fainted, the doctor said. You didn't tell me you were going to faint. She sounded annoyed. She told me I could get dressed slowly. Since I was less than sixty-three days pregnant, I could take the medication that had finally been made available in Australia, she said, though it had been used for years in other countries. I was to take one tablet now and one twenty-four hours later. The procedure would be completed at home.

The drug replicates a spontaneous, natural expulsion, she explained. In other words, it stimulates a miscarriage. For all intents and purposes, it will seem like the blood came of its own volition. You can expect bleeding, and some cramping, maybe a bit more than you're used to. You'll want to start taking this, too, she said, offering me a tight-lipped smile and a prescription for the birth control pill.

I don't need it, I said. The father. I mean, the man. We're not—

There'll be others, she said, insisting. You're only twenty-four.

Because I'd fainted, I was required to sit in the examination room until my blood pressure returned to normal. The clinic had also called my emergency contact and so, when I finally emerged, there was my mother waiting for me, reading an old issue of the *Australian Women's Weekly*. Her lipstick a bright red beneath the white artificial light. I felt touched that she'd applied makeup, knowing it was a sign not of her vanity but of her fear. I'd watched her do this many times in the rear-view mirror in car parks out the front of the doctor's, parent–teacher meetings—it marked the occasion as significant, something she needed her public face for, to feel composed.

I hate these places, she said, though this one could be worse. Lucky I was only at the museum, so I wasn't far away. How are you feeling?

In some old maternal instinct, she laid her hand on my fore-head like she did when I was sick as a child. I would always be my mother's daughter, I thought. How could I have been a mother when I was still my mother's daughter? It was fundamental to who I was. I had always understood myself in relation to her.

This is only one thing that will happen to you, she said to me in the car, as we passed by the bridal shops and motorcycle dealerships that lined the old gritty freeway that would lead us away from the city, back to her house. One thing, out of so many things.

But nothing had really happened yet, I thought. What I'd lost, it seemed it was and would only ever be imaginary. What was I crying for, except the loss of one vision of what my life might have been, one I'd lived out in dreams? As all lovers learn, when love ends, you lose the future as well as the past.

I rested my head on the window, closed my eyes and drifted as my mother drove us home. Jude and I never would have lasted, I knew that. And then where would that have left me? On the road again, a daughter riding shotgun while I sat behind the wheel.

Maybe my mother and the doctor were right, I thought, and someday there would be others—other men, other children, other dogs—that I'd come to love and call mine. But not his. Never his.

I had the neighbour's baby on my hip when the bleeding started, the weight of her gently grounding as we moved from room to room. She accepted me readily now, smiling on my arrival each morning, reaching out, launching herself willingly into my arms and fitting herself around the shapes that seemed designed for that purpose. Her head was resting on my breast and her tiny fat legs were bent like a frog's and kicking lightly at the air around my waist when I felt the twist of my stomach like gears turning or something being wrung out. Slow, crippling waves.

Clutching and releasing. In the bathroom, dark and greasy clots of blood. Once, I'd thought of it as something abstract, no more than a symbol, but there was blood on my thighs and my hands now, as I rinsed my underwear out in the sink. Thinking of what my grandmother said, *My body took care of it.* All my life, I'd pictured my grandmother as some distant gothic figure, but her blood was mine.

White-knuckling it down the road, fingernails digging into palms as I inched my way back to my mother's house later that afternoon, wearing one of the thick maternity pads I'd found in the bottom of my neighbour's bathroom cupboard. I tried to think of it as something ancient and medical, a bloodletting, as I stood crouched beneath the hot stream of the shower, rust-coloured water washing down the drain.

On the last day of the year I took the train down to the city, met Bonnie for drinks and fell asleep beside her in my old room, where she let me sleep close against her back and hold on to her, as if we were sisters or lovers. I was free, but empty.

My mother had been twenty-four when I was born and so part of me had always assumed I'd be a young mother too, as if the course of her life might prefigure mine. It was only that summer that it really occurred to me that I could make different choices, and I felt it stirring in me—the desire for a larger life.

Still, it was hard at first not to see that monthly blood and think of loss. Cycles of loss and letting go. My body like an hourglass, moving time in blood instead of sand.

These days, the ache for a baby is like a bruise. It hurts, that kind of longing. It is the truest form of unrequited love, the most pure, because the object of desire is only imaginary, not yet born.

I didn't go to Europe, as I had once thought I would. I went, instead, to America. Perhaps some part of me remembered the voice of my mother's lover on the phone all those years ago, the one she had left my father and me to follow. I would travel further away than she ever did, towards my own vision of a different kind of life in a place where I belonged to no one. Although, as my mother and I both discovered, it's not so easy to forget, to leave the past behind. It follows after, like a loose hem or a wake in water. You drag it with you when you go.

It wasn't until two weeks before I was to leave that I heard the real story about the night of the fire. Already by then, Jude had been staying with the woman with the white apartment, the one whose cabinet he'd restored in the winter when we'd lived together—there were always women, I knew, willing to take in a man and make a pet of him. But that night, after King died, Jude went back to the Old House alone. He started drinking. He had been thinking of selling the place, but he'd accumulated so much junk over the years, he didn't know what to do with it.

And so, he started breaking up old furniture for firewood—the scrap and broken pieces first, three-legged tables crooked and splintered. He lit a match. Maybe he added a little liquor to the flames. Watching the paint peel and blister, oily black smoke from the burning varnish coiling up towards the ceiling, staining the walls, like water. The fire leaped and he felt heat on his face. Briefly, he was hypnotised by the sudden rush of it. The force of the flames like another body pressing against his. The way the fire moved, he'd said, and the sound, it was like snapping a blanket against itself, shaking it out, before it settles, spreads. Smoke got in his eyes, stung his throat, his lungs. Toxic, he'd worried, the fumes coming off the lacquered wood, and he'd stumbled blindly outside into the yard for air. Looking back, he saw windows full of flames, fire multiplied in the glass. At first, he'd thought it was an illusion—a mirror image, the flames reflected back, doubled. And then the windows popped, shattered. Blown-out glass on the back porch. It looked, he'd said, like hell. Not an empty underground of devils and brimstone but a place where everything you love is burning. A place you used to recognise, and call home.

It was Maeve who told me. Near to nine months after I'd seen Jude for the last time, the bell rang in the middle of one afternoon and there she was, standing on the doorstep of my mother's house, baby strapped to her front, facing out at the world. No longer an abstract sign or symbol but a pink and wriggling creature dressed in an orange knitted suit. Fine dark brows like her mother's, a wet trail beneath her nose where the wind had made it water. Both their cheeks flushed red. I was so surprised by her presence and by the fact of the baby that at first I said nothing, and she had to ask if it would be all right if they came in because outside it was very cold.

Why was Jude making a fire in the house, in the middle of summer? I asked her. We were sitting in the living room, late afternoon light filtering through the stained-glass bay windows. My mother's house was dark before she renovated it, as many Australian houses used to be, built facing away from the sun, and it made everything feel vaguely hushed and sacred with the muted light of churches. The baby was crawling on the rug between us—Edie, Maeve had called her, from Edith, the name of her mother's mother.

I don't know, Maeve said. He just said that he'd been drinking. He was lucky, you know. There'd been rain the night before. The ground soaked with it. Damp wood, wet leaves. Slow to burn. A neighbour smelled smoke and called it in right away. They managed to put it out. It was the water that did the most damage to the house, in the end. Even so, I don't think he could have stayed there. The thing about a once-burned house, he said, is that you can never get the smell of smoke from the walls. Are you going somewhere?

She looked across at where my suitcase was propped open against the sofa, surrounded by piles of books and clothes.

I told her that I was moving to New York for a graduate program. Classes started in September and soon I would be leaving. I was going to study writing, I said.

She nodded, her face showing neither approval nor disapproval nor surprise.

I didn't know you wrote, she said, and I realised then how little I'd shared with her about my desires and ambitions outside of my life with Jude, all our conversations revolving around, circling back to, the two men.

I kissed him, she said then, that night on the beach. I kissed Jude. It won't matter now, but I wanted to tell you, you weren't imagining things. I know I'm supposed to say I didn't mean it, that it was all an accident, but I did. No point in lying about it now. I wasn't thinking about you, then. I was thinking of myself, of the baby, of being alone. I was so afraid. And Jude had always been there for me over the years. I'd never been the type to think you needed a man for anything before, I'd always lived alone, been independent. It wouldn't have spooked me, five years ago, to think of raising a child on my own, if I ever even thought of it at all. But how to explain it? It felt, in a way, primal. This urge. And I do think he would make a good dad if he wasn't so hung up on his past. I think he always felt as a father he'd be illegitimate. He didn't have any good models, you know. His father died when he was still a boy, and all his mother's boyfriends after were real bastards. But he really did love you.

I thought it would've been better if he told you the truth, rather than pretend nothing happened. I mean, it was only a kiss. But he didn't think you'd believe him. That it was all me.

Was it? I said. When you kissed him. Did he kiss back?

She hesitated. Yes, Maeve said, after a pause. But it wasn't love, or passion. It was comfort. The way it can be between old friends. A gesture. There was a lot of sadness in it, that kiss, knowing, I think, that we couldn't really help each other the way we wanted to. And then he said that he couldn't, that he loved you, and I said I know, and that was it. God, she said, and she turned her face away, and spoke her next words quietly, as if she didn't want her daughter to hear. Do you hate me?

Her head bent, the late light catching the outline of her dark hair, she looked like a religious painting. I remembered then the way Jude had moved his hands through my hair on those afternoons of early love, sun behind my head, haloed. We shared something, Maeve and I, beyond her kiss with Jude on the beach, and in the years that followed I would often think of her as a kind of sister, a double. A vision of what my life might have been.

I might've, back then. If I'd known, I said. But now?

I looked at her, her face softened, creased around her lips and eyes, though the contours of her body had sharpened. When she bent down, her shoulder blades stuck out like folded wings, and there was space around the back of her same old jeans, though I could see that her arms were strong from lifting and carrying the baby. She looked so tired, as if everything about her had been crumpled and smoothed back out again. Even the way she spoke seemed different, halting and unsure.

And though a part of me wanted to hold on to that resentment until it curdled, what I felt was a kind of gratitude that she cared about what I thought of her at all. I had been granted the power to absolve, to forgive, and I was benevolent when perhaps I should have been angry. But I wanted to free myself as much as Maeve from the night on the beach and everything that happened after, to pack it away neatly with everything else I planned to leave behind. It couldn't be as simple as its all being her fault. It had to mean something more than that.

No, I can't hate you, I said. How's things with Willy?

Oh, you know, she said. The same. It is what it is.

The baby shrieked then, a spontaneous trill of delight, waving one of my shirts up and down like a flag, *surrender*, and I saw Maeve's expression crack open. The sheer joy of it.

It's this new thing, she said, her little dolphin noises. It means she's happy. Or at least I think it does. She's seven months now. We're doing all right, the two of us.

And I felt she understood me then as she had not before, for now she had known happiness whose underside was loss. We'd both gambled on love, Maeve and I, and neither had got exactly what she had wished for. Maybe life would deliver all the things we wanted, I thought, just never at the right time or with the right person.

You look happy, I said.

I am, she said. I am.

In New York I fit comfortably back into the life of a student, the boundaries of which were familiar to me. The rituals of scholarship allowed me to be the way I was—quiet, solitary. Not that I didn't go out with the girls in my cohort at first, get drunk and fall down in the street, skinning my knees to two bloody bulbs. Not that I didn't kiss strangers. Searching for Jude's face, rearranged in the features of other men. A once-broken nose, changeable eyes. Or the smell of smoke and oranges and alcohol. Warm, dry hands and fingers deft at undressing. Men who spoke with a kind of rough grace. I had a type.

In the first few years after my abortion, I would take jobs with plants and animals and children, like my mother once had. House sitter, dog sitter, nanny. Those were the ones that were available to me and wouldn't compromise my student visa, though sometimes I thought about what Maeve had said of her own work with teenagers, and wondered if there was a part of me that felt I had to make up for something too.

For a while, Maeve and I kept in touch. She would send me an email with a picture of Edie, but it was difficult not to look at her small face and fine brows and think of the child I could have had, who would have been around the same age. For so many years I marked time this way. At first, babysitting the sons and daughters of my professors in graduate school, I found it hard not to see them as symbols—especially if the ages aligned. Thinking, as I stood in a blue polyester gown on the steps of the library on commencement day and watched a woman from my year pose for a picture with her little boy, By now I could be the mother of a five-year-old. And then it passed, and I could look at children again and see them for what they were—just kids, representing nothing but themselves.

Maeve would also write to me if there was any news of Jude. In the years after the fire, he had left the mainland and all but disappeared. There'd been money from the house, enough for him to start over, and so he moved as far south as he could go—to Tasmania—and for some time nobody heard from him. Days and then months and eventually years would pass without a thought of him, and then I would surprise myself by waking up sobbing from a dream that he had died and no one had thought to tell me. This is when it began, my habit of tracking him. In this way my love for him mirrored my mother's love for my father, which, despite their separation, had endured—call it habit, call it time, call it memory, the memory of love. It's not so easy, after all, to cut that invisible thread. How many years after I left Sailors Beach—was it seven?—did I wake up one morning, taste salt in the air, Jude's name on my lips, before I opened my eyes to discover

I was not back at the Old House but in a shack on an island in the middle of the Atlantic, where I was spending the northern summer on a residency. Memories washing back as I walked in my gumboots through the scrub picking wild blackberries instead of sitting at my desk, mind wandering as I held a book in my hands, or steamed clams in a can of beer on the stove. *Sharkbait*, he'd called me, and after all these years he is still circling.

Seeing the picture of Jude had brought back an old grief. There he was, so familiar to me, even with the child in his arms and that new softness to his expression. The look of a man made gentle by the love and weariness of parenthood.

I thought it would be enough just to know he was alive, but life contained more possibilities than I had allowed for. He was no longer that same orphan boy, belonging to no one. Here was proof: the little girl in his arms. Looking again at her dark and serious eyes, which must have been her mother's, her lips so like Jude's, I found I could not wish that it were otherwise.

It was a beautiful photograph.

A man strikes a match and starts a fire in the house of love. A woman takes a pill to make herself bleed. Or maybe it's gin and horses, or a plane ticket to a place that makes you think of summer, where every day might be a holiday—at least from the life that you've been living.

What continues to surprise me, and what I still don't understand, is not the reasons that love ends but the way that it endures.

My mother has lived in this house for fourteen years, longer than she's ever lived anywhere other than her childhood home. I left for America, and Henry moved to the city after high school, but she stayed—though she still searches for places online, properties for sale. It never really goes away, the longing for the life not lived, because isn't that part of how we come to know ourselves too? Through what we lack as much as what we have, all we dream but do not hold. Some desires have no resolution.

Through the bay window in the spare room, I see it is growing lighter. I close my computer and sleep for a long time.

When I wake, later in the day, I go into the kitchen and find my brother sitting at the table.

Henry, I say.

He is shy at first, ducking his head as he nods and says, Oh, hello, with a teenager's awkwardness he hasn't quite let go of, even at twenty-five. But when we hug, his grip is strong, both arms wrapped around my back. He is so much taller than me now, he can rest his chin on my head. I've lived apart from him so long that it is always a shock at first to remember that my once-baby brother has grown. I'm glad he has become a gentle man, a man who hugs and holds on, that we raised him that way.

Let me look at you, I say, standing back. Your hair's long now, isn't it? It's almost as long as mine.

He shrugs, shakes the hair out of his face. It falls around his shoulders in an old style that's recently come back into fashion. It all comes back, I think.

Where's Mum?

I don't know, he says. Down at the shops, probably. I let myself in.

Have you eaten? I'm going to make breakfast.

French toast, soaked in milk with honey, his favourite when he was a boy. Twelve years between us, I loved him in a way that was part sister and part mother and this has never really settled, even as we have both become adults. We don't talk much, seeing each other only every other Christmas since I moved away, but it is still in his company that I feel most at ease.

In the afternoon, the three of us go walking on the bush track overlooking the valley. Galahs and butcherbirds careening high above. Dirt and eucalyptus, the scent of my childhood.

There's no shame in coming home—how many times has my mother said that to me over the years? I agreed with her, but after I left Sailors Beach, it was not clear where that was, if it could be anywhere at all. I thought that if no place could ever house everyone I loved, whatever home I hoped to make could only be shaped by absence. It didn't occur to me that perhaps a home is never a fixed or stable thing but something that can be carried with you and remade.

Two years ago, there were fires in this region, burning along the sandstone spine of the Mountains. The trees are still blackened in places, but new growth is beginning to show through.

As we walk, I think of what Jude once said about how the bush is like the ocean: it is easy to go astray. But today, there is my mother up ahead, holding back the branches, and my brother following behind me. We make our way, a family of three. We lose sight of each other briefly, when the brush grows thick or the path winds round a bend, and then we find each other again.

Acknowledgements

Writing is thought of as a solitary pursuit, but bringing a book into the world requires the belief and dedication of so many. Thank you first of all to Samantha Shea for her invaluable guidance, patience and faith in my work from the beginning. Thank you to Masie Cochran for being an ideal reader and intuitive editor for this book, and for the insights and long phone conversations that improved it. Thank you to everyone at Tin House: Win McCormack, Craig Popelars, Nanci McCloskey, Elizabeth DeMeo, Alyssa Ogi, Anne Horowitz, Allison Dubinsky, Beth Steidle, Alice Yang, Becky Kraemer and Jae Nichelle.

Thank you to Jane Palfreyman, Angela Handley, Clara Finlay and Sandy Cull at Allen & Unwin for bringing this book home to Australia, and to Juliet Mabey, Polly Hatfield and the whole team at Oneworld Publications for giving it another home in the UK. Thank you to Caspian Dennis for sound advice from across the pond.

This novel owes an enormous debt to many writers who came before me, most especially those I was lucky to learn from during my time at Columbia University. Endless gratitude to Rebecca Godfrey, Leslie Jamison and Heidi Julavits for the conversations that greatly influenced my thinking through this book, and for offering generous encouragement at every stage along the way. Thank you to Elissa Schappell for telling me I didn't need permission, and to Hilton Als, for inspiring courage and style on and off the page. Thank you to Diane Williams, for giving me a sharper eye.

I am also grateful for the creative companionship of my classmates and early readers, in particular Liza St. James, Madeleine Watts, Zach Davidson, Francesca Giacco and Will Augerot, who made the writing process feel less lonely.

Thank you to my oldest friends, who feel like family: Phaedra Collins, Aristea Kaydos-Nitis, Rosie Short, Daisy Gibbs, Hannah McManus, Pia May Courtley, Sami Sweeting, Lauren Curtis, Ellie Hayes O'Brien, Holiday Sidewinder. And to Mia Pinjuh and Patrick Ewing, who feel like old friends already.

This book would not have been possible without the love and support of my family. To my parents, Amanda Meares and Steve Lucas, the first artists I admired: thank you for raising me on stories and paintings and songs. Thank you, John Butler. Thank you, William and Edward Butler: being your sister is one of the greatest gifts. Thank you, Russell and Sue Meares. Thank you, Annette and Ron Irish. Thank you, Joey Lucas.

Finally, thank you to Pancho, a tail-wagging reminder to stay present and playful in the world every day, and a constant source of joy. And to Robert, my first and best reader: I couldn't have done it without you. Our life together is the creative collaboration I am most proud of.

Notes

I owe the title of this book, *Thirst for Salt*, to a line from the Robert Hass poem 'Meditation at Lagunitas': 'I felt a violent wonder at her presence / like a thirst for salt'. It is this poem that Jude reads in the garden.

Petra's idea that the body is 'activated by touch' was inspired by Nick Flynn's poem 'The King of Fire'.

The artist who invites people to cut a piece from her clothes is a reference to Yoko Ono's 1964 performance work *Cut Piece*.

The drawing *Two Sunken Lovers Bodies Lay* is by Australian artist Joy Hester and it lives at the Art Gallery of New South Wales, not in New York.

The haunting image of 'a small child, hair androgynously long, alone in a tin boat, gripping the tiller in one hand beneath a red sky, respirator strapped to their face' describes a photograph taken by Allison Marion in Mallacoota on 31 December 2019 during the 2019–20 Australian bushfires. Although the bushfire season in *Thirst for Salt* takes place several years before this photograph was taken, the reference to this image is deliberate.

A short story that later became part of this novel was published in *The Australian Book Review* as 'Ruins', as the winner of the 2018 Elizabeth Jolley Prize.

© Kylie Coutts

Madelaine Lucas was born in Melbourne in 1990 and raised in Sydney as the daughter of a visual artist and a rock 'n' roll musician. In 2015, she moved to New York to complete her MFA in fiction at Columbia University, where she now teaches in the graduate and undergraduate writing programs. She is a senior editor of the literary annual *NOON* and lives in Brooklyn with her husband and her dog, Pancho. *Thirst for Salt* is her first novel.